A CASE -OF- MAJOR MURDER

A Quinn Flitcroft Mystery

By J C Williams

Copyright © 2024 J C Williams

All rights reserved. No part of this book may be reproduced in any manner without written permission except in the case of brief quotations included in critical articles and reviews. For information, please contact the author.

All characters appearing in this work are fictitious. Any resemblance to real persons, living or dead, is purely coincidental.

Cover design by Drew Clarke

Interior formatting and proofreading & editing by Dave Scott

ISBN: 9798341218215

First printing November 2024

You can subscribe to J C Williams' mailing list and view all his other books at:
www.authorjcwilliams.com

Books by JC Williams

The Flip of a Coin

The Lonely Heart Attack Club

The Lonely Heart Attack Club: Wrinkly Olympics

The Lonely Heart Attack Club: Project VIP

The Seaside Detective Agency

The Seaside Detective Agency: The Case of the Brazen Burglar

Frank 'n' Stan's Bucket List #1: TT Races

Frank 'n' Stan's Bucket List #2: TT Races

Frank 'n' Stan's Bucket List #3: Isle 'Le Mans' TT

Frank 'n' Stan's Bucket List #4: Bride of Frank 'n' Stan

Frank 'n' Stan's Bucket List #5: Isle of Man TT Aces

Frank 'n' Stan's Bucket List #6: Las Vegas

The Bookshop by the Beach

The Crafternoon Sewcial Club

The Crafternoon Sewcial Club: Sewing Bee

The Crafternoon Sewcial Club: Showdown

Life's a Pitch

Life's a Pitch: Rock the Rock

A Reluctant Christmas Novel

A Case of Major Murder: A Quinn Flitcroft Mystery

Cabbage Von Dagel

Hamish McScabbard

Deputy Gabe Rashford: Showdown at Buzzards Creek

Luke 'n' Conor's Hundred-to-One Club

Chapter One

A young girl of six or maybe seven years of age twirled her blonde pigtails around like a skipping rope attached to either side of her head. Slowly, she leaned forward, moving her face closer to what she was examining until the tip of her suncream-covered nose came to rest against the cold glass, leaving a smear as she subsequently took a step to her right, inspecting further what was held in the display case before her.

"Oh, I just... hrm, I just don't know..." she said, releasing her pigtails and placing her palms on the glass now as well, adding in a lovely set of handprints to complement the impressive snail trail already left by her nose.

"Tabitha!" the girl's mum scolded her through the side of her mouth, utilising a corner of her beach towel to promptly remove as much of the greasy blemishing as possible while praying nobody would notice.

"It's no good, Mum," Tabitha complained, shoulders drooping. "I just— I just can't choose," she said, sounding like she was on the verge of tears as she was wracked by indecision.

Just then, an older, grey-haired chap wearing a white apron appeared, having moved from his place behind the business side of the counter and offering Tabitha's mum a reassuring smile. "Okay, young lady," the man said, crouching down to address the frustrated Tabitha. At first, she recoiled slightly, worried she was about to be on the receiving end of a serious tongue-lashing for besmirching the shop's previously immaculate and smear-free glass. But then, comforted by the fellow's genial smile and kind eyes, Tabitha soon warmed to the man who'd presented himself before her.

"My name is Chester. I'm the proprietor here," Chester said by way of introduction, extending a hand towards his new friend which was then graciously received. Tabitha, for her part, also admired the oversized ice cream embroidered on the centre of Chester's crisp white apron.

"Ah, you like my apron?" Chester asked, thrilled to see a smiling face looking back at him. Encouraged, he regarded the young one carefully. "And unless I'm very much mistaken, you also love ice cream, like me...?" he ventured, receiving an enthusiastic nod in response. "Well, do you know what this important symbol on my chest means, young lady?"

Tabitha at first shook her head, setting her pigtails flailing. "Ehm... that you work here?" she ventured a moment or two later, correctly putting two and two together, the perceptive little tyke that she was.

Chester briefly glanced up, conscious of the queue forming behind, who, to be fair to them, thankfully didn't appear to mind the slight delay which allowed them additional time to consider their own selections. "Indeed I do," Chester then cheerfully advised to Tabitha. "Work here, that is. However, this image on my apron also means I have a *very* special qualification that can *only* be obtained by working exceptionally hard in the frozen treat industry for over fifty years."

Tabitha, mouth agape, looked on in awe, wondering what sort of mystery talent or skill this older gentleman might lay claim to. Tabitha's younger brother must have been thinking along the same lines, even mistaking the large symbol on Chester's chest for some sort of superhero logo.

"Can you fly...?" her brother asked, emerging from behind the protective shield that was his mum.

Chester laughed at the suggestion, although not in an unkind way. "No, I can't fly," he answered, accompanied by a weary sigh, almost sounding slightly disappointed. "At least not *anymore*," he quickly added, with a mischievous undertone to his voice and a flurry of his bushy eyebrows that left the young'uns wide-eyed in wonderment. "However," Chester continued, playing up to his captive audience. "What this embroidered badge on my apron actually means is that I, Chester J Flitcroft, am a certified, quantified, bona fide, ice cream authority and specialist," he proudly announced, much to the amusement of the other customers in the queue listening in. "Now!" Chester said abruptly, in an unexpectedly loud voice, while clapping his hands together smartly and startling a giggling Tabitha in the process. "If my years of training at Ice Cream University have taught me anything..." he said, now caressing his chin thoughtfully, "the rather troublesome issue you're experiencing at present is that there is simply too darned much to choose from, and you don't wish to get such an awfully important decision wrong. Am I correct...?"

Tabitha bobbed her head so fervently that it was as if it were attached to her neck and shoulders by a spring, with her both captivated and amazed by this frozen-treat purveyor's seeming mind-reading capabilities.

"I suspected as much," Chester replied. "So," he added with a finger held in the air, "that's why you, my new young friend, will have The Bucket 'n' Spade Ice Cream Emporium's most splendid, most wonderful, most blinkin' *delightful* ice cream creation that's ever passed or will ever pass your lips. So, Tabitha, what do you say? Should I go and dig out my bestest, my favouritest, and my most tremenderest scoop reserved for special missions such as this?" he asked, creating several new words in the process, much to his young audience's satisfaction.

Tabitha carefully considered this offer for all of about half a millisecond. "Yes, please," she said, salivating at the prospect of the chilled wonder about to stimulate her taste buds. "What's in it?" she enquired, briefly flicking her eyes to the glass cabinet where an array of multi-coloured and multi-flavoured ice cream options waited patiently for their moment in the sun, quite literally in this case, because the weather outside was balmy and beautiful.

Having received the required approvals, Chester pushed himself upright, which was no easy feat when your knees and other joints were as worn out as his were. "Well," he said, addressing

Tabitha's question about the ingredients while he returned to the other side of the shop's counter area. "First, we place two scoops of chocolate cookie crumble into a chocolate cone. You do like chocolate?"

"Oh, I just adore chocolate," Tabitha was keen to stress, now sounding like she was floating on a cloud in dessert heaven.

Chester held his ice cream scoop aloft, presenting it like the mighty Excalibur after procuring it from the Lady in the Lake. Then, after dipping the scoop in a bit of warm water to ease the ice cream extraction process, he rapidly thrust it towards the tub labelled "choc cookie crumble" located in the back left of the chiller cabinet.

With a polished, practised precision—and much to watching Tabitha's amazement—two balls of deep brown ice cream, dotted with bits of protruding cookie pieces, soon sat on a delicious-looking cone, ready for the finishing touches to be applied.

"Next, it's a quick dunk in crushed Smarties," Chester advised, dipping his creation into a glass bowl filled with the aforementioned topping. "And then, the flakiest of Flakes..." he announced dramatically, standing there with his right arm extended like he was expecting it to magically appear out of thin air. However, it didn't. Appear in a puff of smoke, that is. Rather, one of Chester's able colleagues—well versed in this procedure if her precision timing was anything to go by—appeared with one solitary and alluring strip of Cadbury Flake chocolate presented on a silver platter for Chester's consideration.

"Perfect!" Chester declared, having given it the once over and determining that it was exactly to his liking. Ever so carefully, he picked it up, ensuring none of the exquisite, delicate Flake was inadvertently broken off and left behind. "Et voilà," he said, right after skilfully inserting the Flake into the uppermost ball of ice cream so that it was sticking out at the jaunty one o'clock position, rather like a wonky chimney pot.

Finally, the finishing touch on this brain-freeze, headache-inducing masterpiece was a liberal drenching in Chester's own custom-blend extra-chocolatey chocolate sauce. Then, after one final quality check where he confirmed that everything was precisely as it should be, Chester proudly handed it over to a captivated Tabitha. "That's for you," he said with a smile. "And I hope you enjoy eating it as much as I enjoyed making it."

It was about this time that Tabitha's younger brother, seeing what his sister now had in her possession, pushed out his lower lip. It wasn't that he wasn't impressed, because he was. The problem, rather, was that his sister's hands were now gloriously full, and his hands weren't. A worrying, dreadful state of affairs, to be certain.

"Young man!" Chester called out, spotting the boy's distressed demeanour.

In response, the lad cautiously raised his head until his eyes met with Chester's. "Do you think I'd forget about you?" Chester asked, tilting his head to one side and offering a comical frown.

Hearing this, the boy perked up, hopeful that the answer to this particular question was going to be in his favour.

"Of course I wouldn't!" Chester assured him, reaching down somewhere near his feet, to perhaps some hidden compartment, and then miraculously producing another, identical and equally wonderful-looking ice cream concoction as his sister was presently enjoying.

How Chester managed to pull a proverbial rabbit from his hat like this, and from where, exactly, was anyone's guess.

"What– I mean– how did you...?" the boy asked, reaching up and accepting his very own cone from a grinning Chester.

"A magician never reveals their tricks," Chester advised with a wink. "Never."

With her two kids now beyond happy, Mum declined the option of a frozen treat for herself, instead ushering her children over to the till a short distance away. Once there, she reached into her handbag, no doubt wondering just how much this pair of elaborate chocolate delights were going to lighten her purse by.

"Ah, you shan't be needing that today," Chester advised, moving to the till and tipping his head in indication of Mum's purse.

"I won't...?" she asked, appearing uncertain as to how she was meant to be paying for her purchase if she couldn't reach for her cash or possibly her debit card.

Chester shook his head, hooking his thumb over his shoulder towards a sign hanging on the wall directly behind him.

"What does it say?" Tabitha's brother asked between licks, becoming intrigued by the adults' conversation, as he liked to know what was going on. "I can't see what it says from down here."

"But you can't even read yet, either," big sister Tabitha felt the need to gently point out.

"Oh, yeah. That too," the boy happily admitted.

Mum read the information displayed on the slightly cracked, ageing porcelain sign that appeared like it'd been hanging in the same position for decades. "Well, the sign says every hundredth order comes with the compliments of the proprietor," she related for her son's benefit.

"So you may keep your money for today," Chester reiterated, along with a warm smile. "Because—"

"Because I'm your hundredth customer?" Tabitha ventured, both shocked and delighted. "Wait, hang on. Only you've given us *two* ice creams," she noted. "So that means my little brother..." she said, looking over at her brother. "Well, wouldn't he be one hundredth and *one*...?"

"She's right. And you really don't need to do that," Tabitha's mum insisted, pulling some cash from her purse.

Chester gently waved away the offer of payment. "Oh, don't worry, these two don't get their ice cream for free. Not entirely," he said conspiratorially.

"We don't have to wash the dishes, do we?" a worried Tabitha asked, having heard a similar line of discussion on a television programme, and certain this must be the way things worked in the real world as well.

Chester considered this option for a moment or three. After all, it'd been a particularly busy day in the shop's café area, with plenty of dirty dishes building up in the kitchen as a result.

"Nope, not at all," Chester said eventually, putting Tabitha at ease. "But when you kids leave my shop," he said, delivering the details of his plan, "what you then need to do is make sure and

A CASE OF MAJOR MURDER

tell everybody outside about how utterly splendiferous your ice cream creations are, okay?"

"Okay!" Tabitha and her brother said in unison, relieved that they didn't have to go and get their Marigold gloves on to start working in the kitchen. "Udderly splendiferous!" Tabitha's little brother added, unsure what Chester's words had meant, but appearing to like the sound of them.

"Come on, you two," Mum said, herding the pair of them up. "And what do you say...?" she prompted.

"Thank you, Mister Chester!" they both said, raising their partially eaten ice creams up, ready for potential inspection by any would-be customers outside the shop.

"You're welcome, and do call again," Chester said, returning to his station to help his industrious colleagues attend to the queue that was now stretching through the shop and spilling out onto the pavement beyond the front door.

"Okay, who's next?" Chester asked brightly, directed towards the group of faces staring back at him from the front of the line.

"Uhm, me, I think...?" an uncertain-looking fellow with an inflatable dolphin under his arm said tentatively. "I think I'll go for..." he began to say, extending a finger from his free hand. "No, wait, instead I'll..." he continued. "In fact, you know what, how about the ones you just made for those kids a moment ago?"

"The Bucket 'n' Spade Ice Cream Emporium's most splendid, most wonderful, most blinkin' *delightful* ice cream creation that's ever passed or will ever pass your lips?" Chester suggested, scoop poised and ready for action once again.

"Yep, that's the one!" the owner of the inflatable dolphin said. Or in fact it could've been a porpoise, as both mammals were equally to be found in the waters off the coast of the Isle of Man. "I'll take four of them, please."

Chester smiled, delighted to see his marketing exploits working wonders so soon, even if the fellow had already been in the queue to begin with. "Coming right up, sir."

For a little over fifty years now, Chester J Flitcroft had played a pivotal role at this particular location—pivotal, in fact, for any seaside town worth its salt, for that matter—the dispensing of delicious, delectable ice creams to both tourists and locals alike.

Located in Port Erin, a charming and historic town in the south of the Isle of Man, The Bucket 'n' Spade had, over the years, served more customers than there were grains of sand on the golden, crescent-shaped beach located only a stone's throw away from the shop's front door.

Centred around a sheltered bay overlooked by the imposing cliffs of Bradda Head, Port Erin had been a mecca for visitors ever since the tourist boom at the start of the last century. Boasting towering hillside views in every direction and crystal-clear water lapping the inviting beach, it was no wonder that the area was so popular with folk eager to kick off their shoes and sink their feet into the sand. Indeed, during the summer months, the town enjoyed a vibrant atmosphere, with many visitors arriving courtesy of the magnificent Isle of Man Steam Railway where Port Erin was the final southernmost stop along the scenic route.

And it was at that very final stop, as it should happen, that Chester's foray into the world of retail was first entertained. As a young lad growing up in Port Erin, he was acutely aware of the regular influx of tourists ready and willing to part with their money to make their visit just that little bit more special. And, so it was, following a visit to the region's cash-and-carry wholesalers, that a fresh-faced and jug-eared Chester waited patiently for the next train to arrive at the railway station armed with his cooler box jampacked with delicious, locally made ice cream, refreshing chilled drinks, and whatever else he was able to cram in there, hoping to tempt them after their extended journey.

Soon enough, it was perhaps no surprise that the bricks-and-mortar establishments—who paid out wages, rent, tax, and other expenses—weren't entirely thrilled to see this young whippersnapper diluting the amount of cash available from the tourists' pockets. But there wasn't really too much they could do about the town's newest entrepreneur. Fortunately, however, there was still plenty of business to keep everybody happy and a constant demand for ice cream on a sunny day.

It was from these humble beginnings, then, that Chester, by reinvesting every spare penny into his fledgling enterprise, was eventually able to scrape the funds together to place a deposit on a tired, seafront property, with accommodation for himself upstairs and room for his ice cream emporium downstairs. Sure, it was tough at times, with the building requiring a complete renovation (hence its very reasonable purchase price), but one thing Chester wasn't afraid of was rolling up his sleeves and regularly putting in twelve-hour shifts to make his dream happen.

In the subsequent fifty years, there wasn't a time, at least not that he could recall, when Chester didn't make the short commute to work down the stairs without a huge smile on his face, looking forward to the day ahead. There were many highlights over the years, as he'd often fondly recall, but chief among his biggest pleasures was serving youngsters each summer on their annual family holiday, only to see many of them return as adults with their own children years later, hoping to recreate the magic of their first visit to this wonderful island.

"Okay, Chester, my dear," Doreen—one of the shop's most vital and longest-serving employees—said after the conclusion of another busy day at the office, stretching out a crick in her shoulder. "That's the floor mopped, and the machines all wiped down," she advised, joining her boss as he stood quietly at the front doorway, staring outside. "Should we come back and do it all again tomorrow?" she asked with a grin.

"That sounds like a marvellous plan," Chester agreed. "And thank you for all your hard work, Doreen," he told her, as he did each and every day.

Doreen stepped out onto the pavement, offering a wave over her shoulder. However, she'd only taken a step or two when she stopped, turning to face the shop again. The door was still ajar, as Chester had held it open for her as she'd exited. "You're okay, Chester?" she asked.

Chester offered her a spirited, double thumbs-up in return. "All's good with me, Doreen," he added. And then, "Oh! I almost forgot," he said, a thought occurring. "Wait there a second, would you, if you don't mind?" And with that, Chester navigated gingerly over the floor that'd just been carefully mopped, returning a moment later with a carrier bag in his hand. "Here," he said, passing it over to her.

"What's this?"

"It's for Alfie's birthday tomorrow," Chester explained, referring to Doreen's young grandson. "When he was last in the shop, I'm sure I heard him talking about Lego Star Wars," he told her. "I just hope that's one he hasn't already got, as I believe his space fleet is already rather extensive."

"You're a lovely man, Chester," she said, reaching out and giving Chester's hand an affectionate squeeze. "You do know that, don't you?"

Chester waved away the compliment. "Don't be telling everybody, or they'll all be wanting a discount," he joked.

With Doreen soon on her way, it was this precious time at the end of the day, with the beach now virtually empty, that Chester so enjoyed. He loved people, of course, but with peace and quiet restored, he'd usually stroll across the road (often with a glass of wine in hand for company), taking a seat on the promenade wall and soaking in the stunning coastal view—getting the sense that this idyllic slice of seaside was his own personal front garden. Well, at least until the masses returned once more, the following morning, to lay down their towels for an additional day of lazing in the sun.

Life was good, Chester considered, struggling to decide if he fancied a glass of red or a glass of white this evening.

***

"Bleedin' heck," Bert Harper moaned, staring into yet another empty hole in the sand he'd excavated. He shook his head, giving his metal detector a dissatisfied scowl. "You beeped and told me there was something buried there, you useless heap of junk," he complained. "Do you just like seeing me digging holes for no reason, is that it?" he then asked, once the hole was refilled and patted down. "Look, you don't beep unless there's coins, jewellery, Viking treasure, or something else valuable in there, otherwise you're going in the skip. Do you hear me?"

A CASE OF MAJOR MURDER

The detector, an unexpected gift from his loving wife, was so far proving to be something of a love-hate relationship for Bert. In a little over a week, he'd managed to uncover about a hundred or so aluminium ring pulls, twice as many empty holes, two rusting horseshoes, and a medal of some sort awarded for the Isle of Man's finest sandcastle. At times, Bert felt like an unpaid beach cleaner, but at least it was getting him out of the house, he reasoned. Indeed, on reflection, he wondered if the surprise present from his spouse was intended to do precisely that and give Mrs Harper some time to herself. Plus, as she had said when the gift was handed over: *"A walk up and down that beach each day will do wonders to get rid of your beer belly, dear."*

Initially sceptical on the idea of owning one of these devices, Bert conducted some extensive and detailed research on the detecting hobby (basically, he'd mentioned it to the barman of his local pub) and realised there was some serious dosh to be potentially made with his new battery-operated piece of mechanical wizardry. Especially on a popular beach where clumsy tourists were known to become parted with their various personal possessions on a regular basis. However, he'd enjoyed no luck so far. But the thought of a misplaced Rolex watch or an expensive ring sure had a way of motivating a man to keep on going.

And keep on going he did. Just now, Bert checked the settings on his detector again. In truth, he didn't really have too much of a clue what he was doing or looking at. As such, as he often did, he dropped a coin from his own pocket and passed the machine's coil over the general area to make sure it was still working.

Originally, he didn't have any specific plans of heading out with his detector on this particular evening. But he found that his new hobby, rather like having a dog that required its regular walks, was the perfect excuse to leave his home for a little bit—with the lure of a pint or two to toast his achievement after a bit of successful detecting, or perhaps more likely, to happily drown his sorrows after not locating anything especially of value. Sometimes, of course, he'd simply skip the detecting on certain occasions and just head straight over to the pub!

Satisfied at present that his machine was operating as the designer intended, and with the daylight now starting to seriously fade, Bert glanced up the length of the shore, deciding a slight adjustment in location might improve his luck. And where better spot than opposite The Bucket 'n' Spade, he reckoned. After all, it was a busy section of beach where countless numbers of beachgoers would routinely have been pestered by their children for ice cream and as a result very easily distracted as they rummaged for change. Net result, lovely coins in a variety of denominations dropped in those sands that Bert was hoping to uncover and rehouse in his own pocket.

Bert progressed onward, sweeping his new toy from right to left as he advanced forward like he was scything hay. "Come *on*," he willed the machine, drilling his eyes into the sandy beach as well, as if this might aid in the detecting process. But nothing. A big fat nothing. Indeed, it was at this point that his eyes wandered over to the nearby Bay Hotel, wondering if a pint or two of something cold might be a more worthwhile and satisfying present course of activity.

However, as he approached the section of beach directly in front of the ice cream shop, he felt a renewed focus. "Give it ten more minutes, Bert," he told himself, adjusting his earphones.

However, with the tide now fully out, there was a considerable area in which to focus his efforts in only the short time remaining before it got too dark. He scanned the beach, giving it a quick visual inspection, trying to figure out which patch of sand would have been the most popular with the day's tourists.

"Oh, *hello*," he remarked, spotting the outline of something in the shadows near the retaining sea wall running along the inner edge of the beach. "Has someone left a bag?" he wondered aloud, although it was difficult to clearly see exactly what it was from his current distance.

Hoping it might be something that could attract a generous reward for its safe return, Bert set off, tucking his detector under his arm and picking up the pace. Something that wasn't too easy in a pair of Wellington boots, as he'd soon discover.

"Hell's bells!" he complained, as he stumbled in the soft sand, coming to rest on his knees, almost in the prayer position. After several more expletives were issued, Bert looked up and over towards the sea wall now that he was a little closer and his view a little bit better. "What the...?" he said under his breath, narrowing his eyes in the fading light. "That's not a bag," he muttered, pushing himself up onto his feet again. Cautiously, he ventured closer and, as he now suspected, it wasn't a misplaced handbag or even anything remotely similar. He was looking at the soles of a pair of shoes. "Erm, hello, mate," Bert offered, now able to see that the outline he'd spotted earlier was actually that of a male figure (judging by the large shoe size) lying flat on his back with a multicoloured beach towel draped over his face.

"Look, I don't mean to bother you, yeah?" Bert called out from a few paces away. "But if you're hoping to enjoy some last-minute sunshine, I think you might be a little bit too late. So..."

With no response or movement offered, Bert moved a step closer. "No offence, mate, but have you been on the sauce all day or something?" he asked, wondering if the chap was sleeping off having one too many brewskis in the afternoon sun.

Now standing directly over the man, Bert could see that he was fully clothed, wearing long trousers, a white shirt, and a dark blazer—not exactly dressed for a day of frolicking on the beach. "Ere, mate," Bert said, crouching down beside the fellow, "you can't sleep it off here, yeah? Believe me, I've tried. Several times in fact, and the police aren't too keen on it."

Bert laid his metal detector down on the sand and extended an arm, nudging the fellow in the shoulder. "Oi, wakey, wakey," he offered, hoping to rouse him. But nothing.

"Wakey, wakey, eggs and bakey...?" Bert attempted further. But still, there was no movement or response.

Unsure what else to do, Bert grabbed hold of the beach towel over the man's head and slowly tugged on it. *"Aargh!"* he shouted as the face was revealed, with Bert falling backwards in horror. He dug his heels into the sand, desperately trying to put as much distance between the man and himself as he could. Except each time he kicked out, the soft sand gave way, making any sort of purchase impossible and foiling his attempts at escape.

Panic-stricken, he had to get away. But with no clear idea on how to accomplish that, he ended up rolling onto his ample belly, wriggling away on his stomach like he was at army boot camp. Once eventually at a safe distance, Bert struggled to his feet, at which point he unzipped a pocket in his trousers to retrieve his phone. With a shaking finger, he pressed several buttons on the screen before placing the mobile to his now-sweaty ear.

"Yes, this is Bert Harper," he said when the call was promptly answered, identifying himself with an unsteady voice. "I need... I need the police to come to the beach... I'm at the beach in front of The Bucket 'n' Spade in Port Erin..." he explained. "Please come *immediately*," he stressed. "Why...?" he said, in answer to the question posed to him. "Because I think there's been a murder, that's why...!"

Chapter Two

Eleven p.m. Location: an unremarkable industrial estate on the outskirts of Manchester, England.

"You've dropped one," Quinn remarked, placing a hand on her forehead and slightly kneading her temples. She was fond of her partner, but he could be somewhat exasperating at times.

Toby, sitting in the front passenger seat of their nondescript white Ford Transit rental van, swirled his hand around to try and circulate the air. "Did I...?" he said, opening his eyes. "Sorry, I think I sometimes do that when I'm dozing off," he explained. "You might take it as a compliment, though, that I'm that relaxed in your company...?" he suggested.

"What? No," Quinn replied, sounding decidedly unimpressed. "When I said you've dropped one, I meant literally," she told him, tipping her head towards the passenger footwell. "You let one of our emergency rations roll out of the bag."

"Ah. On it," Toby replied, now fully awake. He leaned forward, putting his head between his knees in the brace position, scanning the area around his feet. "Which way did it go?"

"Dunno, but it's down there somewhere. I heard it land."

Toby rummaged around for a few seconds without locating anything. "Can you put the overhead light on?" he asked without looking up, still leant over like he was in an aeroplane about to crash. "A bit of illumination might help," he offered. "Although I'm a bit worried about what else I might find down here, really, because I don't think it's been cleaned in years."

"Turn the overhead light on? Are you daft?" Quinn admonished. "Need I remind you we're on an undercover surveillance operation, trying to remain entirely unnoticed? Switching the overhead light on would be like setting fireworks off and—"

"Found it!" a well-chuffed Toby announced, cutting his partner off mid-sentence. "Look," he added, straightening in his seat and holding up the sugar-coated doughnut that'd temporarily eluded him. "Hmm, although I think there might be some fluff stuck to it," he considered, moving it closer to his face for further inspection. "Oh, and hairs as well, if I'm not mistaken."

"Right. That one's yours now, mate," Quinn insisted. "You'll be fine with it, I'm sure," she declared. "Keep in mind that helpful five-second rule that applies to all dropped food."

Toby contemplated this important point of food hygiene law. "Erm, I dunno, I think it was actually there on the floor for more like twenty seconds," he considered. "And have you seen the state of this van? If I eat this I might end up with diphtheria, listeria, or something else equally nasty," he put forth. "Hmm. Still, then again..." he decided.

Quinn glanced across the cabin of the van with a look of both incredulity and vexation.

"What? You told me to eat it," Toby said, as he nibbled around the outer edge of the doughnut like a field mouse munching on a sunflower seed, skilfully avoiding the fluff and other detritus, as he was not satisfied to let the doughnut go to waste.

"I'm not bothered if you catch diphtheria, listeria or any other sort of *theria*, for that matter," Quinn replied. "You just said you were dozing off, correct?" she asked, reminding him of his comment from a minute or so earlier.

"Yeah, so?"

"Toby, need I remind you that we're on an important surveillance mission, and you're sat over there apparently trying to get in a nice little *snooze*...?"

Toby pulled the front of his baseball cap down, lowering his head like a naughty pet dog who'd just been caught chewing up one of the cushions on its master's sofa.

"Sorry," Toby then offered after a brief silence. "It's just that I didn't get much sleep last night due to the blazingly hot vindaloo I bought for dinner yesterday evening, and... well, I won't trouble you with the details, but let's just say it burned as much coming out as it did going in."

"I thought you said you weren't going to trouble me with the details...?!" Quinn pointed out.

"Oh, right. Sorry," Toby answered, apologising again.

Quinn offered him a smile of forgiveness, while attempting to keep her eyes trained on the object of their surveillance operation—a sprawling factory unit about sixty metres or so from where they'd parked up.

With his sugar-covered, doughy snack soon polished off, Toby released a contended sigh, wiping away the excess sugar crystals that'd fallen onto his lap. "Is this how you imagined it...?" he then asked a moment or two later, by way of conversation.

"Imagined what?"

"Life at the age of forty," Toby remarked, leaning the back of his head against his seat's headrest as he considered that very circumstance just mentioned.

"Oi, I'm not as old as you! I'm *nearing* forty, but not forty *yet*," Quinn stressed. "Not for another few months," she advised. Not that she was counting down the days before her mid-life crisis should officially commence or anything like that. "Anyway, are you referring to work?" she asked, in response to Toby's question.

"Yeah."

Quinn mulled this over, drumming her fingers atop the steering wheel as she did so. After some due consideration, she said, "Well, if you mean did I for one moment imagine I would be sitting in a clapped-out van on a Friday night, investigating insurance fraud outside Europe's largest knicker manufacturer? Then no. No, this wasn't quite how I imagined my career panning out."

Following this admission on the part of his trusty associate, Toby tried and failed to stifle a guffaw.

"Oh, thanks for laughing at my pain, buddy."

"No, it's not that," Toby answered, wiping away a happy tear. "You know when we were first assigned to this investigation?"

"Sure."

"Well, when I looked over the case notes, yeah? I'd read it as Europe's largest knicker manufacturer. As in, I imagined they made the hugest pair of knickers in all of Europe. And then I thought, blimey, how many women can there possibly be who would need a pair of knickers that large?"

Quinn offered an amused smirk. "I think they're probably the largest on account of the great number of items produced each year, although I'll happily stand corrected if proven wrong," she said. "Still, if I keep eating all this greasy, sugary, unhealthy surveillance food we keep purchasing for ourselves, I may just end up being one of those plus-sized ladies you mentioned that need to buy the biggest knickers possible," she put forth.

And Quinn was right about her initial point, which Toby very likely already knew. The case that Quinn and her sleepy sidekick had been tasked with was investigating Europe's largest knicker manufacturer (by volume) over a few recent, sizeable insurance claims. In these, the company owner had stated that several lorry loads of inventory had been stolen in transit, resulting in the loss of hundreds of thousands of pounds worth of stock.

The police were involved, of course, conducting a thorough and complete review—but ultimately drawing a blank, with no arrests made and none of the missing knickers recovered. As a result, Quinn and Toby's employers were left with no option but to pay the hefty insurance claim without delay. However, some weeks later, when a disgruntled employee at the knicker factory enquired if a reward was on offer if it could be proved the claims were spurious... well, it didn't take too long to figure that "something was very *thong*," as Toby had quipped at the time.

According to the information obtained from said disgruntled employee, the company wasn't in such rude health as it was perceived to be. As such, a substantial cheque from the insurance company was just the ticket needed to keep the owner in the lavish lifestyle he presently enjoyed. Further, it appeared that several employees were also involved in the ruse, no doubt in return for a generous contribution to their monthly pay packet.

A CASE OF MAJOR MURDER

According to the details received from the 'mole,' a few times a week the company loaded up a lorry full of stock intended for onward delivery to clothing wholesalers across the UK. Unfortunately, as had happened on a number of separate occasions during the course of the past twelve months, some shipments were occasionally intercepted en route—sometimes resulting in the driver copping an unwelcome bruise on the noggin, and always with the contents of those lorries disappearing into the night. And, apparently, the greedy boss was busy putting plans in place for another unfortunate robbery in the very near future, again, with the same modus operandi. The only problem for those investigating was that the whistleblower couldn't be sure of any precise date for when this next inside job was set to take place.

Due to this uncertainty around timings, the police, understaffed as they were, could only do so much. They simply didn't have the available resources to stake out a factory for weeks or even months on end, hoping to get lucky at just the right place or time. As such, the insurance company's leading investigative duo were dispatched to solve the case of the stolen knickers with police assistance only a phone call away should the need arise.

And so, after seven arse-numbing days spent festering inside an increasingly filthy surveillance vehicle, they sincerely hoped that tonight was going to be the night when something might finally happen.

"Do we really think the owner is going to be stupid enough to do it again?" Toby asked, reaching into the brown paper bag for another doughnut. "I mean just how arrogant, or desperate, do you need to be to imagine the police and insurance company are that thick that—"

"Hang on, something's happening," Quinn cut in, leaning forward in her seat and perching her chin atop the steering wheel. "Pass me the binoculars," she said, holding her left hand out in Toby's direction. "There are two lorries this time," she remarked. "Why are their *two* lorries?"

"Ehm... the binoculars?" Toby asked in a slightly higher pitch than usual.

"Yes, the binoculars you told me you were bringing after you somehow managed to misplace mine last night, despite the two of us sitting in a closed van with nowhere for them to go."

Toby swallowed hard. "Uhm, sorry, they're still in my car," he revealed.

"You mean your car that's currently parked up outside of our office?" said Quinn. "Miles away from here? *That* car?"

"The zoom on my phone is pretty impressive," Toby offered as an alternative. "Here, I've got it," he said, snapping a few shots of the approaching articulated lorry while securing the doughnut he'd just taken between his teeth.

"Fine. Just keep taking pictures," Quinn suggested, making a mental note to purchase a replacement pair of binoculars for herself. "This doesn't feel right," she added a few moments later. "Something's fishy here. For every other delivery we've observed, there's only been one lorry, correct?"

"Correct."

"So why is there a second one on the scene tonight?"

Toby shrugged. "A double order, maybe?"

The pair of them continued their surveillance operation with an inkling that tonight could be the night they'd been anxiously waiting for. Over the next half hour or so, they saw a flurry of movement and heard the characteristic *beep-beep-beep* of several forklift trucks kept busy transferring a large supply of shrink-wrapped pallets from the warehouse dispatch bay and loading them into the belly of the waiting lorries.

"Should I put our police contact on standby?" Toby asked, still snapping evidential pictures with his mobile phone.

Quinn paused for a moment, giving the suggestion a brief bit of thought. "Hmm," she offered, reflecting on the various potential outcomes of doing so. "I suppose we don't want the cavalry arriving if we're not certain anything is happening."

"I could just send them a quick text instead. Tell them there's movement and be prepared to round up the troops if required?"

"Good idea," Quinn said, reaching for the door handle.

"Where are you going?" Toby said in a whisper, even though nobody outside the van could possibly hear him, even had there been anyone about. "Quinn? What the hell are—"

"I'm just going to stretch my legs," she advised. "If I'm spotted, I'll just say I'm out for a jog after dinner to burn off some calories," she added with a wink, climbing out of the van. "Make sure you stay here, yeah? So you can call it in if need be."

"But you're wearing a skirt, and Doc Martens boots," Toby pointed out to the slamming door. "Ladies don't usually go running at night in a skirt and Doc Martens," he said to himself, on account of now being alone in the van. "Quinn!" he shouted in a loud whisper, as loud as any surveillance operative on an active mission might be permitted. But it was too late, as she was already gone by now, making her way towards the knicker factory.

With most of the workers now likely at home at this point in the evening and enjoying the start of their weekend on a Friday night, the industrial estate was relatively quiet apart from the activity at the knicker factory's loading dock. Indeed, all Quinn could mostly hear at present was the rhythmic pounding of her pulse in her ears and the dull thud of her boots each time they made contact with the tarmac.

"Have a look, see what's going on, and get out again," Quinn told herself, progressing up the side of the road nearest to the factory. There appeared to be a lull in the proceedings just now, Quinn noticed, with the forklift drivers on their tea break if the lack of activity was anything to go by. Or maybe they were simply finished by now, she wasn't sure which.

Quinn came to a temporary halt, resting her hand against a lamppost while she stretched out her hamstrings and quads to cement the illusion of being a jogger engaging in some evening exercise. However, all she could really see from her present vantage point was the front of the two lorries, which didn't offer too much assistance to their ongoing investigation. Quinn knew she needed to be nearer the business end of the operation, and that involved her being up close and personal to the loading dock.

Following a bit of running in place, a series of awkward star jumps, and then a set of further stretches, Quinn wandered casually across the road towards the parked-up vehicles, as if she were just cooling down now from her exercise routine. And even though she couldn't possibly hear Toby from where she presently was, she could see him, in her mind's eye, yelling at her to *"not be so bloody stupid."* Still, she pressed on. "Oh, bugger," she muttered to herself, upon realising she'd left her mobile phone in the van. No matter, because she knew Toby would be poised and ready to make a call to their reinforcements if anything should happen.

Quinn pressed her shoulder's back, projecting a sort of confident nonchalance, as if it were not at all unusual or in any way out of the ordinary for her to be currently strolling around where she decided to be currently strolling around—a tactic she found often worked well on previous investigations. Fortunately, as she soon discovered, though, the area was clear of people, and if the well-stuffed lorries were anything to go by, the packing-up job was nearing completion.

"Hmm, strange," Quinn said, having first peered through a narrow gap into the trailer of one lorry, and then the other one parked up a short distance away. And her confusion came about as one trailer was crammed with shrink-wrapped pallets, each comprised of dozens of carefully stacked boxes displaying the manufacturer's logo (the company name in bold, above a stylised image of lacy knickers).

The second trailer, however, contained a collection of loose, individual boxes that appeared to have been thrown in with far less care and consideration. Curious at this, Quinn checked that the area was still clear and, with as much dignity and modesty as she could muster wearing a shortish skirt, climbed up and into the back of this second trailer, at which point she crouched down beside the nearest box. She then rummaged for her Swiss Army knife stashed inside her bra (uncomfortable, perhaps, but practical), using the blade of the knife to cut into the sealing tape securing the carton shut.

"What on earth...?" she mumbled to herself once she'd benefitted from a glance inside the box, a box which most certainly did not contain knickers, as she could now clearly see. But before she could explore further, Quinn heard the sound of approaching footsteps. Heart racing, she closed over the cardboard flaps, jumped to her feet, and took up a position of cover behind a pile of boxes in a far corner of the trailer. The footsteps halted, and Quinn held her breath. A second or two later, a head popped into view at the end of the lorry.

"Toby? Is that you...?" Quinn whispered, with his face barely just recognisable in the darkness.

"Oi, you scared the living daylights out of me when you disappeared for so long!" Toby said. "I couldn't see where you'd gone and thought you'd been bloody kidnapped or something!"

"Well you scared the daylights out of *me*, when you appeared from nowhere just now!" Quinn countered. "I thought someone that worked here had found me!"

Toby looked over his shoulder for a tick. "Come on," he said. "The coast is still clear."

"Help me down?" Quinn asked, after walking to the back of the trailer and wriggling between the narrow gap between the end of the lorry and the padded frame of the loading dock's bay door. With Toby's assistance she leapt to the ground, her boots making a satisfying thump when they once again made contact with the tarmac.

"I think this second lorry is a dummy of some sort," Quinn said, starting to fill Toby in on her findings. But then, and taking Toby entirely off-guard, "Kiss me!" Quinn suddenly demanded, puckering up and swiftly leaning in.

"Kiss you...?" Toby replied, wondering if he must've misheard her, as the two of them were friendly of course, but definitely never had that sort of relationship. "Did you bump yourself on the head while you were in the back of that trailer...?"

But before he could find out the answer, Toby found himself in the middle of a passionate embrace outside an undergarment factory, as Quinn had pulled him in close and locked their lips together, along with the quick, whispered instruction to him to "just play along."

However, their unexpected smooch was soon interrupted by a burly security guard with a shaven head and not too much of a neck to speak of, appearing close to their position outside of the loading dock. "What are you two doing back here?" he growled, walking towards them at pace and armed with a fierce look that would turn milk sour.

Quinn removed her lips from Toby's. "Oh! Bloody Nora!" she said with a laugh, attempting to make light of the situation for the guard's unique benefit. "I thought you were my husband for a moment!" she lied.

"You shouldn't be here," the security guard answered, waving his torch at them menacingly. "I asked, what are the pair of you doing skulking around back here?" he demanded, now joined by two more equally intimidating colleagues.

"Oh, we *shouldn't* be here...?" Quinn offered, trying to sound as innocent, and as ignorant of the stated prohibition, as possible. "Sorry about that, we didn't realise," she added, taking Toby by the hand and attempting to lead him away from the factory. "In that case, we'll just get out of your hair, yes?" she promised, which was perhaps ironic considering the three security guards didn't have even a single follicle between them on their scalps.

"I said what are you doing back here?!" the fierce-looking chap demanded again, moving around to block their escape route.

"What, here? You mean *here*, here...?" Quinn said, trying to buy some additional thinking time to work out what she was going to say, exactly. She then looked over her shoulder conspiratorially, as if she were making certain they'd be able to speak in confidence. "Well, you see..." she whispered, offering another quick glance over her shoulder for good measure. "Me and my friend," she indicated, nodding at Toby. "You see, me and my friend both work together on the other side of the estate. Unfortunately, so does my *husband*, if you catch my drift...?"

It took a second or two, but the security guard gave them a cockeyed grin as he eventually caught on to Quinn's meaning. "Ah, out for a romantic stroll together, are we?" he said, flapping his eyebrows. "Far away from the husband's prying eyes?"

"Yes, that's it exactly," Quinn responded. "So if you should ever happen to see me with my husband," she added, tapping the side of her nose. "Then mum's the word, yeah?"

"You can trust us," the burly chap said, stepping to one side to allow the pair of them to be on their way. "After all, who are we to stand in the way of true love?"

However, one of the fellow's more recently arrived colleagues didn't appear quite so satisfied with the alibi that was provided. "Alright, if all that's true..." he said, expanding his body mass like an agitated pufferfish. "Then tell me which factory you two and your husband all work at."

Quinn stared back, beginning to feel her mouth dry out with her jaw being held open. "Pardon me?" she said, hoping to buy a smidge more time so she could try and formulate some kind of convincing response.

"Listen, luv. It's not a difficult question. If you work around here, as you say, then tell me the name of the company you work for," he said sternly.

Quinn's mind went horrifyingly blank. They'd been parked up near the industrial estate for days on end, ostensibly observing, and yet she couldn't think of one single business other than the knicker factory. "Erm..." she offered as a placeholder. And then, momentarily, "Firstly, I don't like your aggressive tone, young man," she scolded him, figuring attack to be the best form of defence (along with a bit of flattery mixed in as well by calling him "young," even though he wasn't, especially). "And, secondly, if you must know, we both work at Topham's Tile Factory. Over there..." she said, waving vaguely to the indeterminate vicinity, slightly off in the distance somewhere, the precise location not in any way clear. "It's next to the stationery wholesalers and behind the plumbing outlet store," she insisted, trying her utmost to sound convincing, even though everything she uttered was a complete fabrication in all respects.

The three guards looked at each other. "Okay, fine. But you can't be back here," the meathead who'd posed the question said, without a flicker of emotion. "So, on your way," he instructed.

Quinn didn't need asking twice, tugging her partner Toby's hand and leading him away until they were well clear. "Don't look back," she advised through the corner of her mouth, picking up the pace but not so much as to make it obvious that they were frantically trying to make good their escape.

Taking ragged breaths and on the verge of hyperventilating, Toby did as he was asked. "I should have taken a pair of knickers from the back of that lorry," he said, resisting the urge to break into a full-on sprint. "They may not be my style at all, but after that unpleasant encounter I'm pretty sure I now need to change my underpants."

"Just keep smiling and walking," Quinn said calmly. "Keep on walking before the three stooges back there realise there's no such business called Toppingham Tiles, or whatever fake name I came up with just then."

Quinn and Toby eventually returned to their van via the long route, taking several detours through the vast industrial estate, keen to ensure they weren't being observed or followed. Which, fortunately, they didn't appear to be.

"Sheesh, that was a close call," Quinn remarked, once sitting safely back in their dirty, slightly squalid surveillance vehicle.

"I take my hat off to you," Toby remarked, doing exactly that with his baseball cap. "The old fake kiss routine worked a treat," he said, impressed with his partner's improvisation skills under pressure. "And coming up with those fictional business names," he added, shaking his head in amazement. "Where any of them actually real?"

"Nope. I made them all up," his partner replied with a laugh.

"Quinn, you really are as good as everyone says you are," Toby offered.

"Oh? Like who?" Quinn replied.

"Well, mostly me right now. But others also, before," Toby said.

"Well, if you're impressed now, I can go one better."

"You can? How?"

"I know what that gang of knicker thieves are up to," Quinn advised.

Toby returned his hat to his head. "I'm all ears," he said, encouraging further explanation.

"It's the old double bubble deception," Quinn explained. "It's something I've seen probably dozens of times down the years, and I was certain of it the moment I clapped eyes on the identical lorries each displaying the same number plate. You've heard of this scam?"

"What? Yes, yes of course. The old double bubble!" Toby immediately replied, doing his best to sound convincing. "But if you could maybe just refresh my—"

"The company packed up two lorry loads, yeah?" Quinn began. "One lorry is full of the genuine article. Knickers, in this particular case. And the other lorry has just a bunch of empty cardboard boxes inside."

"Okay, so how does that work? Because it's been a while..."

"Well, conveniently placed CCTV in the loading area records the valuable cargo being moved out of the warehouse and then loaded onto a lorry for subsequent delivery. Then, at some point down the road, the lorry is broken into while en route to its destination. That usually happens in a motorway refuelling station or some similar area where, again, there's plenty of CCTV to capture the action and back up the fraudulent insurance claim. All with the crucial time stamps on the footage to substantiate the timeline of events."

Toby nodded, slowly putting the pieces of the jigsaw together. "And I imagine the one that looks as if it's being burgled is the one that's actually got the empty boxes in it rather than the one filled with the valuable cargo?"

"Yep. Just a bunch of dummy boxes being cracked open and tossed about, all made to look as if there was something in them when there wasn't," Quinn replied. "But there's nothing but air inside them. Which is what I discovered when I snuck into the rear of that lorry back there, just before you found me inside."

"I see," said Toby.

"And meanwhile, the genuine load is diverted to some type of storage facility somewhere off the beaten path, maybe out in the countryside, so there won't be any CCTV cameras about, where it'll sit and wait for things to settle down before being sold on again. It's quite a clever scam when you think about it. And the police never smell a rat because they would have watched the CCTV footage each time, showing a lorry load of knickers being loaded up and sent off, all with the correct paperwork and time stamps, only to be robbed by a ruthless gang of masked thieves a short while later. Albeit, a gang of thieves who were essentially paid actors, not actually stealing anything, and giving the lorry driver a few lumps on occasion only to make things look properly authentic."

"So the company gets a big insurance claim paid out and still maintains possession of their merchandise to sell on at some point a bit further down the line…?" Toby marvelled, sounding very much like this was the first time he'd actually been made aware of this form of scam. "Erm," he then added, hastily shifting gears. "I mean, of course that's how I might explain the double bubble as well, if somebody were to ask. You know, if they'd never heard about it before," he said confidently, as if entirely familiar with this particular type of swindle the whole time. "So, what do we do next?" he asked.

"We wait to follow the lorry with the genuine load, and hopefully, discover the location of the company's hidden warehouse. And if we're really lucky, we might even locate and recover a portion of stock from the previous, false robberies, as some of that inventory might still be stashed there for safekeeping."

Toby liked this plan. "I'll text our police contact and tell them we might be calling for the cavalry shortly?"

"Splendid," Quinn said, staring intently at the knicker factory and praying to the insurance gods that their cover hadn't been blown. Because if it had, Quinn knew it was unlikely they'd get a second chance to capture the gang red-handed. "Oh, and for what it's worth, Toby," she added, "you're a bloody good kisser."

"Well, I didn't know what was happening there at first, but once I'm in character, I do give it my all," Toby replied happily, as he reached for his phone. And then, "Hang on," he said, a thought occurring to him if his puzzled expression was anything to go by. "There are two identical lorries with the same number plates.

A CASE OF MAJOR MURDER

Are we sure we know which one is which down there? What if we get the two mixed up?"

Quinn held up her Swiss Army knife. "X marks the spot," she declared with a wink.

"You scratched the bodywork of the one we need to follow?" Toby said, putting two and two together and getting what he was confident enough was four. "So, a case of blatant vandalism?" he asked with a laugh.

"Absolutely, my young padawan. Not an actual X, of course, as that would be far too obvious. But I scratched up the lorry's rear bumper pretty good, which could happen easily enough by accident in any number of ways. I wonder if they'll put in an insurance claim for it as well, once they finally notice it?"

Just then, Quinn's own phone, sitting in a cubby on the dashboard, started to ring. Initially, she ignored it. However, being on an active mission, it could easily be one of their team back at the office checking in. As such, and in case the lorries moved and they needed to make a sharp exit and pursue, Quinn went ahead and activated the mobile's speakerphone function.

"Yes, hello," Quinn said, her eyes still fixed on their target.

"Is this Quinn Flitcroft?" the caller asked in a serious tone.

"That depends," she replied cautiously, the voice unfamiliar to her. "Who's this?"

"This is the police calling."

Quinn was confused. "But you've not texted them already, have you...?" she said quietly over to Toby, receiving a firm shake of the head in response.

"How can I help?" Quinn asked of the caller, though not entirely convinced of their identity, as she was always sceptical in her line of work.

"Ms Flitcroft, this is PC Bennett and I'm calling from the Isle of Man Constabulary."

Quinn rolled her eyes, assuming this to be some sort of scam hoping to extort her credit card details or some such thing.

"That's where your dad lives," Toby reminded her.

"Oh. The Isle of Man. Okay," Quinn said to the caller. "And what is this about...?"

The caller went quiet for a moment. "Ms Flitcroft," they said a moment later. "I'm awfully sorry to have to deliver distressing news over the phone."

"Wait, is it my dad?" Quinn asked. "Are you calling about my dad? Please tell me you aren't!"

"Unfortunately, I am, Ms Flitcroft. I regret to advise you that there's been an incident."

Chapter Three

A friendly little bird swooped down onto the balcony of Quinn's fourth-floor flat, looking for its breakfast as it did most mornings for the past few months. Spotting its expected arrival from her kitchen window, Quinn stepped outside gingerly, with no sudden movements, so as not to startle the wee thing and possibly frighten it away.

"Three months we've been friends for, now, and I still don't know what make and model you are," she said softly, armed with a handful of birdseed. "Hang on, did I just say make and model? I meant *breed*," she added with a gentle laugh, correcting herself. "Sorry, I reckon I've spent too much time spying on vehicles and such. No offence there, buddy," she offered to the bird, who had now landed on her hand, pecking happily away and not appearing in any way fussed about how it was being referred to as long as its belly ended up full.

Currently living in the vibrant city centre of Manchester, with concrete towers in every direction, it was often easy at times to forget, occasionally, that a greener and altogether slower, more sedate world existed outside of this sprawling metropolis. Sure, it was exhilarating living in a bustling city, with all of the basic staples of life a single person might need so close at hand, with coffee shops wherever you looked and cuisine from every corner of the world only shouting distance away. And it was this general sort of existence that Quinn had enjoyed for nearly ten years. But she never really had an opportunity to call any particular place home, not for any great length of time, what with the transient nature of her job going wherever her employer required her to go at relatively short notice.

Of course, she could always complete a series of very lengthy daily commutes. But the thought of having to spend hour upon hour on the road each morning and evening didn't offer much appeal. Therefore, the option she chose was to move between a variety of cities in the UK and Ireland several times each year, resulting in yet another rented apartment each time.

Obviously, this lifestyle was not without its particular charms, always offering her exciting cities to explore, diverse cultures to embrace, and new friends she'd not yet met. Well, this is what Quinn told herself each time she received the call to pack up and head to the next destination. Sadly, the unfortunate truth of the matter was that she often didn't stay long enough in one place to even say hello to her neighbours and rarely had enough time to step out of her apartment to go and explore her new surroundings. At least not properly. It was tough at times, Quinn reflected, and even though she was compensated handsomely for this nomadic existence, having lots of money in the bank wasn't much use if you didn't have any time to really spend it.

Then, out of the blue, after flying solo for so long during her work, Quinn's employers decided it would be preferable for her to team up with another investigator, particularly on the more challenging cases involving unsavoury characters where being a lone female wasn't exactly ideal. (Not that Quinn couldn't handle herself, however, as she would happily wade into the middle of a Wild West barroom brawl, as she liked to imagine, and emerge, eventually, with nary a scratch or a hair out of place.)

So that's how, following an extensive and rigorous recruitment process, Toby Haddock found himself working alongside one of Great Britain's most tenacious, innovative, and successful insurance fraud investigators.

Quinn wouldn't mind admitting that she didn't take to him at first, finding his quirky, childlike enthusiasm frustrating at times—including his insistence on adopting silly disguises when on active duty, with a seemingly endless array of false beards and moustaches, prosthetic noses, and other such paraphernalia at his disposal. Still, there was no doubting his integrity and willingness to learn, which was evident in spades. And, as the weeks went by and they enjoyed a few positive results at work, Quinn started to value both his company and input. Although she'd still not forgiven him for turning up to a surveillance operation in the dead of night wearing a mask designed to make him appear like a very old senior citizen, frightening her half to death. *"It'll help me blend in,"* he'd insisted at the time. But, in truth, it made him look more like his face was melting, like something out of a horror film, rather than giving him the appearance of an older gentleman as intended.

Now, having been granted a leave of absence from her work following her recent phone call with the IOM Constabulary, it wasn't just her feathered friend she would miss when returning to the Isle of Man. She would also miss her newish colleague, the absolute goofball that was Toby Haddock.

Outside on the balcony of her soon-to-be-vacated flat, Quinn raised her hand closer to her face, with her bird friend still there in her palm. "I won't be here tomorrow, little fellow," she said regretfully, as the bird tilted its head and ruffled its feathers a bit, almost as if it was directly responding to what she was telling it. "It's not that I don't like you anymore, or anything like that," she promised her small companion. "It's just that I'll be going home for a while, you see. And by the time I come back, I'll probably take up residence in another city. But where I'm off to today isn't too terribly far away. Not if you've got a good tailwind. That is, if you want to come and visit me...?"

Quinn slowly turned, trying to figure out in which direction home was, exactly. "I think it's over that way," she said, pointing with her free hand to a spot somewhere in the distance. "If you're unsure where you're going," she added helpfully, as she mapped the journey out in her head. "Just head over to Liverpool, and you can follow the Isle of Man ferry from there across the Irish Sea, yeah? I'm sure they wouldn't mind if you even landed on deck and hitched a ride. That way, if you wanted, you could give your little wings a rest during the crossing."

Just then, a voice could be heard calling from inside of the apartment, alarming the bird and causing it suddenly to take flight. "Knock, knock!" the visitor had just announced. "The door was unlocked, so I let myself in," they announced further.

It was Toby.

"Hiya. I'm out here on the balcony," Quinn answered.

"Morning, partner," Toby said brightly, offering one of the two takeaway coffee cups he was carrying with him. "You okay?"

"Just saying goodbye to someone," Quinn replied, accepting the coffee as she watched her avian friend rise up towards a particular section of grey in the murky, overcast sky. She then adjusted her gaze, peering down on the hordes of office workers scurrying to their various places of employment below. "I think I'll miss this view," she confessed.

"But not the traffic noise, surely?"

"That I won't miss," Quinn had to admit. "And don't call me Shirley!" she quipped, to which Toby allowed a bit of a chuckle to escape. "And thanks for this," Quinn added, raising her cup in salute and then taking a sip of her coffee.

"Not a problem," Toby replied. "Right, so I've already looked online and your flight's running to schedule," he added, before examining his watch to check the present time. "By my reckoning, if we're on the road within the next twenty minutes or so, you'll be at the airport in good readiness."

"What am I ever going to do without you?" Quinn responded, smiling fondly. "And you promise you'll keep me updated with the ongoing cases, as well as what weird and whacky disguises you're deploying?"

"Weird and whacky...?" Toby said, placing a hand against his cheek in feigned offence. "I'll have you know my disguises are of the highest quality," he insisted.

"Oh, I'm quite sure," Quinn said, with a kind of amused scepticism. "Anyway, have you heard any updates from the police about our 'Operation Knickers' stakeout?" she asked, offering up a sleepy yawn. "What was the aftermath?"

"A handful of men in custody now, from what I've been told," Toby advised. "And a good chunk of the missing stock recovered, with our help of course. Also, the police tailed the second lorry carrying only the empty boxes. Apparently, it pulled over into a service station near Stockport, and that's when the staged robbery commenced for the special benefit of the onsite CCTV cameras. There were two masked raiders who broke into the rear of the lorry, making it look as if they were helping themselves to its contents, while the driver was very conveniently inside enjoying a fry-up. The police were suitably impressed with their acting skills, even thinking of nominating them all for Oscars."

"You must give the company full marks for ingenuity," Quinn commented, along with a wry smile. "But why don't these types of people ever think about possibly quitting while they're ahead? Because now, since they've been too greedy, they'll need to pay back all of the previous insurance claims they'd taken advantage of, *and* face a lengthy stretch of time behind bars on top of it."

"My heart bleeds for them. A real tragedy," Toby said, rubbing his thumb and forefinger together in order to play the world's smallest violin. "Anyway, about your dad," he then said, moving the discussion away from matters of fraud and onto events more personal. "Do we actually know what happened...?" he asked, his tone one of genuine compassion now.

"All they can tell me at this stage is that it was an accident," Quinn said, holding her coffee cup to her lips, without drinking, as she looked off into the distance. "An awful accident."

"But how, exactly? Do they not have any sort of inkling?"

"The police constable did suggest it might have something to do with him being a nosey old bugger," Quinn answered, allowing herself a little half-laugh as she said it, despite the present situation they were discussing.

"What? How so?"

"Well, there was a major incident declared at Port Erin Beach last night, according to the officer I talked to. Helicopters, sirens, coastguard, and nearly the entire Isle of Man police force were in attendance. And the officer wondered if my father might have been distracted by all the commotion going on outdoors."

"You mean they think he might've been having a bloody good nosey and not looking where he was going?" Toby ventured, with a kind-hearted smile.

"Right. And it wouldn't surprise me," Quinn replied, shaking her head in a mixture of affection, amusement, and plenty of concern added in. "My dad's the chairman of the neighbourhood watch committee," she explained. "So, he'll likely claim he was carrying out his civic duty as a diligent member of the community, rather than a curtain twitcher simply heading to the window to catch a glimpse of what the fuss was outside."

"Ah, so that's where you get your inquisitive nature from, eh?" Toby suggested. And then, "Oh! If your father ever needs to use a disguise during his neighbourhood-watching duties, well, I'm your man," Toby said, pressing an assured thumb into his chest.

Quinn rolled her eyes. "I'll be sure to send him your way," she said with a smirk.

"All joking aside," Toby added. "The old man's going to make a full recovery, I very much hope...?"

"It's still early days, and he's still heavily sedated. But the medical staff sounded confident when I'd spoken with them," Quinn advised, suddenly fighting back the tears. "But the injury list, as far as they've been able to assess so far, consists of a nasty bump on the head, a broken left arm, and a damaged hip from his fall down the stairs," she said, wiping a tear away now that was making its way down her cheek. "I just dread to think what could have happened if he didn't have his mobile with him to phone the ambulance before he lost consciousness. He could have been lying at the foot of his stairs for hours, or even days."

"From what you've told me, your father sounds like a fighter. I reckon he'll be up and running around Port Erin again, helping to preserve law and order, in no time at all," Toby said cheerily, hoping to raise Quinn's spirits. "Oh, hey, so did you hear what the major incident was all about last night?" he added, giving the impression, by the sound of it, that he may have some important information to impart if Quinn wasn't already aware of it.

"Go on..." Quinn answered, nodding for him to continue.

Toby offered his most sinister-looking of expressions. Which, truth be told, appeared more as if he simply had a case of trapped wind, really.

"There's... been... a *murder*...!" he revealed, saying it slowly, to build the tension, with only a crack of thunder missing at the end to enhance his dramatic delivery.

"Oh...? Oh, I see," Quinn answered, not sounding in any way convinced.

Quinn then headed into her flat, standing herself in front of her hallway mirror, deciding she best start making herself look presentable before departing for the airport. "If you say so," she told Toby, who had followed her inside. She wasn't persuaded by what he'd said to her, assuming it to be some kind of joke—a joke she didn't have an awful lot of time for at the moment.

"You've not seen the news?" Toby asked, slightly offended that this revelation he'd imparted relative to her isle of birth hadn't received the shock and awe he was expecting.

But Quinn wasn't paying too much attention to him, as she'd set down her coffee cup and was focussing more on the crow's feet around her tired eyes that required a little bit of extra assistance from her makeup bag.

"I'm deadly serious," Toby assured her, trying to get her to believe he was telling the truth. "Honestly!"

"Toby, as much as I love you, which I do, I need to try and work wonders on my face," she said, while looking at her reflection in the mirror. "And I've only got so many available minutes left to do it in. So..."

Quinn knew what he was saying must be rubbish. Yes, something big, something troubling, had occurred over there on the isle. But murder...? *Obviously* not. That kind of thing just didn't happen on the Isle of Man. Not ever.

"Right. I'll show you," Toby said, delving into his pocket to retrieve his phone, before furiously tapping away on it. "There!" he said a moment later, attempting to show her the news headlines and accompanying images now displayed on the screen.

Quinn offered him only a sideways glance. "Toby, I'm not sure what you're—"

"Look!" Toby insisted, waving his phone around in circles, in front of her eyeballs.

Quinn did as instructed, as she had little choice at this point. Plus, she figured it'd be the quickest method of reaching the impending punchline of Toby's joke, in order to finally get it out of the way. She thus allowed her eyes to fall upon the phone's display, where she was greeted by an image of a large white tent erected on a beach. "Why are you showing me a photograph of a campsite...?" she asked, even more confused now than before.

"It's not a campsite, it's a police forensic tent," Toby informed her. "Look at the headline and read the article," he suggested.

Quinn used the tip of her finger to pinpoint the link, opening up the article in question. And there, accompanying the image of the forensic "camping" tent, the horrific and disturbing headline was more obvious now:

Police confirm a murder investigation is underway after a man's body was discovered in Port Erin, on the Isle of Man

"Holy macaroni," said Quinn, once she'd finished scrolling through the article. "It's no wonder my dad was scrambling to get a better view, if he had a ringside seat to all of that."

"I know," Toby said, retrieving his phone and popping it back into his pocket, mission accomplished. "And I bet you can't wait to get your magnifying glass out for this one, am I right?" he joked, although not without some degree of seriousness attached.

"It's been years since I was a police officer on the Isle of Man before trading in my hat for my present work," Quinn reminded him, returning her attention to her liberal application of foundation. "The police are more than capable without little old me sticking her beak into their investigation," she insisted. "No, my priority is to make sure my dad is well looked after and up on his feet as soon as possible, that's all."

"And you won't stick your investigative beak in just a teensy little bit...?" Toby teased.

"Nope, not even the least little bit," Quinn declared. "Now, if you're looking for something to do, can you double-check that I've emptied everything out of the kitchen cupboards while I turn myself into an exotic glamour puss? That would be most helpful."

A CASE OF MAJOR MURDER

***

Quinn peered through the rounded window the moment the plane descended clear of the dense cloud cover, tipping its wing for a moment before it straightened itself up ahead of the final approach into the island's Ronaldsway Airport. And there it was, her first glimpse of home in quite a good while. Enjoying a bird's eye view, Quinn offered a contented sigh, drinking in the vision of undulating fields below, a medley of vivid greenery in various, alternating hues, interspersed with large swathes of lovely yellow as well from a farmer's impressive crop of rapeseed. And for the next couple of minutes, as she waited for the plane's wheels to make contact with the runway, she tried to remember the last time she'd returned to the island.

It'd been three years since her mum sadly passed, but had she been over to the island since? she wondered, frustrated that she couldn't immediatcly recall for some odd reason. "Ah! Of course!" she said aloud, waking up the middle-aged businessman seated next to her as she did so. She smiled to herself, happy to finally recollect that she'd flown over for her dad's birthday the previous year, albeit staying only briefly, flying in and out the same day. She was a trained investigator, after all, so she ought to be able to remember such details.

It wasn't that she wasn't close to her dad. In fact, nothing could be further from the truth, as she adored him. And rarely a day went by that she wasn't on the phone with him to have a bit of a chin wag and see how he was doing. Further, the island she knew as home was, to her, simply paradise. But try as she might, and she often did, Quinn just couldn't forgive those people from ten years prior who were *supposed* to be her friends, but who had let her down so badly when she'd needed their support the most. Other friends at the time suggested to Quinn that upping sticks and leaving the isle, as she had ultimately done, would simply be cutting her nose off to spite her face, as it were.

She knew, both then and now, that this advice was probably correct. But that distressing period in her life left a bitter taste in her mouth that would still take some time to recede. However, with all that said, it was the fact that she could no longer see her dad every day, in person, which bothered her the most.

Once safely on the ground and her luggage collected from the baggage carousel, Quinn jumped straight into a taxi, her next stop being Nobles Hospital located in Douglas, the isle's capital, which only took about fifteen minutes or so to reach.

"Good afternoon," Quinn whispered on arrival at the Ward Six reception desk, not wishing to disturb any of the residents who might be convalescing nearby or otherwise trying to rest.

"Can I help?" a nurse with a pleasant, gentle expression asked, looking up from her stack of paperwork.

"I'm here to see my dad who was admitted last night?" Quinn answered. "His name is Chester. Chester Flitcroft."

Quinn held her breath as a wave of anxiety surged through her body. She scanned the nurse's face, dreading that she might see the genial smile give way to a compassionate tilt of the head preceding the start of a potentially difficult conversation.

"I see," the nurse said, lowering her pen. "And are you a family member?"

"I'm his daughter, Quinn."

Then, to Quinn's immense relief, the nurse offered a beaming smile. Something, Quinn reckoned, medical staff didn't ordinarily do if they were about to deliver devastating news.

"I'll show you through," the nurse offered, while pushing back her chair. "Now, I must tell you your dad is a little bit bruised, and he's been hooked up to a monitor," the nurse cautioned, once she had emerged from behind her desk. "So, I don't want you to get too much of a shock when you first see him."

"Is he awake?" Quinn asked, grateful for the warning.

"Yes, but he's still very drowsy. So don't be upset if you aren't able to get an awful lot of conversation out of him at this point," the nurse kindly advised, escorting Quinn the short distance to her father's private room. "Can I just tell you..." the nurse added, once outside the door. "Nearly everybody on the medical staff is immensely fond of your dad, Quinn."

"You know him from The Bucket 'n' Spade?" Quinn presumed, that being the case with many of the island's residents.

The nurse nodded. "Oh, absolutely. Many of us have been enjoying his ice creams and charming personality since we were young ones," she said warmly. "He's a wonderful man, and just know he really is receiving the very best attention possible," she added, taking hold of the door handle.

Quinn felt herself welling up. "Thank you. Thank you so very much for saying that."

"Right, then, Mr Flitcroft," the nurse said, as she eased open the sturdy wooden door. "Look who's here to see you."

Even though the sight of her father lying there bashed and bruised was harrowing, Quinn adopted her most sunniest of dispositions, sitting beside him for the entire afternoon and most of the evening, talking to him even though he probably couldn't hear what she was prattling on about. Stroking the back of his hand, she told him all about her latest adventures in cracking insurance fraud cases across the UK, including about her newest work partner Toby and providing an in-depth analysis of their recent OPERATION MISSING KNICKERS.

And funnily enough, it was during this talk of knickers that Chester peeled open one eye, and then, a moment later, the other one followed suit.

Quinn leaned forward, unsure if she should call for someone or not. "Oh, so I start to talk about women's knickers and that's when you decide to wake up, eh?" she joked, overjoyed to see him conscious and looking quizzically around the room.

"Quinn?" he said with a dry, gravelly voice.

"Yes, I'm here, Dad."

Chester groaned in pain, looking down at the plaster cast on his left arm. "What am I doing here?" he asked, his heavy, drowsy eyelids in danger of closing over again.

Quinn pressed the button to call the medical staff. "You're in the hospital, Dad," she told him. "You had a bit of a tumble down the stairs, remember? But don't worry, okay? The team are doing an amazing job in looking after you."

Chester wrinkled his brow, looking straight ahead, down towards the foot of his hospital bed. He appeared to Quinn like he was perhaps hearing her words but not really registering them.

Concerned, she pressed the call button again. "Dad," she said gently. "Dad, you had a nasty fall, but you still managed to phone the ambulance. Do you remember...?" she asked, concerned that his injuries might extend beyond those that were clearly visible.

Gradually, her father turned his head, until suddenly his eyes directly met hers, locking into place.

"Oh, I remember, all right," Chester said, just as the nurse, responding to the call button, was rushing in. "But you're wrong, Quinn. I didn't *fall* down those stairs, honey... I was *pushed*."

Chapter Four

For Quinn, one of the many pitfalls of living a hectic life, flitting from one city to the next in performing her particular job, was the distinct lack of any sort of regular routine. It wasn't that Quinn was complaining, necessarily, as she liked her job. But she'd noticed that her oft frenzied and chaotic lifestyle—often eating on the hoof, and not being able to choose the healthiest of meal options while engaged on a stakeout, for instance—was beginning to catch up with her. Because trousers that were previously a comfortable fit were now a little bit too snug and in real danger of cutting off her circulation.

As such, with a comfortable place to finally settle into for a while—a familiar 'home base,' as it were—and a daily routine that was far less constantly in flux, Quinn decided that now was the ideal opportunity to part ways with her uninvited excess weight and also give her old running gear an outing for the first time in years. First up, she needed to rummage through several boxes of personal possessions that were kept at her dad's when she'd originally moved away for new adventures in England.

Having eventually located her old running shorts and top, she offered them a cautious sniff. "Not too bad," she remarked, impressed by the absence of any noticeable musty aroma considering that they'd been shoved in a box for about a decade. "But the rest of you are going straight into the washing machine when I return from my run," she said, addressing the pile of her other recovered clothes now lying in a crumpled heap on the floor.

Soon dressed and ready for action, Quinn first checked her phone instinctively, almost as if she were looking for any sort of distraction to further postpone the start of 'OPERATION GET FIT.' Spotting the notification for an unread message on the screen, she couldn't help but smile as she took note of the sender's name. "Toby," she said fondly, unlocking her phone to read the details:

> Presently on my way to investigate machinery theft at a sewerage works in Blackpool! Then it's a case of fly-tipping! Enjoy your new life by the seaside, you wretched hag... ☺xxx

Quinn chuckled away, typing her reply:

> And who says the life of an insurance investigator isn't full of glitz and glamour? Just take care where you step. Anyway can't talk now, there's a beach chair currently waiting with my name on it ☺xx

Of course Quinn was only teasing, swapping banter with her work chum, because it was still before seven o'clock in the morning and likely still a couple of hours before the first of the beach chairs would be unfolded and laid out onto the golden sands. So, a perfect time to go for a run, she reckoned. Not only because it would still be fairly cool outside, but also the fact that there'd hopefully be nobody around to see her start puffing like a steam train after only a hundred yards or so. An outcome she believed to be a distinct possibility considering her lack of any kind of proper physical exercise to speak of lately.

Quinn stretched out her various leg muscles while walking through the living room of her dad's decent-sized flat, stopping briefly to admire the view from the living room window as she'd done countless times over the years when she was a little bit younger. Positioned directly above the ice cream shop, the flat boasted a sweeping panoramic view of the entire bay, with the view also encompassing the rugged, rising promontory that is Bradda Head, where the iconic Milner's Tower—a sturdy, stone spire memorial constructed in the late 1800s—overlooked the seaside village like a proud custodian.

In imminent danger of putting the kettle on and unfastening her trainers, Quinn dragged herself away before she talked herself out of a run. "Lingering at the window isn't going to get you back in shape, Quinn Flitcroft!"

The living accommodation, separated from the popular ice cream shop below, was accessible via a private doorway at street level, inside of which introduced a steep staircase providing admission to the upstairs flat. And it was standing at the very top of these stairs, looking down them now, that Quinn felt a wave of anxiety surge through her body again. Because this would've been the exact spot her father was standing just before being shoved down them with such a horrendous lack of regard for what was certain to be the terrible and obvious result. And from where her feet were presently placed, it was an awfully long way to the bottom.

Furthermore, while her father's injuries were extensive, Quinn couldn't help but see, considering the distance he'd fallen, that they could have quite easily been exponentially worse. And what made it even more frustrating for her was the fact that the police still had no idea who might have pushed him, or for that matter *why*. At this stage, all they did know for certain was that the tumble occurred shortly before nine-thirty in the evening—the time her dad had managed to phone himself an ambulance—and that there were no obvious signs of a forced entry into the flat.

With nothing concrete to go on, the authorities were working on the theory that Chester's assault was somehow linked to the awful tragedy on the nearby beach, as the timing of the two incidents, as well as the physical proximity, could hardly be a coincidence. So far, the deceased party remained unnamed to the public, and with little information available for the authorities to release just yet, it was no surprise that both the residents of Port Erin and the island's wider population were on tenterhooks about such a heinous affair in what was ordinarily a tranquil community with hardly any crime to speak of, and certainly no violent crime. The only consolation at this challenging time, if anyone should be searching for one, was that a single murder could have very easily been two and yet very gratefully wasn't.

Fortunately, by now, the elder Flitcroft, being such an affable, amiable character, was busy charming the pants off the medical staff at Nobles Hospital after several days of recovery, with his discharge scheduled for the following morning. Of course Quinn was delighted about the prospect of having her dad back home. However, she now had to figure out how to get him comfortably up and down a steep staircase—no easy feat for a man who'd be in a wheelchair for the next few weeks. But with plenty of offers of assistance already received from friends and other assorted well-wishers, she knew there'd likely be plenty of help available to lug him up the stairs when needed.

Back where 'Operation Get Fit' was concerned, Quinn had ultimately overcome her various distractions and finally managed to drag herself out of doors into the fresh air. When performing a series of deep lunges on the promenade walkway, Quinn would have looked to all the world like an experienced athlete warming up before a vigorous bit of training. That belief, however, would have been shattered little more than thirty seconds later as she stood hunched over, gasping for air, using her hands to brace herself against the back of a bench for dear life.

"Oh... my... god...!" she said between ragged breaths, her cheeks already turning an exerted shade of crimson. Thankfully, at this early hour, at least, there was nobody to bear witness to just how unhealthy big city life had made her. Or so she believed...

"Quinn...? Quinn Flitcroft, is that really you?" an upbeat voice could be heard from across the road, a short distance away.

Quinn groaned, not feeling exactly company-ready just now. She attempted to make her gasping-for-air posture appear like some form of purposeful endeavour by throwing in a few strategic leg raises. Then, with as much of a perky, energetic performance as she could muster, she straightened herself up, raising her hands skyward, arching her back, while tilting herself this way and that as she stretched—all in an effort to complete the illusion that this was some sort of intentional routine she'd been engaged in from the start.

"Quinn Flitcroft!" said that same voice, its owner sounding much closer now. "I *thought* that was you."

Quinn spun around to find the uniformed figure of her former police colleague, Megan Stonehouse, standing before her.

A CASE OF MAJOR MURDER

Megan extended both arms, using her tentacles to pull Quinn into a warm, squidgy embrace. "I'd heard you were back on the island!" she said enthusiastically, before releasing her grip. And then, "Oh, you look absolutely pooped, Quinn. There's even a vein throbbing on the side of your forehead," she remarked.

"Pooped? Ah, well I've just been for a... uhm... That is, I've just returned from a five-kilometre run..." Quinn replied with a very slight embellishment on the truth, as it had been merely thirty metres at best. "I see you've been promoted," Quinn then added, quickly steering the conversation away to something else as she noticed the three chevrons attached to Megan's epaulette.

"Yes, it's Sergeant Stonehouse now," Megan proudly advised, despite this being something Quinn had just commented on and could obviously very clearly see for herself.

An awkward silence ensued where the two of them grinned clumsily at each other. During her time working for the Isle of Man Constabulary in years gone by, Megan was just one of those people that Quinn could never take to, despite her best efforts. A rare occurrence, as Quinn tended to get on well with very nearly everyone she encountered. But Megan always reminded her of that snidey girl at school who'd keep stealing your favourite pen or something, and then make it sound like it was *your* fault when you eventually told the teacher.

With her being a talker by nature, Quinn wasn't too good with awkward silences, always feeling the overwhelming urge to fill the void. "Well, I'm sure the promotion is very well deserved," she said, opting to remain magnanimous. With little else she could think of to say, though, she started to turn away, thinking some form of exit might be in order.

Megan held out an arm, thus preventing Quinn's immediate escape, however. "Before you go, I just wanted to say how sorry I am about your dad," she said. "Rest assured that we're doing all we can to bring the perpetrator to justice at the earliest opportunity," she promised. "Hence, why we're out following up on enquiries at this time of the morning," she added, flashing a smile that seemed to be sincere and genuine.

"And the fact that you've got a crazed murderer on the loose?" Quinn asked bluntly.

"Rest assured we're leaving no stone unturned in that regard either," Megan promised again, just before her chest-mounted radio crackled to life. "Anyway, I'll leave you to warm down, as that vein in your forehead still looks like it's about to explode, Quinn. Oh, but before you go?"

"Yes? What is it now...?" Quinn asked, wondering why Megan wasn't answering her damned radio.

Megan tilted her head, giving the impression she was simply bursting with compassion for what she was about to say. "About that unfortunate incident when you—" she began.

"What, you mean the one that got me forced out of the job I adored?" Quinn cut in, smiling through the obvious annoyance. "What about it?"

"I was going to say that you were always an excellent police officer, Quinn," Megan answered. Though whether it was a comment delivered with any degree of real sincerity, Quinn couldn't say for sure.

"And what happened to you back then," Megan added. "Well, it was a mistake that any of us could have made."

"A *mistake?*" Quinn replied, resisting the urge to jab a serving police officer in the chest with the tip of her finger. "No, the only mistake I made was in trusting—"

But Megan had turned away, appearing slightly uninterested at the current moment in what Quinn was trying to say, as she was finally paying attention to her police walkie-talkie instead, listening to what was presently coming through over her radio's earpiece. "Sorry," she said, still somewhat distracted. "Duty calls and all that," she advised, while raising a hand to acknowledge the approaching police van now slowing to a crawl ahead. "And we simply must meet up for a coffee, yeah?" she added, glancing back over her shoulder at Quinn. "Oh, and you should go easy on the exercise. You look absolutely shattered."

Quinn took a sip from her water bottle, watching as Megan walked towards the waiting police van. "Yeah, I'll look forward to that coffee," Quinn called after her, offering a wave with next to no effort in it. "And make sure that van doesn't run over your feet, Stonehenge," Quinn advised, making sure to mutter this part under her breath, of course, only to herself. "Or better yet, Stoneshed, let's hope that it does."

On the basis that she was already self-conscious about exercising for the first time in close to a dozen years, Quinn didn't really relish the prospect of breaking into a jog with Megan still within potential viewing range. And as Megan was probably under the impression her morning jog had come to its conclusion anyway, Quinn saw no real reason to continue, instead conducting several neck rotations for appearance's sake—in case anyone might still be looking—and then strolling back towards her dad's flat, exercise over for the day. "Oh, we simply *must* meet up for a coffee, *yeah?*" she mocked, mimicking Megan's annoying voice. "Yeah, I don't flippin' think so, Stonebreath!"

Upon reaching and opening the front door, Quinn immediately realised she'd left it unlocked earlier. Probably not the best thing to do, she reckoned, considering there was still a murderer on the loose out there. Once inside, she looked up the steep stairs, giving some thought to sprinting up and down them a few times to at least register some meaningful activity on the Fitbit exercise tracker she'd just purchased for herself recently. She stood there wavering, however, as the sight of that stairway still made her fairly uneasy.

Before she could commit one way or the other, though, something shiny on the floor, down near her left foot, caught her eye. At first glance, she wondered if it might be a sequin, or perhaps, more likely, a small coin. But after crouching down and plucking the item from off of the small area rug at the base of the stairs, she soon realised it wasn't.

"Jiminy Cricket!" she exclaimed, while holding up what she'd retrieved and moving her face in for a closer inspection. Because there, pinched between her thumb and forefinger, was a small, shimmering diamond refracting the natural light streaming in through the panel of glass on the front door. How she'd managed to spot something so small nestled amidst the fibres of the rug was something of a miracle, but she was pleased that she had. It's not just that diamonds were valuable; it was also that it presented a mystery as to what it had been doing there, and Quinn liked mysteries. Was there an innocent, benign explanation for it being there? Or was it instead a clue of some sort?

Intrigued, Quinn revised her schedule for the rest of the early morning, spending the next hour or so on her hands and knees, picking through the carpet to see if her new discovery perhaps had any company.

***

With the ice cream shop currently down one key member of staff for the foreseeable, Quinn was on hand to not only take care of her dad when he returned home but to also pitch in behind the counter as and when needed. In her younger days, especially during school holidays, she was often found rocking her white apron and putting in a shift for some extra pocket money, so she knew the ropes. Of course it had been a fair few years since she'd wielded an ice cream scoop with purpose, but like riding a bike, there were some skills that do not diminish with the passage of time. At least that was the feeling on her part.

However, it was only a little over two hours into her first shift when Quinn was on the receiving end of her first complaint.

"But I thought you'd pointed to the tub of mint choc chip...?" a harassed Quinn asked, holding a freshly filled cone aloft with that flavour of ice cream inside of it.

Quinn's current customer, a teenage girl with an unpleasant disposition, folded her arms in protest. "No!" she said, scowling across the countertop. "No, I'd pointed to the one *beside* it," she insisted. "*Obviously*. Butter pecan, yeah?"

The girl's dad shook his head in embarrassment and dismay. "I'm sorry about her attitude," he said on his daughter's behalf. "She's been in a stinking mood since we told her we're all going hiking this afternoon."

Quinn waved away his concerns. "No apology necessary. It was entirely my fault, and I'll have one butter pecan ice cream ready in just a tick," she promised, overlooking the teenage girl's surly manner in favour of the more gracious, 'customer is always right' type of approach.

In response to this unlucky faux pas on Quinn's part, Doreen, silver-haired deputy shop manager extraordinaire, offered her a friendly tut-tut. "The first error of the day and it just so happens to be your favourite variety...?" she remarked with a chuckle, as she attended to her own customer. "My, what are the chances. I assume mint choc chip is still your favourite?"

Quinn couldn't deny it. "Yup, still my favourite. And of course you're right, it would be a shame to see it go to waste..."

Doreen was in complete agreement if her eager nod was any measure. "Oh, it would. Although, I'm not sure if that new fitness regime you mentioned could cope with too many similar such mistakes."

As there were only a couple of customers remaining in the queue, with Doreen assuring Quinn that she could take care of them, Quinn capitalised on the temporary lull to step outdoors and enjoy her serendipitous mistake. Once outside, a warm and gentle breeze ruffled her fringe. She smiled as she tucked into her cone, spotting two children on the beach opposite to her squealing in delight as their respective kites weaved erratically through the air, with the multi-coloured ribbon tails dancing behind in seeming hot pursuit. For Quinn, it was a happy scene that brought back fond, nostalgic memories of her own carefree summer holidays. A precious time when the only worries she could recall were about whether to spend her time on the beach, taking a dip in the clear blue sea, or exploring the various coves dotted around the rugged coastline. And despite being an only child she was never alone, for there was always a constant supply of visiting children, both local and tourists, with whom to while away the halcyon days.

Shifting herself back to the present, Quinn popped what remained of her cone into her mouth, turning her attention to the now infamous point a little further up the beach. With the macabre police forensic tent since removed, it was still difficult to comprehend the tragedy that had recently occurred in such close proximity to where so many families were now out on the sand enjoying the glorious weather.

From her current spot, at street level and positioned directly in front of the shop, it was difficult to see the precise area where the murder victim was discovered on account of the edge of the promenade—where the retaining sea wall drops down to beach level—presently obscuring her view. Curious, Quinn moved a few steps forward, turning to look up to the living room window of her dad's flat that she knew provided an unhindered view of the entire beach. She had to wonder, did he see something from up there that he wasn't supposed to...?

Of course Quinn had already spoken to her dad about the day of the murder at some length. But as he'd related to both her and the police, he couldn't recall seeing anything unusual on the day in question in the hours leading up to the body being discovered, other than the usual types of comings and goings one would typically expect to see on a popular beach.

Frustratingly, their shop's CCTV system—which might have provided vital clues, perhaps revealing something her dad had failed to notice—was, according to Doreen, damaged during a heavy storm a few years back. Because of the limited crime rate in the area, her father had apparently considered a replacement system a nonessential expense. While it was indeed true that her dad maintained a position on the neighbourhood watch committee, that role was more symbolic than anything else given the distinct lack of any serious law-breaking. According to Doreen, Chester mostly just liked the spiffing hat he was allowed to wear.

Sadly, with a murder, and then a vicious assault on his person on the very same day, even Chester would have to admit that the crime rate had suddenly, recently gone up. And as such, a working CCTV system would've been rather helpful right about now.

Conscious that several new customers had just made their way into the shop, Quinn figured she'd better head back inside before she was sacked from her current place of employment before lunchtime had even rolled around. However, she'd only taken a few steps in that direction before the phone in the rear pocket of her jeans started ringing. Soon noting the caller ID was identifying the number as originating from Nobles Hospital, she quickly answered. "Yes, hello...?" she said anxiously, hoping that it wasn't any sort of bad news from the medical staff. However, a smile emerged when she immediately recognised the familiar voice on the other end of the line.

"Dad?" she said, now at the shop's entrance and holding the door open for a lady trying to manoeuvre a child's buggy inside. "Hiya, Dad. Everything okay?" she asked, stepping inside where she made her way over to the serving side of the counter. But her smile dissipated when she listened to what her dad was telling her. *"What?* Dad, please tell me you're joking?" she said. And then, "Okay. I understand. Look, I'll take your car and get there as fast as I can, alright? Yes, I'll be there soon."

Concerned by the small segments of the conversation she was able to hear, Doreen glanced across. "Quinn...? Is Chester okay? What's going on? Quinn...?"

"What? Oh, sorry, Doreen. No, it wasn't a call about his health, if that's what you're asking. Rather, it was about the unexpected visitors he's just had."

"Visitors? I don't follow."

Quinn was struggling to process what she'd just been told by her dad. She shook her head, incredulous. "The police have just been to see him..." she began.

Doreen presumed this to be positive news about their investigation as to how he'd ended up in the hospital in the first place. "Ah. Have they found out who assaulted him?"

"You might think so. But, no," Quinn replied, scarcely able to believe the information she was about to relate. "Apparently, if what my dad just told me is true, the police weren't there about him being assaulted. They were there to speak to him about who *he* might have assaulted."

"Huh? Has your dad been given too many painkillers, by any chance? Is he thinking clearly? Because who on earth would the police think he assaulted?"

Quinn stared down at her feet, still shaking her head in utter disbelief. "Doreen, I don't know how or why. But somehow the police have got it into their heads that my dad participated in that awful incident on the beach."

Doreen didn't know whether to laugh or to cry at what was, in her obvious opinion, a completely ludicrous suggestion. *"What?* They think your father had something to do with that *murder...?* Are they mad? Have they lost their marbles? Please tell me you're kidding! Quinn...?"

Chapter Five

The often cheerful, buoyant members congregated inside the Castle Rushen Bowling Club HQ were understandably subdued considering the awful news filtering around their ordinarily sleepy town. A hushed, respectful silence greeted their duly elected chairman, Derek Ogilvy-Pratt, as he pushed himself up from his chair and adjusted his tasteful dark green tie, a tie which was slightly and uncharacteristically askew today for one so usually well presented.

As the proud and dutiful current leader of this fine organisational establishment—the oldest crown green bowling club on the isle, tracing its heritage back nearly a hundred years—Derek cut an impressive, commanding figure in his crisp white shirt and tailored suit in classic brown tweed. He ran a steady hand over his hair—parted neatly on the side and dyed a deep black, like squid ink—making sure it was all arranged perfectly, with nary a strand out of place.

Derek called the room to order by clearing his throat. About to speak, he initially paused for a moment instead, casting his eyes around the interior of the clubhouse like a preacher surveying his loyal flock, before then nodding approvingly, apparently satisfied. "Club members..." he said, addressing them solemnly, while turning slightly and directing a quavering finger towards a framed picture hanging on the wall behind him.

The photograph he was drawing everyone's attention to was a head-and-shoulders image of a similarly well-groomed fellow boasting a luxuriant walrus moustache, and a steadfast, determined gaze which oozed an air of noble authority.

Derek bowed his head for a bit, with the raw emotion of the occasion in danger of consuming him and cutting his address short before he'd really begun. He paused a moment longer, and then, in a slightly trembling voice, he bravely carried on. "Club members," he said again, drawing their attention to the portrait on the wall once more—this portrait being just one of many that formed an impressive timeline gallery of the club's social committee, from the past all the way up until the present, who had served tirelessly since the organisation's inception. "Ordinarily, it would be my distinct pleasure to stand before you and update the membership on our vision for driving this respected and historic club forward," he continued. "However, today, it is my awful duty to confirm the ghastly news about our beloved long-serving treasurer, and dear friend, Major Vincent Goodacre."

Derek briefly lowered his head yet again, clearly struggling to keep his feelings in check and to maintain some semblance of a proper stiff upper lip. "Many of you here today are already aware of the terrible event that claimed the life of the man we all knew fondly as the Major," he said, soldiering on. "And I, like you, share a collective sense of disbelief that such a generous, selfless soul could fall victim to such a hideous, wicked crime."

The various members sitting around the tables of the packed clubhouse remained silent and respectful as Derek then launched into a carefully considered eulogy that was heartfelt, poignant, and filled with charming anecdotes about Vincent Goodacre's eventful life and career. Indeed, there was scarcely a dry eye in the house as Derek reached his powerful crescendo with a lovely summary of the late Major's extensive charitable endeavours.

After sensing the eulogy was approaching its imminent conclusion, the bar staff had already circulated and replenished the glasses of those in attendance ahead of the formal toast, as previously instructed. "Ladies and gentlemen!" Derek called out to everyone who had assembled, reaching for his own champagne flute. "Although it's somewhat earlier in the day than I'm accustomed, I should like to propose a toast," he declared, holding out his crystal glass for all to witness.

The club members raised their own glasses in response, taking to their feet in full readiness to offer their respects to a fallen friend and dear colleague.

"Here's to a unique, and benevolent man, who will..." Derek started to say. Until, that is, he spotted an embarrassed-looking lady returning from an unfortunately timed trip to the loo.

All eyes fell on poor Brenda, caught like a rabbit in the headlights as she hovered in the doorway, appearing uncertain about whether to retreat to where she'd just arrived from or to simply shuffle back over to her seat. "Erm, should I just...?" she asked, pointing towards her vacant chair, and with her face turning an ever-increasingly vivid shade of red. "Or rather, should I..." she then asked, hooking a thumb over her shoulder in the direction of the bog, probably hoping a giant sinkhole would open up and swallow her instead.

"Yes, do come in!" Derek instructed. "Don't just loiter in the hallway, Brenda, standing there in some kind of limbo," he said, along with a less-than-subtle rolling of the eyes, irked that his emotionally charged words had been so rudely disrupted.

Brenda, a petite woman with a cloud of white hair and a timid disposition, attempted to return to her seat with the minimum of disruption. However, her attempts at being discreet—which largely consisted of her taking exaggerated, stealth-like steps as a cartoon burglar might—served only to tickle the funny bones of those tracking her progress and resulted in several people now giggling like unruly school children.

"We'll have some order!" Derek cut in with a frustrated shake of the head, eager to restore discipline before the giggling should become contagious and spread to the entire group. "Yes, do come along, Brenda. My shoulder is getting tired," he advised, his arm still held in a raised position in delayed anticipation of his toast.

With Brenda eventually returning to her table and her glass now in hand, Derek picked up roughly where he had left off, seizing his opportunity before there could be any other untimely interruptions made. "Ladies and gentlemen!" his deep, baritone voice sounded across the clubhouse. "Please join me in remembering a trusted and valued friend. To the Major."

"To the Major!" the club members all said in unison. This was followed by a moment of quiet reflection where most were lost in their own thoughts about their fallen comrade. Although, the occasional and stifled bout of tittering suggested that a few were still tickled by Brenda's 'walk of shame.'

The horrific demise of Major Vincent Goodacre had yet to be formally confirmed by the isle's authorities who were, according to local press reports, still investigating "an unexplained death." However, in such a close-knit community like Port Erin, where most folks knew what you'd had for breakfast, keeping the identity of a murder victim under wraps was always going to be a considerable challenge. And so that proved to be the case, with rumours of the victim's name soon spreading faster than an outbreak of head lice at a primary school.

And if reports of a murder on the isle weren't already shocking enough by itself, the whispered identity of the unfortunate victim made things even more unfathomable. Major Goodacre's cheerful smile was a common sight around the town. The decorated military veteran was known to many not only on account of his tireless charity work, but also by virtue of his marvellous moustache, which never failed to impress. So splendid and magnificent was it that it was almost famous in itself, often producing a host of admiring glances whenever the Major should be out enjoying one of his regular strolls.

Following the toast in Major Vincent Goodacre's honour, and with other official functions of the meeting eventually out of the way, the various club members were free to relax as well as they were able and do fairly much as they pleased. With his seventy-ninth birthday having only been several days away, the Major's family had already organised for a celebration lunch, a subject Derek Ogilvy-Pratt was just discussing with Primrose Ellis, the club's social secretary and official lady's team captain.

Derek, with an elbow resting on the granite top of the club's bar, took a sip of his pint of Okell's bitter, a local Manx brew and his regular tipple of choice. "A dreadful affair, Primrose," Derek offered as his critical assessment of the unfortunate situation in general. "A complete and utter waste."

Primrose, standing nearby at the bar, stared in the vague direction of her designer shoes as she examined her set of manicured fingernails as if either distracted or bored.

Derek waited patiently for a response that didn't immediately arrive. Figuring he hadn't been heard over the ambient noise and assorted chatter in the room, he felt the need to repeat himself. "I said it's a complete and utter waste, Primrose. An awful business," he reiterated.

Primrose snapped herself back to the present. "What? Oh, yes. Yes, it's a complete waste. The family have already paid for the birthday catering, and I very much doubt they'll get their deposit back on the cake and such now that it's no longer required. An awful business, as you say."

Derek offered a wry smile, unsure as to whether Primrose had understood the point he was trying to make, or if she was simply engaging in a bit of gentle gallows humour in an attempt to perhaps lighten the mood. "You don't appear to be your usual self today," he observed, offering his stylishly dressed companion a concerned look. "Although I suppose we're all a bit shaken up by the terrible news."

Primrose narrowed her eyes, taking a small, discreet step to her left, slightly reducing the space between them. "Derek," she whispered, while glancing around and about her, concerned that those sitting at the nearby tables might be within eavesdropping range. "Derek," she said again, doing her best to appear calm and casual to anyone who should happen to glance over in their direction.

However, it was now Derek's turn to be somewhat distracted and not pay attention, as he appeared to be focussing more on his drink just now than anything else, really.

"Derek!" Primrose exclaimed, after receiving little reaction to her subtle approach.

"What's that...? Oh, yes. I'd love one," Derek replied to a question that wasn't asked, while checking the contents of his pint glass and observing that it would very soon be empty. "I was just going to have the one... But I think I'll leave the car here and have another tipple or three for the Major. He'd expect nothing less."

Frustrated, Primrose nibbled down on her bottom lip before forcing through a smile, signalling to anyone possibly observing that all was well, with absolutely nothing untoward going on.

"Derek, I've been sending you messages all day but you haven't been answering me," she said through gritted teeth, speaking to him from out of the corner of her mouth just like a ventriloquist. "I nearly tried phoning you at one stage. You see, we need to talk about a pressing matter..."

Derek was horrified. "We don't talk on the phone, Primrose!" he reminded her in no uncertain terms. "We have no idea who might be *listening*," he stressed. He then put what he was saying to Primrose on hold for a moment as Finlo, a club member who didn't like bowling, necessarily, but appreciated the discounted bar prices, started to make his way past them on a journey to the 'little boy's room.'

"I've had a few cheeky snifters in honour of the Major," Finlo cheerfully announced, while almost staggering straight into a coat stand.

Derek tipped his pint glass approvingly. "Erm, yes. Jolly good show, Finlo," he said. "Although I think you've had rather more than a few?"

Derek waited a moment longer until Finlo was gone and there were no other pending interruptions. "Apologies, Primrose, for not responding to your messages. My wife Virginia has had me traipsing around that bloody B&Q DIY centre for most all of this morning, buying all sorts of things I don't believe we genuinely need," he explained. "And by the time that was sorted, I knew I would be seeing you here very shortly anyway. Why, whatever is so urgent that we need to discuss...?"

But before unburdening herself, Primrose first felt the need to check their immediate surroundings once more. Slowly, she twisted the cervical vertebrae in her neck, rotating her head first one way and then all the way over in the opposite direction, as far as it would go, making her appear like an overly cautious owl. Indeed, if she continued in this action much longer, she was in danger of ending up with a serious crick.

"Derek, I received a letter today," she then revealed, doing her best to appear unflustered, even offering a playful titter to indicate that she was engaged in some form of jovial chit-chat with her fellow club member.

"It wasn't a credit card statement, was it, my dear Primrose?" Derek asked. "We both know how it gets thrashed when the old shopping itch needs a good scratch, eh?"

However, Primrose wasn't in the mood for what seemed to her like an unfunny joke. A fact confirmed when her jovial persona gave way to a frosty glare that could chill molten lava. "Well, yes, there was a credit card statement, as it should happen. But that's not the delivery causing me concern. It was the *other* one," she advised. Primrose took a deep breath to compose herself before continuing. "Derek," she said, "the other letter that landed on my doorstep was sent by Major Goodacre..."

Derek, who was presently glancing about to locate any available bar staff, shifted his attention slowly back towards Primrose. On the basis that they had all congregated to celebrate the life of their former, deceased treasurer, he could easily be forgiven for sounding a mite confused just now. "You what?" he asked. "You've received a letter from a *dead* man?"

"Well, he obviously wasn't so dead when he'd typed it, Derek!" Primrose was quick to point out, as she assumed the communication surely hadn't been drafted from somewhere beyond the grave. Primrose fidgeted with her expensive necklace, gradually building up the courage for what she had to say next. "He *knows*, Derek," she then revealed. "Or, rather, he *knew*."

Like a tap had just been left opened, the blood rapidly drained from Derek's face, leaving him looking a sickly shade of pale. He ran a finger under the collar of his shirt, giving the impression it was slowly strangling him. Alarmed, Derek loosened the knot in his tie before he keeled over from asphyxiation, taking several deep breaths once this was accomplished. Then, concerned that anyone present might've developed secret lip-reading abilities, he used a hand to shield his mouth from view before replying.

"What...? He knew about us...?"

Primrose simply nodded in response.

Derek emptied the remaining contents of his glass, eager, it would appear, to calm his elevated heart rate. "Gordon Bennett," he muttered, nervously shifting his weight between each of his feet. "So was he trying to blackmail you, then? Or us...?" Derek asked, struggling to work out the possible motive for such a letter being sent, upon which he received a further nod of confirmation. "Good lord. I didn't think our Vincent was the type to engage in that sort of thing. But why would he—"

"Does it matter why? All that matters is he somehow found out about us," Primrose answered. "Although, he did give some nonsense excuse about being concerned we'd bring the club into disrepute with our 'salacious activities' as he referred to it."

"Disrepute?" Derek scoffed with an indignant sniff. "And yet avoiding disrepute was hardly what was foremost on his mind, it would seem, if what the greedy old duffer wanted was to shake you down for money. Knowing just how wealthy your husband is and the cash you have access to, our good Major must've been contemplating a significant payday."

Derek was furious, but he resisted the overwhelming urge to flourish an angry fist, as it may have been noticed by his bowling club associates. "The bloody cheek of the man!" he remarked. "It's just not cricket, I say. Especially coming after all of that glowing praise I'd just delivered in his eulogy."

Having had most of the morning to consider the letter she'd received, Primrose had also reached a similar conclusion. "One would have to imagine that money was the primary motivating factor for him reaching out, as opposed to anything else. But as there wasn't any opportunity to follow up on this message of his after he, well, you know... then we can't know for certain."

Derek contemplated for a moment the unwelcome situation they both found themselves in. While engaged in deep thought, he was nevertheless briefly distracted by the wonderful aroma wafting over from the hot buffet being laid out on the opposite side of the clubhouse. Then, with a smile emerging like he'd just had a result on the horses, he offered the benefit of his wisdom. "You've heard of the saying 'dead men can't talk,' I suppose?"

This sinister-sounding pronouncement did little to appease Primrose, whose reddened cheeks were starting to show through her generously applied makeup. "Yes, of *course*. I *know* that," she replied, perhaps a bit louder than she'd intended. "But just think about it, will you? The very person attempting to blackmail me about our... our *thing*... then conveniently turns up murdered on Port Erin Beach. If the police should find out about this connection, how long do you think it'll take them before they're banging on our front doors demanding answers?"

Up until this point, Derek had only considered the potentially expensive, possibly physically painful, and definitely thoroughly inconvenient prospect of his wife finding out about yet another illicit affair. She'd already become aware of one or two previous marital wanderings over the course of their years together, but he didn't fancy the idea of her finding out about one much more current. However, the gravity of how this situation might look to the authorities was an altogether more sobering thought than even that of dealing with Mrs Ogilvy-Pratt's dire wrath.

"You've destroyed the letter?" asked Derek.

"Of course I've destroyed the letter. Its remnants are probably still smouldering in my log burner," replied Primrose.

Derek's shoulders relaxed, as he was never keen on loose ends. "Ah! Marvellous," he said in a well-that-takes-care-of-that sort of manner, wondering what all the fuss was about, then, and why old Primrose didn't appear to be sharing in his newly found sunny optimism at the moment. But with a rumbling belly, his attention was being drawn towards the buffet queue that was presently increasing in length with each passing second. "We'd better get a wriggle on," he advised. "Otherwise we'll be left with those awful, soggy mushroom vol-au-vents that Edwina always insists upon inflicting on us."

Primrose placed a firm hand on Derek's arm, preventing his immediate departure. "Wait, hold on. What if the Major had told somebody else about us...?"

"Then it'll be our word against that doddering, now-dead fool, won't it?" Derek pointed out with a satisfied grin. "All we need to do is keep a low profile for a couple of weeks and all of this nonsense will disappear faster than the contents of the buffet table," he added, casting a hungry eye across the clubhouse. "Oh, bother. That greedy oaf Brian has just picked up a dinner plate. Come on, otherwise the only thing left will be crumbs."

"So you don't think we need to worry...?" Primrose asked. "Not about the food. I mean about receiving that letter?"

Derek puffed out his chest and pressed back his shoulders like he was on a military parade. "Nothing at all to concern yourself with, my dear," he assured her. Then, leaning in closer, he added, "The only person who knows about the two of us is now in the morgue having the Port Erin sand brushed off him," he said with an amused grin. "So relax. Nobody will ever be able to connect us to that unfortunate incident. And besides, it's not as if there's any genuine connection to be made anyway."

Derek eyed his empty pint glass, wishing he could've had an additional refill by now. But as there were currently no available bar staff to serve him for some reason, he decided that making a beeline to the food table was the best course of action right now. He thus charted a course and set out that way, full steam ahead, with Primrose following behind. Heading in the opposite direction, club members Kirk and Lyle were escorting their swollen plates of buffet towards the bar, looking for something to wash their lunch down with.

"You'll do well to get served," Derek offered, as both groups crossed paths, briefly coming alongside each other. "It's like the bloody Mary Celeste behind that bar," he grimly advised.

Undaunted and thirsty, however, Lyle was the first to come to port at the granite-top bar, wondering, just like Derek had before him, where the staff had buggered off to. "Cindy, are you back there...?" he called out, suspecting she might be hanging out the back door having a crafty fag, as she often did. "Come on, Cindy, we're spitting feathers out—"

"Oh, I'm here!" Cindy immediately replied without revealing herself, confusing Lyle in the process. Because as far as he could tell, there was a Cindy-like voice, but no Cindy to go with it.

A second later, the auburn-haired bartender raised the crown of her head so that it was now slightly visible to Kirk and Lyle, both standing on the other side of the bar and now looking down on her.

"Sorry, boys," she said, springing upright and fully into view like a wound-up Jack-in-the-Box, while simultaneously moving her hand towards the beer pump with an empty glass for a pour. All of this was accomplished in one fluid, practised motion, as if this precise routine was performed multiple times throughout the course of the day. "I was just on my knees cleaning up a spill when talk of a rather interesting postal delivery had captured my attention. The usual, I presume?"

"Flippin' heck, Cindy, I didn't see you hiding down there!" Lyle commented, chuckling happily away to himself. "And, yes. Yes, the usual, please."

"You know, it's funny," Cindy remarked, as she expertly angled the glass in her hand in order to form the perfect head on Lyle's pint. "Because you weren't the *only* one who failed to notice me hidden back here. And it's amazing what you hear people talking about when they think nobody is listening..."

Chapter Six

With an initial quote to install a temporary stairlift in Chester's flat coming in at an eye-wateringly expensive four thousand quid, it was decided that a preferable, and significantly cheaper, option was to simply engage the services of four strapping locals and carry the recovering patient up his flight of stairs when he returned home from hospital.

Moreover, with the significance of his injuries, it was unlikely he'd be able to wander too far from home on a regular basis in any case, and therefore any further excursions up and down the staircase would be kept to a bare minimum. Until he was on the mend, at any rate. Not that Chester had any distinct desire to go anywhere, really, considering the current scrutiny directed his way from the police.

But now safely at home and trying to get comfortable in his favourite armchair, positioned to afford him a pleasant view of the bay to watch for ships drawing near, Chester's patience levels were already beginning to be tested. "Quinn," he said, using his good arm to adjust the cushion behind his lower back for maximum lumbar support. "Quinn, could you stop? You're in danger of wearing a hole straight through the carpet and floor and into the ice cream shop below us if you don't stop pacing back and forth like a crazed bear." Then, seeing the sort of reaction he was receiving, he tried softening his approach to her a little, adding, "Pumpkin, having you home again, here with me now, is wonderful, okay? But you need to relax, yeah?"

Quinn came to an abrupt halt next to her dad's vintage record player, giving the impression she was about to slam its lid shut as she searched for something, anything, to physically abuse in an attempt to alleviate her obvious frustration. Fortunately she held off, as it was a very nice phonograph indeed and one that Chester was quite fond of. Plus, a vinyl George Harrison LP was playing on the turntable, with the former Beatle singing, at the present moment, one of his lovely old songs that was all about love, and peace on earth, and that sort of thing.

"Relax?" said Quinn. "You want me to *relax*...?"

Like many fathers might have done in similar situations over the years, Chester was now regretting his choice of words. "All I'm saying, honey pie, is that fretting over something neither of us can really control is fruitless, isn't it?"

Quinn approached her father's chair, placing her hands down on both armrests, elbows locked, with her face only about a foot away from his, like some sort of interrogation was about to take place. "Dad, need I remind you that the police have you firmly in their sights in a murder investigation?!"

Despite the gravity of the situation, Chester couldn't help but laugh at the circumstance he'd found himself in. "That's a small matter I'm acutely aware of," he advised. "But surely it won't take them long to realise how utterly absurd of a notion that is, right? I mean, *me*...? Murder...? It's bloody ridiculous is what it is."

Quinn threw her hands in the air, before promptly lowering them so that she could use the tips of her fingers to knead her temples. She then resumed her back-and-forth pacing as she set about pondering the recent chain of events. "I'm just concerned about this investigation and its possible consequences for you," she said. "Of course we both know full well that you absolutely did *not* murder anybody," she added. "Wow! There's a sentence I never thought I'd have to flippin' say."

Quinn offered a frustrated, what-the-hell-is-going-on sort of sigh before continuing to share in her current thought process.

"But as it stands, I can completely understand why the police now have you earmarked as their prime suspect," she said with some degree of worry. "I mean, with the evidence they have, it's the closest thing to a smoking gun. A smoking gun with your fingerprints all over the grip and the trigger."

"But the Major wasn't—" Chester started to protest.

"I know he wasn't shot, Dad, if that's what you were going to say. But you take my point, right? Because now, my overwhelming fear is that with the seemingly damning evidence they have on you, will the police even bother to invest any time and energy in seeking out the *real* party responsible? After all, they probably already think they've got their man, and have their champagne chilling on ice! And it could be only a matter of time before they formally arrest you for the crime."

The 'smoking gun' that Quinn was referring to was, in actual fact, a piece of crucial evidence recovered from the body of the victim. A significant discovery, and one that directly implicated one Chester J Flitcroft in the vicious murder of Major Vincent Goodacre. Utilising her contacts still working within the Isle of Man Constabulary to good effect, Quinn had been made aware of the specific reason for the dark raincloud of suspicion now hovering ominously above her father's head—a brief handwritten note found inside Major Goodacre's blazer pocket, detailing the following information:

C Flitcroft – £7k poker debt now overdue

Unfortunately, for Chester, this incriminating snippet of information strongly suggested that he was very heavily indebted to the victim following a noticeable streak of bad luck at the poker table. A significant gambling debt indeed, and one which would conveniently expire at the moment of Vincent Goodacre's *own* expiration. A compelling reason, then, for the police to consider Chester a credible and entirely viable suspect.

For operational reasons, the authorities were largely keeping their own set of cards, figuratively speaking, close to their chest concerning their ongoing murder investigation. So much so that even the official cause of death still remained undisclosed to the public. Although Quinn, again via her sources, understood that it was blunt force trauma to the back of the head.

And no matter how much Chester protested his innocence, the fact that Vincent Goodacre's corpse was found within virtual spitting distance from Chester's front doorway, and with a clear motive concealed inside the victim's pocket, it was likely that he would continue to feel the heat for the foreseeable future.

By now, Quinn was sitting slumped on the sofa, leaning forward with her head cradled in her hands, trying to make sense of this mess and figure out how that spurious note had ended up in the victim's pocket, as her father had made absolutely clear to her that no such debt existed.

"Look, why don't you go and see if Doreen needs a hand down below in the shop...?" Chester proposed, suspecting his daughter might benefit from a change of scenery, and also to protect his carpet from becoming threadbare when she inevitably reverted to pacing mode again. "Maybe the distraction will help you come at this problem from a different perspective?"

However, Quinn steered right around the suggestion, instead removing her head from her hands and gazing across at her dad. "So, you do..." she said. "Or, rather, you *did*," she corrected herself, "play poker with Mr Goodacre, right?"

Chester rolled his eyes, even though he knew his daughter's probing was for his benefit and ultimately his liberty. "Quinn, I've already gone through this previously, both with you as well as the police."

"Yes, I know, but humour me once more, Dad, okay? Please."

"Of course," Chester replied, seeing no harm in obliging. "Yes, we all enjoyed a friendly game of cards about once a month or so, rotating the location between each of the players' homes."

"Players...?" Quinn prompted.

"Sure," Chester replied, repeating what he'd already explained previously. "We'd usually have six or seven players at each game. Although it wasn't always the same faces each month, as people might be on holiday or simply not in the mood for cards at that particular time or what have you. It just depended."

"And the stakes were never excessive?"

Chester considered this question for a second or two, uncertain what would be considered "excessive," as the answer would likely vary from person to person depending on their risk appetite. "Well, it wasn't the sort of money you'd ever lose your shirt

A CASE OF MAJOR MURDER

over. But on the same token, it was pleasing enough if you occasionally won," he advised.

"But never seven-thousand-pounds excessive?"

"Good heavens, no," Chester replied instantly. "No, if I lost fifty pounds then I'd be upset. Look, it was always just a friendly game of cards with no serious amount of money ever changing hands. A fact that any one of the other regular players will hopefully be verifying to the police to help clear this nonsense up."

Quinn contemplated this from the point of view of the police, wondering if it would be that easy. "Hmm," she thought out loud, narrowing one eye to aid in her thinking process. "But the other players would only be able to account for the games they actually participated in, right? What I mean is, they could never confirm that you and Major Goodacre didn't have a separate game from time to time with higher stakes involved, see? A game where you might have lost seven grand, for instance."

"But we didn't. Not ever. I wouldn't be that stupid."

"I know that, Dad, and you know that. But it's what the police know and think that really matters, right? And at this moment in time, they think that you owed a shedload of cash to a man who subsequently turned up dead. So, you can see how that looks from where the police are standing...?"

Quinn continued questioning her father for clarity on points that he'd already answered both to her and the constabulary. It wasn't that she didn't believe him, because she absolutely did. All Quinn was doing was covering all the bases and hoping to glean some nugget of critical information that may have been missed on the first time of asking.

However, her efforts were fruitless, with no new knowledge obtained that she wasn't already in possession of. Her father, as he'd already explained, did not observe anything in any way out of the ordinary on the beach that fateful day, either during the course of the afternoon or on into the evening. Or even directly prior to his tumble down the stairs, for that matter. But a point he was sure of, however, was that if he had witnessed a murder, that was the sort of traumatic event that would without doubt stand out in one's mind.

"*Argh!*" Quinn exclaimed once they'd finished talking, giving the impression that she wanted to strike something in frustration again, but was of course restraining herself. "You're missing something, Quinn," she then added, admonishing herself aloud. "*Think*, dammit..."

Chester kept his mouth closed while Quinn processed all the information rattling around her head. She meandered over to the front window, looking down to street level where a driver was struggling to reverse into a parking space that looked to be a few inches shorter than the length of his vehicle. The poor driver appeared distinctly flustered, Quinn observed. But that didn't prevent several beachgoers from watching his failed and hopeless attempts at parking with amusement nonetheless. Just then, the sun's rays reflected off the frustrated driver's front windscreen, dazzling Quinn in the process.

"Aww, bloody hell," she said as her pupils constricted, squinting as the defeated driver pulled away, apparently unable or unwilling to continue entertaining those mirthful observers presently questioning his driving abilities. "I reckon that's what I get for being a nosey so-and-so," she remarked.

Quinn rubbed her eyes, shifting her gaze away from the road and towards the gentle waves breaking against the beach. The same sunlight that'd just temporarily blinded her now danced on the water like millions of tiny diamonds glinting off the surface. "Oh, wait, hang on!" she said as the watery vista brought a memory flooding back.

"Quinn? What is it?"

"Dad, have you had any lady friends visiting you recently?" she asked, turning to face her father with her thinking finger raised.

Chester considered her blankly.

"Dad, I'm serious, and it's important. You see when you were in the hospital, I spotted a small diamond hiding in the carpet at the foot of your stairs. The type you might find in jewellery, or embedded in a fancy watch, maybe."

Chester shook his head. "There haven't been any lady friends," he said. "The only women that have been in this flat since your mum passed, as far as I can recall, are you and Doreen."

"You're certain?"

"Yes, quite certain!" he said, although it wasn't clear to Quinn if he sounded disappointed by this revelation or not. "You should check to see if Doreen is missing a diamond," he suggested.

Quinn retracted her thinking finger. "I think I'll do that now," she agreed. "Because if Doreen isn't missing one, which I hope is the case, then there's every chance the diamond belonged to an unwelcome visitor to your flat who either shoved you down the stairs or knows who did."

"And perhaps the same person who smashed the Major's skull in like an overripe cantaloupe...?" Chester added, though possibly not as delicately as Quinn would have liked if her disapproving look was anything to go by.

"You'll be okay on your own for a bit?" she asked him, reaching for her handbag lying next to the sofa, and then receiving a spirited thumbs-up from her father. "Alright. I need to go and speak with Doreen, and then..."

"And then?"

Quinn remained rooted to the spot for a moment like somebody had pressed the pause button on her. After being motionless, she suddenly clicked her fingers, reanimating herself. "Dad, somebody is clearly out to frame you for the murder of Vincent Goodacre, yes? On that, we're agreed. Otherwise, how and why did that handwritten note turn up inside his pocket, suggesting you owed him a boatload of cash when you didn't?"

"It's certainly looking that way, yes," Chester replied. "And I couldn't help but notice that the police, so far, don't appear too concerned about who pushed me down the stairs, I might add."

Quinn sucked in air through her teeth, giving the sort of expression one might exhibit when eating a lemon, lime, or some other type of equally tart citrus. "Dad, if the police think you're involved in the murder, then I suspect they also don't especially believe you were pushed," she had to remind him.

"Eh? They think I somehow managed to hurl *myself* down the stairs? Why the devil would I bloody do that?"

However, Quinn didn't have all the answers, instead merely trying to see how things may appear from the outside looking in.

"Perhaps the police think you were injured in a tussle with the Major...?" she offered. "Or maybe falling down the stairs was self-inflicted, just a convenient smokescreen to suggest the presence of a mystery assailant when there wasn't one?"

These alternative realities, ludicrous as they sounded, served only to rile Chester, who now appeared intent on rising from his seat in protest. "I didn't invent a mystery assailant, and I wasn't involved in any sort of wrestling match with the Major!"

"Dad, I know that. When I say things like 'mystery assailant,' it's not because I think you're making it up. It's just that I know what the police could be thinking. It's imprinted on them to consider all possibilities, no matter how far-fetched they might appear to us."

Sensing he'd got himself severely flustered and needed some reassurances, Quinn leaned over, placing a peck on his cheek. "I'll make sure to prove your innocence, Dad, I promise. And until I do, I'll be stuck to this case like a barnacle on the hull of a ship."

Chester unclenched his jaw and settled back into his chair, although with the seriousness of the situation not lost on him. "Thank you, Quinn. I don't know what I'd do without you."

"Well, you're my dad, Dad," she replied, as this fact alone was motivation enough for her to instantly go the extra mile for him without question. "Now, there's simply too much at stake to miss something in this investigation. For that reason, I think it's time for me to enlist some additional, expert help," she declared.

"Help? Help from whom?" Chester asked.

The corners of Quinn's mouth curled up into a knowing smile. "From quite possibly the most diligent, tenacious, hardworking and professional detective I've ever had the pleasure of working with, Dad. That's who. Well, when he's not dozing off in the van, at any rate." She rubbed her hands at the prospect of smashing this mystery wide open. "And with the two of us on the case, it's not a matter of *whether* we'll find the true murderer of Vincent Goodacre. Rather, it's a case of *when*..."

Chapter Seven

Despite the presence of a moderate breeze, the heat of the midday sun remained stifling. Indeed, it was the sort of summer's day that was best suited to sitting in your garden, wearing your shorts and t-shirt, with a glass of something cold for company. Unfortunately for Toby Haddock, this was an ideal and enviable scenario that was probably light years away from his current reality, where he was presently crouched inside a rusting skip, dressed head to foot in a homemade ghillie suit—a camouflage outfit he had used, with various degrees of success, on previous surveillance operations. It was, he now reflected, a considerable advantage when deployed to an active investigation where there was, very specifically, dense undergrowth to blend into. Alas, sitting in a partially empty metal skip in the midday sun without the slightest hint of greenery about, it served only to increase his core body temp to potentially critical levels.

"Will you clear off!" he complained in a loud whisper, swatting his hand furiously but to negligible effect, as the persistent fly that had been plaguing him for the past fifteen minutes or so was winning their pitched battle if its feisty, unrelenting efforts were anything to go by. Further dampening Toby's overall spirits was the scent filling his nostrils—a heady cocktail of what reminded him of rotting salmon with subtle undertones of wet dog blended in, a nauseating combination of odours lingering indecently from the last several times the skip was used in anger.

Undeterred and ever the professional, Toby set aside his personal discomfort and peered through his military surplus binoculars (also camouflaged) for another visual sweep of the surrounding area. "Oh, come on," he said with a sigh, after finding nothing of significance since his last view precisely ten minutes earlier. Indeed, it was a similar regimented pattern of searching that had frustrated him since the present operation had commenced some hours previous. Although as his stomach—made queasy by the foul odour of the skip he was positioned inside—would attest, it felt significantly longer than that.

Just then, as the persistent fly returned, this time along with a few of its mates, Toby felt a vibration very near his right nipple. He lowered his field glasses carefully, allowing them to come to rest gently against his chest by way of the strap around his neck, and then removed his mobile from the easy-access Velcro pocket his mum had so kindly installed when originally helping him to construct his covert surveillance suit. And despite being somewhat hindered now by the awkward, sweat-inducing face mask (also camouflaged) that he was wearing, the name of the caller on his phone's display screen still managed to raise an immediate smile on an otherwise miserable day.

"Oh, hiya, Quinn," Toby whispered into his phone, grateful to hear from his former investigative partner. "What? No, sorry, I can't speak any louder, as I'm on active operations just now," he advised, in answer to the question posed. He listened further for a moment, using his free hand to attempt to swat away the flying pests that were still vexing him, though it was a rather half-hearted effort at this stage as he knew there was no real victory to be had. "Am I on a very exciting mission?" he repeated back to Quinn, before releasing a pained sigh. "No, I'm hiding in a skip at the end of a country lane, trying to capture evidence against a team of persistent fly-tippers who've been the blight of the local council. And by fly-tippers, I don't mean people who sneak up on unsuspecting flies and topple the little bastards over, of course, but people who engage in illegal waste disposal. So, no. Not an exciting mission in any way, really. And it's also not lost on me that I could simply be replaced by a cheap CCTV camera at any given time."

Then, repeating her next question back to her as well, "So why am I hiding in a skip, of all things...?" he said, while briefly popping his head up for a look. He looked all around at the depressing, pancake-flat wasteland surrounding him with not even a single bush he might hide behind. "Well let's just say any alternative form of cover is sadly not available," he explained, spotting a previously unnoticed puddle of some unidentifiable liquid in the far corner of his current office as he hunkered back down. Perhaps it was the source of the overwhelming, pungent aroma, he considered, although not brave or stupid enough to stick his nose anywhere near it to find out. "Anyway, enough about me," he said. "Do the local fuzz still think your dad's a ruthless killer?"

With no sign of any discarded old fridges, knackered ovens, or rusting lawnmowers being directed towards his observation point (at least for now), Toby eased back, resting his overheated frame against the corroded interior of the large metal refuse receptacle that was his present home, listening to Quinn fill him in on the details of the Isle of Man murder case. Of course with her being a friend and recent colleague, he'd already been made aware of the predicament her father found himself in with the murder, and he was interested to hear about any latest developments. "What's that...?" he said a short time later, perhaps a little louder than he should have considering that he was still ostensibly in surveillance mode. "You're *serious...*?"

After confirmation, Toby continued, "Quinn, I've got a river of sweat running down into the crack of my... In fact, never mind. Suffice it to say that since you've left, I don't appear to be getting the first pick of the plum jobs. Hence, me standing inside of a glorified rubbish bin right now. So if you're serious about me flying over to the island to lend a hand? Then yes. Yes, I would. I'm owed more holiday time than you can shake a stick at. Although, if the bosses get funny about me taking any days at short notice, then they can stick their job up the same place as where my river of sweat is currently pooling up!"

But before Quinn could say anything further, Toby was distracted by what sounded like the noise of a throaty van engine being carried in his direction over the breeze. Instinctively, he returned his voice to proper surveillance levels, making sure to speak in hushed whispers. "Sorry, Quinn, but I've got to go just now. 'OPERATION DISCARDED CRAP' might finally be about to bear fruit. I'll call you later, okay?"

Toby returned his phone to his breast pocket, eagerly waiting to see what or who was driving up the lane towards him, confident that all his hard work was about to pay dividends. However, it was at that point that he realised the sound of the van's engine was moving *away* from him rather than *towards* him.

Further, it was also at this moment that he noticed a battered-looking chest freezer tipped on its side with several microwave ovens scattered around it for company. "Eh? How the blue bloody blazes did you lot end up there in so short of a time while I wasn't looking...?" he asked, deploying his field glasses to try and catch the van's registration number. But it was too late, as the van was well out of sight by now, having already successfully dumped its latest load of household junk and then promptly buggering off without any interruption or delay. Toby kicked the interior of the skip which, in doing so, released a shower of rusty metal particles, falling gracefully like snowflakes on a cold winter's morning. Or perhaps like ashes falling from the sky after a violent eruption from Mount Vesuvius. Toby wasn't sure which. "Ouch," he said. "Those were my toes."

***

In the Isle of Man, working her early morning job on the ground floor of a tastefully appointed townhouse, Cindy Shuttleworth—the auburn-haired, chain-smoking barmaid from the bowling club—shoved the hoover across the hallway carpet, taking care not to catch the feet of an antique bureau writing desk (as she'd nevertheless done several times prior if the indents in the wood were any indication). She paused for a moment, noticing a thick layer of dust hugging the uppermost surface of the desk. With a frustrated exhale, she depressed the hoover's on/off switch and retrieved a yellow cloth from within her cleaning belt. "Scruffy toffs," she admonished to nobody in particular, as she disturbed the dust with several cursory swipes of her hand. "*Honestly*, these *people*," she added, accompanied by an audible tut-tut.

Evidently, Cindy's uncompromising standards of cleanliness had not been met if her affronted reaction was any measure. Of course, as the owner of the property would no doubt be eager to stress, it was Cindy herself who was the duly employed cleaner of said property, and it was on her watch that the layer of dust had accumulated to such a degree in the first place.

Cindy's annoyed frown soon softened upon hearing footsteps descending the home's elegant spiral staircase. Immediately, her somewhat half-arsed approach switched to that of a rather more conscientious employee, with her now gently caressing the antique wood with her dusting cloth, carefully polishing it. "Good morning, Lady Alcott," Cindy said without breaking focus away from her duties, the impressive workhorse that she was (or was keen to portray, at least).

Lady Alcott, a dour-looking woman with a pallid complexion and tight greying perm, came to a halt directly to stern of Cindy, standing there with one hand on her hip and armed with a fierce scowl. *"Cindy,"* she said in her assured, imperial tone, completely devoid of humour. "Cindy, I've just discovered a lump of *chewing gum* affixed to the frame of my late uncle's portrait," she advised, with clear disdain dripping from every word.

Cindy, still positioned with her back to Lady Alcott, was doing a bang-up job of now appearing engrossed in the task at hand. Although as soon as her employer's words landed, she instantly ceased chomping down on what was in her mouth. "What?!" she said, sharing her outrage while she squirrelled away her current piece of chewing gum, using her tongue to stash it somewhere deep inside her cheek. Lowering her dustcloth, she spun around to face Lady Alcott, sporting her most affronted of expressions and rolling her eyes in solidarity. "Honestly, your Ladyness, some folks have no respect! And that's the truth."

Lady Alcott considered Cindy with one eye narrowed like a butcher trying to work out which stray dog had snaffled a pile of pig's knuckles left out on the counter. "Well, if you could ensure that the foreign object is removed without delay, Cindy. You see I'm hosting the vicar and his wife this afternoon, and standards must of course be maintained."

"Foreign object...?" Cindy enquired, confused by Lady Alcott's peculiar way of speaking.

"The *chewing* gum, girl."

"Ah. Righty-ho, your Ladyshipness," Cindy replied, still uncertain about the correct way to address the landed gentry, while offering a dainty curtsy as well. It wasn't clear if the curtsy was being offered with respect, though, or some degree of petulance.

"I'll give it a good seeing-to," Cindy promised. "Or I'll see to it, is what I think I might mean...? One of those."

Lady Alcott huffed, sidestepping the hoover before continuing her journey, during which she was, perhaps, also considering her future recruitment procedures.

Unfortunately for Lady Alcott, Cindy didn't appear to be quite finished. "Uhm... before you go, Lady Alcott...?"

Lady Alcott came to a very reluctant halt. "Yes, what is it?"

Cindy shuffled up the hallway, for some reason dragging the hoover along behind her. "Sorry, I was meaning to ask you, your LadyGagaNess... That is, I was hoping you could help...?"

"Spit it out, girl. The vicar will be arriving shortly, and I've no time for nonsense."

"Ah, yes," Cindy said, sensing she might be losing her audience if she didn't soon get to the point. "I was wondering if you needed me for a few extra hours. You know, not just for cleaning, but for cleaning and whatnot."

"And whatnot?"

"Yes, ma'am. I've never mowed a lawn, for instance, but I'd be happy to give it a shot if you'd like. Although you might need to teach me how to start the mower. Oh, and how to run it, too. Just that first time, though. I'm a quick learner. Well, maybe show me twice to be sure."

Lady Alcott responded with the sort of look you'd give someone who'd just trampled mud all over your new white carpet. "So I understand, you want me to employ you to mow my lawn, as well as perform a distinctly mediocre job of cleaning my house?"

Cindy took no offence to the critical assessment of her work skills to date. "Yes, that would be appreciated," she said. "You see, my other cleaning gig has just ended abruptly, and there are no extra shifts to be had tending the bar at the bowling club."

A CASE OF MAJOR MURDER

An incredulous Lady Alcott stared blankly. "Cindy, you're just fortunate that competent staff are rarer than hen's teeth on this island."

Cindy offered a wide smile, wondering if another curtsy was in order. "Why thank you, your Ladybug. It's nice to hear that—"

"Good heavens, that wasn't a compliment, girl! Honestly, if you just stopped losing money on that witless bingo game you play on your phone instead of doing what I already *pay* you to do, then perhaps you wouldn't be angling for additional hours."

With that unsubtle decline delivered, Lady Alcott continued on her way to review the spread her head chef had laid out in advance of the vicar and his wife's upcoming arrival.

Cindy glared as Lady Alcott veered left towards the kitchen, before then disappearing from view. "Remove the *foreign object* without *delay*, Cindy," she said, mimicking her boss's voice in a less-than-complimentary fashion. "I'll show you, you stuck-up old cow. Just you wait and see!"

Cindy, by her own admission, had experienced an unfortunate run of luck over the last two months. Having only recently moved out of the family home, her dreams of venturing out into the world to become a globally recognised fashion designer—as she'd told her mum when packing her bags—hadn't, as yet, come to fruition. Perhaps, as her mum might possibly point out to her if asked, because Cindy didn't know one end of a sewing machine from the other.

And so, with fame and fortune on hold for now, at least for the time being, Cindy had instead secured a job pulling pints at the local crown green bowling club. It wasn't a forever job, just something to help pay the rent on her new flat as she assured her ever-sceptical mum. A mum who'd remained doubtful of her daughter's ability to manage in the real world. And soon enough, her mum's concerns started to become apparent as the electricity, gas, and rate bills (for starters) began landing on the doormat that Cindy had stolen from a nearby hotel. But she had a plan, did Cindy. A cast-iron, sure-fire way to pay the bills and keep her in the indolent lifestyle she'd become accustomed to while living at home with her parents. And the gist of her grand plan that would see the big bucks rolling in anytime now? Well, that was in playing online bingo, and was like "taking candy from a baby," she was keen to suggest after some degree of surprising initial success. However, as with all good things, her winning streak had soon come to an abrupt and particularly expensive end—an unfortunate (but not entirely unpredictable) outcome that had an eventual impact on her ability to turn the lights on in her new flat and also stock her fridge. But she wasn't as annoyed as the credit card companies who, as she would discover, didn't seem to appreciate people running up thousands of pounds of debt with no ability or inclination to repay it.

No matter, Cindy was the resilient type, always looking for the next sideline to bring a few quid in and keep the wolf from the door. While working behind the bar over at the bowling club, for instance, Cindy shortly realised that it was frequented by a large assortment of affluent people who, she gathered, didn't much care for doing things for themselves, particularly when it came to any sort of manual labour. So, with a stack of business cards hastily printed up, Cindy started to advertise her services as an experienced, hardworking housekeeper with a list of references as long as your arm, figuring if her potential customers were too lazy to clean their own homes then they'd be too lazy to confirm her references.

And her assumptions proved to be spot on when, in next to no time, she had accepted several offers of employment for her fledgling cleaning business. Granted, three of them ended up 'politely' dispensing with her services after only a brief period. A period in which she'd managed to set fire to an antique grandfather clock, unplug an industrial-sized fridge freezer with the loss of its entire contents, and somehow fill a carpet cleaner with a bleach-based solution that effortlessly destroyed a cherished Persian rug. "Simply teething problems," as she'd relayed to her concerned mother. Still, with two suckers/clients having miraculously remained present on Cindy's cleaning roster, things were becoming improved, financially speaking, to both her landlord and credit card provider's relief.

A CASE OF MAJOR MURDER

Alas, just as things were beginning to pick up, fate, it would appear, was to once again conspire against Cindy Shuttleworth, with one of those two remaining contracts having come to a sudden and abrupt termination. This time, however, it hadn't been on account of her abject uselessness or wilful negligence. No, the reason her credit card company wouldn't be receiving their minimum payment this month was because the troublesome Grim Reaper had intervened—with the name of her only other client none other than Major Vincent Goodacre (now deceased), whose sudden and unfortunate demise had seriously inconvenienced our Cindy, leaving her in something of a financial pickle once again. Not ideal timing, Cindy considered, as she sparked the hoover back into life, giving it a kick as she reflected upon Lady Alcott's haughty, unwelcome attitude.

"Stuck-up old cow," Cindy said again, continuing with her cleaning duties, but with scant regard for the chunk of wood she'd now just taken out of the skirting board with her heavy-handed manner. "I'll show *you*..." she repeated, throwing in a few expletives under her breath as well.

Then, however, the corners of her mouth turned up in the gradual development of a devious, I've-got-a-cunning-plan sort of smile. And it was at that moment that her thoughts moved away from exacting revenge on Lady Alcott and to the conversation she'd recently overheard in the bowling club. That private discussion, of course, was the one between Derek Ogilvy-Pratt and Primrose Ellis that she'd managed to eavesdrop on while down on the floor on her hands and knees attending to a spill for several minutes.

And as a result of this current, glorious lightbulb moment, Cindy allowed her mind to drift away, now daring to dream of a future without any credit card debt, no landlord chasing her for overdue rent, the ability to play online bingo with wild abandon, and finally, the prospect of never having to bother cleaning up after Lady Alcott to pay the bills.

"How much is my silence worth...?" she asked herself aloud, sluggishly proceeding up the length of the hallway carpet as she calculated the answer to that potentially lucrative enquiry.

"Quite a lot, I reckon," she said in answer to herself, offering the gilt-framed image of a pompous-looking bearded aristocrat an optimistic wink. "In fact, this time next year I could be a millionaire," she declared, taking inspiration from one of Derek 'Del Boy' Trotter's famous catchphrases. "Yes, I think I quite like that idea," she proclaimed. "Cindy Shuttleworth... millionairess..."

Chapter Eight

It was another two days until the Isle of Man Constabulary formally confirmed what most of the island already knew—that the identity of the body discovered on Port Erin Beach was that of Major Vincent Goodacre.

Furthermore, the official press release revealed the cause of death to be blunt force trauma to the head. "At this time," as it went on to say, "we are exploring an existing, promising lead, yet all lines of investigation remain open. We would urge anybody possessing any knowledge about this horrific tragedy to please come forward at their earliest opportunity."

Processing this limited selection of information divulged by the authorities, Quinn Flitcroft was able to confidently arrive at the following conclusion: her father was still apparently the only suspect, and the police therefore had zero idea about the *actual* killer's identity.

With the grim and very real prospect of her beloved dad facing serious time behind bars, Quinn was determined to redouble her efforts to ensure that potential outcome should not come to pass. Using her considerable investigative experience, she'd set out to build a complete picture in her mind of the character that was Vincent Goodacre. She'd intended to speak with those who knew him, both personally and professionally. However, similar to how word about the victim's identity had leaked out before official confirmation, there were now many in the community who'd heard whispers that Chester Flitcroft was in the frame as the prime suspect. As such, knowing Quinn was his daughter, there were more than a few people she'd wanted to talk to who either didn't feel comfortable in doing so or flat-out refused, hampering her investigation as a result.

Still, with a thick skin and undeterred, she pressed on regardless. She simply had to. Because not only was she acutely aware that the idea of her father being a cold-hearted killer was quite frankly ridiculous, but with every second the real perpetrator remained at large, there was always the terrible possibility that they could strike again.

Initially, Quinn had wanted to have a good rummage through Major Goodacre's closet, so to speak, hoping to discover a few skeletons hiding back there that might provide a motive for his murder. However, the few people that did agree to talk to her all spoke of a charming, warm-hearted, and generous man who'd go out of his way to help you. A widower with an extended family living down in Australia, Vincent Goodacre spent his time, from what Quinn could gather, working on the board of several charities, keeping the local bowling club committee on their toes, and testing his skills around a poker table from time to time. Asked whether they knew of any enemies, the consistent feedback was that Mr Goodacre was a popular man that nobody had a bad word to say against.

Faced with a consensus that the man was thought of as an all-around good egg, Quinn had to weigh up whether the murder was premeditated, or if there was the possibility of something else afoot. Could the Major have been the victim of a robbery, for example? Or what about a case of mistaken identity, perhaps?

These were just some of the different, various scenarios kicking about inside of Quinn's head. And to fully investigate each of them, with the clock ticking, well, it felt like there simply weren't enough hours in the day. A good job, then, that the cavalry had just freshly landed at Ronaldsway, the Isle of Man's airport…

"Ah, Toby, it's so brilliant to see you," said Quinn, as she drove them on the thirteen-minute journey along the coast-hugging A5 over to Port Erin, a little bit further south on the isle. "And I have to say, the thought of working beside you again has really made me think it's possible that… that… Ehm, Toby…?"

But Toby wasn't really listening just now. Instead, he had his face positioned an inch or so from the passenger window, admiring the dramatic coastline where turquoise-coloured waves were caressing a long shingle beach. He watched on at one particular point where he observed one hardy soul, standing atop a paddleboard, swaying back and forth like a punch-drunk boxer before finally yielding and falling harmlessly back into the water.

"Hey, can we rent a paddleboard while I'm here?" Toby enquired, looking across to Quinn with pleading, hope-filled eyes. "I've always wanted to try it out."

"Sure," Quinn answered. "And if you help find me a murderer, Toby, then I'll even *buy* you a paddleboard, how does that sound?" Quinn then pointed to the folder currently lying on Toby's lap. "In there are all my notes, observations, and outstanding action points," she advised, keen to get her partner up to speed at the earliest opportunity. After all, time was of the essence considering there was a killer on the loose.

Toby dragged his attention away from the action on the waves and began turning the pages within the plastic ring binder that he'd been handed back at the airport. "Impressive work," he remarked, as he advanced through the detailed notes. "Wait, hold on..." he added a moment later, followed by an uneasy laugh.

Quinn flicked her eyes over to the passenger seat. "What is it? You've found something?"

"No, these names you've detailed here on page three..." Toby said, running his finger down the list like he was considering the menu at a fancy restaurant. "They're all people that were associated with our Mr Goodacre, correct?"

"Correct. Well, the ones that I know had dealings with him in the last month or two. But there'll be some that I've missed, so obviously we'll need to keep—"

However, Quinn's explanation was cut short by the sound of a mischievous giggling—the sort that a young boy might offer upon seeing a pair of naked boobies appear on the evening telly. "Uhm, Toby? Need I remind you that you're reading my dossier about a brutal murder and not a book of jokes?"

"Yeah, I know, but some of these names, Quinn," Toby replied. "I mean, seriously... Derek Ogilvy-Pratt, Winfield Bogel, Jesper Spatchcock, Cindy Shuttleworth, and Major Vincent Goodacre himself? They all sound like they came straight from the board game Monopoly or something."

"You mean Cluedo?" Quinn asked. "I think you mean Cluedo."

Toby shook his head. "Nah, it's the one where Colonel Mustard is in the Library with the Candlestick. Like that."

"Yes. That's Cluedo."

Toby considered this for a moment but appeared to remain unconvinced. "I thought Cluedo was that stuff that kids make elephant and giraffe models out of?"

"What...?" asked Quinn, as they approached the *'PORT ERIN WELCOMES CAREFUL DRIVERS'* sign. "Did you possibly get stuck into the complimentary bar on your flight over, by any chance?" And then, thinking about what he'd just said to her, "Wait, are you talking about Play-Doh, rather than Cluedo? That's the modelling clay that kids often use."

"Oh? I dunno, maybe," replied Toby. "I think I'm getting myself all confused. I've been conducting covert operations from a skip for the past week, so perhaps I've been overcome by noxious fumes or bitten by something poisonous. Or possibly both. Wait, did I say that right? Would it be *poisonous*, or *venomous*? I always get those two things confused..."

Quinn couldn't help but laugh at Toby's comical misfortune, which was a real tonic after the last few days. "Ah, Toby, it's so good to be working with you again," she said, reiterating her earlier sentiment. "You're an absolute kook, but you do make me smile," she added, before briefly glancing across. "Although..."

"Although?"

"The jury's still out on the shaved bonce," she said. "What's with the new look? You think you're Kojak now?"

Toby went quiet for a moment, suggesting he may have been a smidge offended by the gentle ribbing. "I wish I could say it was that, actually," he replied. "But, no, did you ever get chewing gum stuck in your hair when you were younger, and your mum had to cut it out with a pair of scissors...?" he asked.

Quinn pressed down on the car's indicator lever, steering the vehicle through the edge of town and down a narrow, twisting road that led directly towards the bustling seafront. "Not that I recall," she answered. "But I know what you're saying, of course. Why, is that what's happened to you? You recently got chewing gum stuck in your hair?"

"Uhm... well, not exactly," Toby said, running a hand across his smooth head. "But on that recent skip-based covert operation I told you about?" he continued. "I was working really long hours, and I may have dozed off on duty at one point. Anyway, I'd been overheating, and I stupidly removed my camouflage ghillie suit head piece. And God only knows what sort of industrial strength adhesive my head made contact with inside the dank confines of that heap. Because when I woke up, there was a load of rusting flakes of skip metal stuck solidly to my hair. *Big* flakes. Big *sharp* ones. Oh, and a fork, also."

Quinn pulled up near the front of the ice cream shop, grateful to find an available, open parking space. "Wait, what? A fork? As in a metal fork?"

"No, it was just one of the blue plastic ones you get from a chip shop," Toby advised. "Fortunately, the fork came off without too much fuss. But as for the large metal flakes... well, I tried everything to get them out when I got home later that night, including butter, baby oil, and even washing-up liquid. Sadly, nothing worked, and each time I ran my fingers through my hair I ended up slicing them to ribbons. My hair did smell quite nice by the end of it, though..."

Quinn applied the handbrake, giving the impression that she perhaps regretted ever introducing the present topic into conversation in the first place. "So that's why you shaved your hair off?" she asked, cutting to the chase in the hopes of bringing his tale to a reasonably swift conclusion, conscious they had the important matter of a murder investigation to focus on. "To get rid of the metallic head lice infestation, I mean?"

Toby sighed at the memory of his fallen locks. "Yeah, that's right. But would you mind having a gander at my scalp for me a bit later? I think there might be a few rogue flakes of skip still embedded somewhere in my skin," he said. "Because when I was walking through the airport security gate, I kept on setting off their metal detector. They must have made me walk through it a good six or seven times before believing I wasn't carrying any concealed weapons. At one point, I was worried I was going to miss my flight after it was taking so long with all the frisking and what have you. In fact, I was terrified they were even going to perform a full cavity search."

Quinn shook her head in disbelief. "I assured my dad that I was bringing over to the isle the most diligent, tenacious, hardworking, and professional detective that I've ever had the pleasure of working with," she related, for her colleague's benefit.

Toby pressed out his lower lip and tipped his head in acknowledgement. "Thanks, Quinn!" he said, sounding well-chuffed.

Quinn opened the car door before placing one foot onto the tarmac. "Yeah, well... after what you've just told me, I think that I'd better manage his expectations," she said, although her wry smile suggested she wasn't being overly serious. "Alright, come on, slaphead. We've got a murderer to catch..."

***

Following a brief pit stop for a cup of tea and a formal introduction to her father, Quinn was eager to get straight to work. But first, she took Toby downstairs for the ice cream she'd promised him as part of the determined negotiation process that had successfully persuaded him to fly over to the isle. Although in truth, his list of demands wasn't particularly high, consisting merely of a room to sleep in and the aforementioned frozen treat. They were friends, after all, and if Quinn needed him, then they both knew he would be there in an instant.

A short time later, sitting in The Bucket 'n' Spade after Toby's debut Manx ice cream was demolished without hardly touching the sides, so to speak, Quinn moved forward in reviewing her plan of attack regarding how best to smash this case wide open. Number one on the agenda, by her reckoning, was to do a deep delve into the background of those people in close, regular contact with Vincent Goodacre in the run-up to his murder. In her mind, this vicious crime was unlikely to be some random act of violence, of that Quinn remained convinced. Her investigative prowess suggested to her that this was a targeted assault, most likely perpetrated by somebody known to the victim.

During a slight lull in their discussion, Quinn looked over at Toby sitting on the opposite side of the table. "So, out of interest, what did the gaffer say when you told him you were taking your annual leave at short notice?" she asked by way of some simpler conversation.

However, Toby was maintaining his focus at the moment in reading through the dossier of case notes laid out in font of him, giving them his full and undivided attention like the diligent investigator he was. Either that or he was just ignoring the question for some reason, Quinn suspected.

"*Ahem*. Toby, I said I was just wondering what they said when you told work that you were heading over to the Isle of Man?"

Toby, in response, slowly raised his head, looking decidedly shifty at this point. "Erm, yeah, about that..."

"You *have* told work that you're taking holiday leave?"

"Nah," Toby said, while returning his attention somewhat to the page he'd just been reviewing. "You know what they're like, Quinn, they'd only have said no. So I figured I'd just leave and worry about it later. Besides, the bosses are always harping on in my performance reviews about 'showing some initiative,' and things like that. So I reckon that's precisely what I've done, yeah? I've shown initiative! If anything, they should be pleased that their messaging hit home, in my humble opinion."

"So the powers that be still believe you're on duty manning your skip...?" Quinn enquired, uncertain about the quality of the logic being presented, but amused nonetheless.

"Yep, probably. And the best bit is that I can still remote access all my employer's expensive-to-access databases to do some digging on *this* little lot," Toby added, pointing his pen towards the list of potential suspects he'd been provided with by Quinn.

Fully aware that her pal had dropped everything in order to stand by her side in her hour of need, Quinn regarded her companion with a gleam in her eye. "Thank you, Toby. You're one in a million."

Toby swatted away the gratitude without lifting his head up from what he was reading, although obviously appreciating the praise. "You just keep those ice creams coming and we'll say no more about it," he insisted.

Quinn pushed her seat back before rising up with the assured confidence of a woman on a mission. "Right, then. I'll leave you to it, partner, to see what you can uncover on that lot, okay? I'm going to go knocking on some doors around the neighbourhood to try and locate any CCTV footage of the crime scene that the police might possibly have missed."

Left to his own devices, Toby suddenly felt a wave of guilt as he was now occupying an entire table on his own when the shop was completely packed out with every other table full, with this becoming especially obvious after exchanging glances with a family hovering close by.

The dad of the family possessed the pained expression of a man who'd just had his wallet drained by his tribe of young ice cream fiends. He approached the table where Toby was stationed with hope-filled eyes and an inflatable beach crocodile secured under his arm. "I don't suppose you're leaving, are you...?"

"What's that? Oh, no, sorry, I—" Toby started to say, as he'd originally planned to use the ice cream shop as his investigative HQ for the day. But looking through the shop's front window to the world outside, the vision of a cloudless sky and glorious sunshine appeared as an altogether more appealing option instead. "In fact, scrap that," Toby decided, closing his laptop and collecting his paperwork. "I think I'll go and rent myself a deck chair and use the sand over yonder as my office for the day."

The dad, currently being pestered to purchase a beachball and other assorted items by three of his four offspring, gave Toby a *do-you-mind-if-I-come-and-join-you* look, before ushering his brood to grab the seats at the newly vacated table. "Cheers, mate," the jaded dad said. "And don't forget your suncream," he added, resting his inflatable crocodile up against the wall. "Because it's flippin' roasting out there."

"Roger that," said Toby. "Thanks."

For some individuals, the sound of people frolicking in the sea only metres away might prove something of a distraction, especially if you needed to get some work done. Moreover, it wasn't just those currently in the waves who were causing something of a ruckus, because Port Erin Beach was also busy with cheerful family members making sandcastles, playing beach volleyball, throwing a frisbee, or doing any number of things to generally make the most of the pleasant weather. But Toby, now stretched out on his rented lounge chair with his laptop lying on his belly, didn't mind the noise one bit. In fact, as he was presently reflecting, it was certainly preferable to crouching inside a decaying skip. Thus, he happily rolled up the trouser legs of his chinos before powering up his laptop.

Fortunately, as he had commented to Quinn just earlier, he was still technically on active duty, and therefore had complete access to his company's extensive suite of databases used to investigate global insurance fraud. With credit histories, electoral registers, criminal records checks, previous insurance claims, and a whole host of other goodies available at his fingertips, Toby had everything he needed to start building a broader picture of the potential suspects on his considerable list.

For the next couple of hours, Toby ploughed his way through the names Quinn had helpfully furnished him with. But it was slow progress, the administrative equivalent of wading through treacle with an adult hippopotamus strapped to your back. And granted, he did manage to uncover a few juicy bits on several of those listed in Quinn's dossier—information that those individuals would probably like to remain private, Toby suspected. But he'd discovered nothing that would entirely raise eyebrows, and certainly nothing of the scale that he'd consider to be a motive to commit murder.

Until, that is, he started reviewing the surnames starting with the letter 'S' on his alphabetised list of people. "Hmm," he said, sitting himself upright in his chair with his interest now piqued. For the next few minutes, he fervently tapped away on his keyboard with his eyes glued to the screen. "Ah-ha!" he eventually offered, gazing up from his laptop, delighted that his efforts had finally been rewarded.

Enthused by what he'd discovered, Toby reached into one of the pockets of his chinos and removed his phone, hastily scrolling through his lengthy list of contacts. Once he'd found the particular name he was looking for, he auto-dialled the number and placed the phone against his ear.

"Oh, hey there, Phillipa. This is Toby. Toby Haddock," he said brightly, once the call connected. "What's that…?" he asked, plugging his other ear with his finger, hoping to drown out the noisy, jubilant celebrations of some young children playing nearby.

"Erm, yeah," Toby replied to the question posed, now that he could properly hear it. "Yeah, precisely, I'm still working on the fly-tipping operation," he said, telling a little white lie—or more like an outright fib, really—to one of his colleagues back at base camp. Then, swiftly shifting the direction of the conversation, "Phillipa, I don't suppose you could help me with something…?" he asked. "What is it? Well, I need you to speak with that friend of yours to access the bank account of an individual. Is that possible? It is? Ah, brilliant. Give me a few minutes and I'll email you the name and last known address. Oh, and Phillipa? I owe you one!"

Armed with a contented grin, Toby eased himself back into his comfortable beach chair, giving thought, if just for a short moment, as to how many domestic appliances might have been tossed at the end of the country lane since he had vacated his skip-cum-office for an altogether more pleasant and favourable working environment.

"Cynthia Britney Shuttleworth," he then announced to himself aloud. "Congratulations, my dear, you have just entered my suspects list at the coveted number one spot!"

Chapter Nine

The sound of desperate whimpering permeated the air in the living room of Chester Flitcroft's flat. The noise was akin to that of a dog secured to a lamppost outside a local shop who was terrified that its owner had abandoned it rather than merely popping in for a loaf of bread and a pint of milk and suchlike.

But the source of this sorrowful snivelling wasn't, as it should happen, an overly anxious family pet...

"Aww, jeez Louise," Toby complained, digging his fingernails into the armrests of his chair, bracing himself for the next incoming assault. With his pain threshold already stretched to the limit, he added mournfully, "I'm not certain how much longer I can withstand this agony..."

With a sympathetic wince, Chester watched on from his cosy position on the sofa, where he was supported here and there by a number of comfy cushions. "*Oof.* That seems like it could scar, son," he noted. "Looks nasty."

Toby appreciated the expressed concern, which only served to reinforce just how much of a brave little soldier he believed he was being. "It really, really does hurt," he insisted.

Quinn, presently standing behind Toby's chair, didn't appear to be quite as pitying of Toby's current plight. "Oh for crying out loud, hold still, will you?" she said, as she squeezed some of the contents of a plastic bottle of salve into the palm of her hand. "Now brace yourself, you big baby, because I'm going in again."

In response, Toby instinctively moaned, like the executioner was just reaching for the lever to let loose the voltage to the electric chair. "It's kinda weird, you know? It feels both cold and hot at the very same time," he reported, as Quinn ultimately applied some additional balm to his skin.

Following a careful massage, Quinn leaned forward a bit to inspect her work, checking that her generous application of aloe vera gel was covering every millimetre of Toby's scorched scalp. "There. Done," she advised, using a tea towel to wipe the gloopy residue from her hands. "And it's probably not as bad as certain other people might think," she added, throwing her dad a look. "Although it's still beyond me why you'd want to sit on the beach for several hours this afternoon without using any sun cream."

Toby's pained expression softened as the cooling effect of the aloe vera gel worked its magic, temporarily dousing the flames. "I forgot I didn't have any hair on my head to protect me anymore," he offered as his defence. "So I reckon my newly exposed scalp wasn't toughened up enough to endure the brutal Isle of Man sunshine."

Quinn moved around to the front of the chair, handing Toby the rest of the aloe vera should a further top-up be required at some point. "Well, if you're going to stick with the shaven look, you should think about buying yourself a hat, yes?" Then, looking downward, closer to floor level, "Oh, and I'm not applying gel to your lower legs, Toby. That you can do yourself."

Toby stared down at the reddened areas on both of his shins and ankles. "I shouldn't have rolled up my chinos. That was mistake," he said, shaking his head in despair. "Honestly, I thought I was on the Isle of Man, not in flippin' Death Valley!"

"You're being melodramatic," Quinn said. "It's never that hot here, you silly thing. You just weren't as prepared as you—"

"Here," Chester cut in with some degree of devilment evident in his smile. "What if there are some metal skip fragments still embedded in your skin?" he asked, agitating the flames again. "You know. Embedded deep inside? Toby, they could be red hot by now."

Toby swallowed hard and was now fearing the worst. "Red hot and *melting*," he said in response. "Blimey, there could be a river of molten metal slowly making its way towards my brain, right as we speak!" he added, urgently pushing himself up from his seat. "I think I'd better go and give myself a cold shower before it's too late..."

Quinn playfully stamped a hoof, like a horse getting ready to charge. "Toby! There are no foreign metallic objects embedded in your skull," she insisted. "Now if you can manage to get ahold of yourself, we could get back to business, yes? So, please, will you just tell my dad what you told me over on the beach?"

Toby had witnessed that foot stamp previously, accompanied as it was now by arms folded across her chest. And whilst it was delivered with a friendly smile, he knew Quinn well enough to do as she said without further delay and regardless of how much personal discomfort he was in. As such, Toby proceeded as instructed, setting forth his findings to Chester. He revealed how he'd reviewed all of the names in Quinn's detailed dossier. Those names were, as he explained, friends, colleagues, associates, and anybody else who'd been in close contact with Major Goodacre in recent weeks leading up to his murder. Or those that Quinn, at least, was able to successfully uncover, of course.

Of those names he had punched into his work databases, the majority of them came back with a relatively clean bill of health. There were a handful of small exceptions consisting of: overdue parking fines, a few drunk and disorderly convictions, some who enjoyed a smoke of 'wacky baccy,' and one individual who'd been caught in a compromising embrace in a secluded car park with an inflatable sheep. But as Toby summarised, there was nothing in these various indiscretions to suggest anybody may have had a compelling reason or motive to want to harm the Major. Until that is, he input the name Cynthia Britney Shuttleworth into his laptop.

"Wait, is that not the young woman Vincent had cleaning for him...?" Chester interjected, having recognised the name. "Cindy. Yeah, I remember her," he went on, after receiving a nod as confirmation. "Whenever I was at his house and she was working, all she appeared to do was chew gum and look bored, as if she'd rather be anywhere else. Though that's not a motive to commit murder, surely?"

"You're right. It's not. But theft most certainly is," Toby replied. "You see our Cindy, as it should happen, has quite the rap sheet, consisting of a rash of petty theft convictions. A number of which, interestingly enough, having been perpetrated against former employers."

"As well as cleaning for Mr Goodacre and others, Cindy also worked behind the bar at Castle Rushen Bowling Club," Quinn pointed out for her dad's benefit. "Probably to help fund her expensive gambling habit, which we found out about."

Toby then picked up roughly where he'd left off, explaining how he'd called in a few favours that provided him with copies of both Cindy's bank records and those of Mr Vincent Goodacre. "Yes. Cindy's account statements were page after page of debits in favour of online bingo companies," Toby revealed, "with her cumulative spend far exceeding the salary of a humble cleaner and barmaid. Fortunate, then, that she was somehow managing to receive regular top-ups to her modest income."

"So she was stealing from the Major...?" Chester asked, arching an eyebrow.

Toby nodded. "It would appear so," he said. "There were regular cash withdrawals from his bank account that had no relation to any payment of her salary. Withdrawals that just so happened to coincide with cash deposits placed into her *own* bank account shortly following each transaction. Over twenty thousand pounds total in the last six months alone."

"She must have had access to his debit card and PIN number," Quinn thought aloud. And then, "We should call the police and give them this information, Toby," she added, promptly reaching for her phone. "Because this is exactly what we need to clear my father's name."

However, Toby didn't appear to be quite so keen on that idea, swiftly raising a palm in the air like he was directing traffic and requesting it to come to an immediate halt. "Quinn, no! Don't call them!" he instructed. "That is... at least not yet."

"Eh? Why not?" Quinn asked, unclear as to why they wouldn't want to hand this crucial piece of evidence over to the authorities straight away.

"Yes, whyever not?" Chester enquired additionally, as he quite liked the prospect of being exonerated for the crime of murder, thank you very much.

Toby, observing their puzzled faces, slowly lowered his hand, laying it to rest by his side. "Look, the way I see it," he explained, "we *could* give this info to the police and hope it's enough to get you off the hook, Chester. Or, we could keep on digging a bit and gift-wrap the entire case with a nice ribbon and sprinkle it with glitter, yeah? We do all the legwork for the coppers, tie up all the other loose ends—like why you were shoved down the stairs, and how that odd note ended up in the Major's pocket, for example—and make it impossible for them not to offer you an apology for ever thinking it was you in the first place."

Toby paused for breath, looking first to Quinn and then over to Chester, hoping to gauge their reactions. But they didn't seem too convinced by his plan of action if their neutral faces were anything to go by. Undaunted, Toby felt a need to fill the silence and continue. "Plus," he added to Quinn, sweeping an expressive hand through the air, "imagine how good our CVs would look if we solved a murder?" And captivated by that prospect, Toby then looked out through the front window, gazing dreamily across the length of Port Erin Bay. "We'd be a famous investigative duo... Like the Isle of Man's very own Dempsey and Makepeace."

Quinn took a moment to consider the merits of this suggestion, weighing up both the pros and the cons of it. "Well, I think more of a Sherlock Holmes and Dr Watson comparison would be preferable," she decided. "But still..."

"Okay, but who would be Holmes and who would be Watson?" asked Toby. "Because, you know, I rather believe that—"

"Oh, I think I know what you're about to say. And yes, I understand where you're coming from," said Quinn. "But hear me out first, because the way I see things, I was thinking that—"

"Yes, *hello*! Once you two have finished finding ways to tickle your egos," Chester felt the need to interject, "need I remind you both that it's not *you* who's potentially facing thirty years in the slammer? For that reason alone, do we not need to tell the police what we know about this shady Cindy character now?"

Quinn had in no way intended to downplay the severity of the situation, as her dad's fate was always present in her mind. But if somebody was trying to frame him, as seemed highly likely at this point, then perhaps digging a bit further as Toby suggested might not be so bad an idea, in that approaching the police with irrefutable evidence in hand could only be a good thing.

"Dad, I know what you're saying," Quinn said in response to her father's concerns. "But with Toby and me effectively investigating, I reckon we might only need another twenty-four hours or so. Forty-eight, max. That should give us the time to do some more digging around and wrap this case up for the authorities, all tied up in a bow as Toby says. So it won't be long before you're off the hook and the real killer is on their way to jail."

Chester appeared to remain somewhat reluctant about this proposed plan of attack, as its failure or success would naturally have a direct impact on his future liberty or lack thereof. "But if before then the police do come calling to drag me away in handcuffs, we'll inform them of what we know...?"

Quinn walked over to the sofa and knelt down, placing an assuring hand on her father's arm. "That goes without saying," she promised. "So, you're happy if we keep picking away at this case for a little bit longer?"

Chester rolled his head back until he was looking up at the ceiling. It was like he was trying to figure out what was the worst that could happen. "Dempsey and Makepeace indeed?" he said with a chuckle. And then, "Fine! But I'd prefer you to wrap this up in twenty-four hours rather than forty-eight, okay?"

Quinn nodded towards the living room door, giving Toby the signal that it was time to set to work. "We'll see what we can do, Dad," she said. "Now, if you'll excuse us, we need to go and speak with one Cynthia Britney Shuttleworth."

However, before the pair had taken more than a step or two towards the doorway, "Oi! Hold on!" Chester called out, delaying their immediate departure. "Before you go, Toby."

Toby spun around. "Yes? What's up, Chester?"

"I need to know something," Chester insisted.

"Okay, sure," Toby agreed with a shrug, although anxious to sally forth and continue on with the investigation, conscious as he was that their countdown clock had already begun ticking. "What is it you'd like to know...?"

"Honestly, this is seriously important," Chester stressed, with a perfectly deadpan expression about him. "And I don't want you sparing me from the details."

"Uhm... alright?" Toby said with some apprehension, wondering what he might be agreeing to but agreeing nevertheless as it seemed very significant to Chester. "Just name it."

"The person you mentioned earlier. You know, the one with the blow-up sheep in the secluded car park?" Chester answered. "You have to tell me who that was...!"

***

If he was being perfectly honest with himself, Toby had been a tad ambivalent about his chosen career path of late. Sure, investigating insurance fraud could be interesting, and exhilarating, even, if you were presented with a juicy case you could really sink your teeth into. Unfortunately, however, he'd had a recent run of assignments that were, in his professional opinion, a bit naff.

Of course this wasn't a new experience, and having to take the rough with the smooth was all part of the job. After all, not every case was going to be something straight out of the movies, like busting a diamond smuggling operation wide open, for example. This Toby knew. But when the occasional snooze-fest had come along over the course of the previous several months, he could always rely on his partner to keep him company and help cheer him up, no matter the nature of their current mission. Indeed, even when he was drowning in pools of his own perspiration inside a rusting skip, Toby couldn't help but reflect on how it probably would have been quite good fun had Quinn been there to playfully bust his chops and keep him in line.

And that was the reason, then, collaborating with his old pal once more, that Toby was presently sporting a huge grin as he struggled not to fall too far behind of his associate—a lady on a mission, if her assured stomp was anything to go by.

Quinn glanced over her shoulder without letting up her pace, ascending a particularly steep set of stone steps leading from the seafront up to a portion of the headland overlooking the bay. "Oi, are you on slow mode back there?"

Toby swatted away her words while taking heavy breaths to force some air into his lungs. "No, I'm just being observant and making sure we're not being followed. You know, like all good investigators should!" he insisted. He was lying, of course. Many months of paying for a gym membership without ever actually attending was starting to take its toll on his overall fitness levels.

One of the joys of working a case on the Isle of Man, at least, was that nowhere was particularly too far to get to on account of the island's relatively small size. Unlike the *much* larger chunk of land back home, where many of the more complicated investigations might mean commuting from one side of the UK to the other, often stuck driving in the car for hours on end. Indeed, on this present occasion, there wasn't even a need to hop into a car at all, with their eventual destination being only a bit less than a mile away. Still, Toby felt he could've used some sort of vehicle just now—a helicopter, maybe?—as he panted like an overheating dog pushing himself up the current path they were on.

Already at the top of the steps, Quinn took the opportunity to admire the slightly elevated view of the beach below, which was nestled in between the two towering headlands on either side. It was a picture postcard backdrop, and one that had been appreciated by generations of visitors to this charming seaside town. In addition, as was evident by the alluring aroma of warm malt vinegar currently wafting on the gentle breeze, it was also popular with good folk eager for a coastal vista to accompany their fish and chips.

A good twenty seconds later, Toby finally joined Quinn, doing his best to regulate his breathing and not give the impression he needed to sit down for five or ten or maybe fifteen minutes. Instead, he placed his hands on his hips, hoping a lungful of the salty sea air might help invigorate him. And he did get that, yes. But he also took in the tantalising scent of a nearby couple's meal as well. "Bloody hell, that smells absolutely delightful."

Quinn cast an eye over to the two ladies tucking into their dinner. "It does. But if the colour of your cheeks just from climbing those steps is anything to go by, I'd give the fried grub a wide berth for the foreseeable," she advised. "Now, come on."

Of course she wasn't being overly serious, just pleased to have somebody on active duty with her with whom she could share such banter. Plus, truth be told, she'd gained a couple of pounds herself over the past several years, a state of affairs that she was actively trying to remedy.

"Also, I was happy enough to drive the car to our ultimate destination, but you insisted on a brisk walk to travel there instead, taking the scenic route, if you recall?" Quinn then reminded her salivating colleague.

Eager to reinforce the idea that he was, in actual fact, a prize physical specimen, Toby launched into a set of enthusiastic star jumps along with a bit of running in place, much to the amusement and bemusement of those sitting on nearby benches tucking into their lovely fried food. "I'm just getting warmed up!" he declared. "Now lead on, Macduff, I'm ready when you are... Erm, in just a second, that is..."

Quinn didn't need asking twice, pressing on while Toby took a short moment to recover from his impromptu exercise session. Then, following a brief glance at the notes she'd stored on her phone, "Right. If our information is correct, Cindy lives in that block of flats over yonder," she advised, once Toby had caught up. "You can see it from here."

Now alongside, Toby raised his forefinger in the air like he was checking which way the wind was blowing. "Quinn, I was just thinking," he said with a thinly disguised smile. "You know when I was conducting thorough investigations and obtaining extensive intel on all of the potential suspects in this case...?"

"You mean lounging on the beach in a deck chair with your laptop perched on your belly and a chilled bottle of Fanta within easy reach?"

Toby couldn't disagree with this assessment, and was amazed that Quinn had so much of it correct, apparently by clairvoyance. "That's right. Although it was Sprite, rather than Fanta," he felt the need to convey, what with precise details being so critical in their shared line of work. "No, but what I was *actually* going to ask is what *you* were doing, while I was busy cracking open this case like a walnut," he added, finger still aloft. "Or maybe like a Brazil nut. You know, those really difficult ones to get open...?"

However, Quinn wasn't taking the bait, at least not entirely, suspecting she was on the receiving end of some gentle ribbing. "Well, I was out knocking on doors, scouring for any possible CCTV footage that might shed some light on what happened to Mr Goodacre," she said matter-of-factly, darting her eyes between the apartment blocks they were now walking towards and trying to figure out which one was their target. "After all, we now know how he was killed," she added. "At least in a general sense, in that he was bludgeoned to death. But what was the motive? And how did the killer go about it? For instance, did the murder take place on the beach itself? Or was the victim attacked elsewhere, and the body only placed there afterwards? Or, let's say, for example, that—"

"Any joy...?" Toby cut in, because these were all unanswered questions that he was already aware of.

Quinn shook her head in the negative, but her sunny expression suggested all was not lost. "The constabulary, to give them their due, had already visited every property that I did. All except for *one*..." she said.

But Quinn had casually drifted off before imparting any possible details of what she may have found. Instead, she glanced at the address stored in her phone and cross-referenced it with the building they were now standing in front of. "Hmm, I think this is us," she noted.

Toby stared at her hard. "*And...?*" he said.

"Hmm? And, what?" Quinn asked innocently.

Toby cast his partner a suspicious look. He knew from experience that she enjoyed meandering off topic if it meant she'd be keeping him in suspense. "I didn't just fall off the turnip truck, Flitcroft. You know exactly what I'm talking about!"

A CASE OF MAJOR MURDER

Quinn's devious smirk suggested he was correct. "Well," she said, steering the ship back on its original course and addressing Toby's question, "I must have visited thirty or so buildings during the course of the morning, residential and commercial," she revealed. "Unfortunately, a good few of them didn't have CCTV cameras, and those that did had already provided their footage to the police."

Now standing before Cindy's apartment block, Toby was still listening, but was also reviewing the name plates under each of the intercom buzzers positioned next to the front door. "Okay, so if the police have all of the available CCTV and your dad is still the prime suspect, we can assume they've found nothing in the footage to change their minds?"

"That's how it looks, yeah," Quinn replied. "Fortunately, that's when I found the vandalised boat."

Toby gave his attention back to Quinn, while arching a thumb over his shoulder. "I can't find Cindy's name listed under any of the buzzers," he told her. And then, with Quinn's words finally landing, "Eh...? *What* vandalised boat?"

Quinn chuckled to herself upon receiving the sort of response she'd been hoping for. With Toby now dangling on the end of her rod, so to speak, she continued with her story. "After I finished traipsing around Port Erin," she said, "I decided to head back and meet you. And it was when I was walking over by the Port Erin Lifeboat Station I spotted a fishing vessel with a giant... Well, an enormous... Erm, that is, a huge..."

"A huge what? Just spit it out!"

Quinn stepped in closer to Toby, looking around to make sure there wasn't anybody within earshot. "A giant willy," she said.

"You mean like Free Willy? A giant okra, or whatever they're called?" Toby asked.

"No, I mean a *phallus*," Quinn clarified. "It was graffitied on there. And it was at least four feet long, I'd reckon."

"What? Somebody swam out and painted a four-foot todger on the side of a boat...?" Toby asked, unsure if he wasn't the only one who'd been exposed to delirium-inducing levels of UV rays recently. "And also, sorry, but what exactly does that have to do with our investigation? I mean I'm not saying it's not interesting or anything like that. It's just, again, what's it got to do with our investigation?"

"The boat wasn't in the water," Quinn explained, smiling as an elderly chap with a walking stick ambled slowly up the concrete path in their direction with the straps of a shopping bag secured tightly in his spare hand. "It was on land, supported on one of those frame thingies they set them on when they're out of the water," she said. "You know, so they don't keel over."

"Keel over? Did you just make a pun...?" Toby asked, wondering if he should be impressed or not. But he still didn't know how any of this might be relevant to their case, so in the meantime he turned his attention to the approaching elderly fellow, offering him a friendly smile. "Can I help you carry that?" Toby called over, concerned if the old boy was perhaps struggling with both a walking stick and a well-stuffed plastic shopping bag to contend with.

"No, but thanks," came the grateful response. "Right now I'm in perfect balance, you see, and if I let go of my shopping while I'm still in motion then I might topple over," the man said with a ragged, staccato laugh that sounded like an old lawnmower engine spluttering to life after the spark plug had been taken out and cleaned with a wire brush.

With his offer politely declined, Toby returned his attention to Quinn and the matter at hand. "Right. Anyway, what number flat are we looking for? Because like I said, I don't see—"

"We don't have the flat number," Quinn had to remind him. "Anyway," she pressed on, not yet finished recounting the details of her boat story. "According to the owner I spoke with—or the captain, rather—his boat has been defaced with inappropriate artwork several times over the last few months or so while it was either out of the water getting repaired or moored at the pier. He reckons it might be a disgruntled former employee. Or former crew member, I guess you would say."

The elderly fellow with the walking stick had by this stage made his way up to the front door of the apartment building and

A CASE OF MAJOR MURDER

placed his shopping down on the ground (somehow managing to successfully maintain his balance), rummaging around in his pocket to locate his key.

Toby, who had politely stepped to one side to afford the chap plenty of room, cleared his throat. "Excuse me, sir. We're looking for somebody who lives in this block of flats," he said. "But we're not entirely certain of her flat number."

The man, who'd recovered his keys by this time, eyed Toby with suspicion. "And you are...?" he asked, looking oddly at Toby's sunburnt head. "You're not those TV licence inspectors, are you?"

Toby laughed. He'd been accused of being many things during the course of his career, but never a TV licence inspector. "What? Absolutely not. No, sir, we're nothing of the sort. We're private investigators, actually, and we're looking for a woman who lives here by the name of Cynthia, or Cindy, Shuttleworth."

The older gent remained captivated by Toby's red, blistered bonce, making no attempt to hide his interest. "Shuttleworth...? What sort of name's that?" he then asked, lowering his attention to Toby's eye level. "Sounds like some kind of American car from the nineteen sixties, doesn't it?"

Toby offered an accommodating grin in return, thankful he'd not yet been told to sling his hook. "It's a particular lady we're looking for. She's got auburn hair, in her early twenties..." he said, not really imagining there were too many flats inside the modestly sized block, and therefore not that many people living there to choose from. "She's a barmaid in the bowling club."

"Hmm, does she smoke quite a lot?" the man asked, lifting his walking stick until he was pointing it at the ground-floor flat to one side of the front doorway. And there, scattered on the grass directly beneath the flat's window, were dozens upon dozens of discarded cigarette butts lying there like fallen soldiers after a fierce battle.

"If so," the fellow continued, "there's a young girl who lives in Flat One that smokes like a bloody chimney and stinks the entire place out. Swears like a drunken sailor as well. As I recall, she once gave me a business card for some new business venture of hers. Cleaning services, I think it was...?"

"Yes! She's a cleaner!" Quinn entered in. A little too enthusiastically, perhaps, as she appeared to temporarily startle the old chap, causing him to wobble for a moment. "Flat One, you say?"

The elderly gentleman nodded, giving Toby's burnt head one more quizzical stare before shuffling forward and inserting his key into the lock. "And..." he added over his shoulder. "If you two *do* turn out to be TV licence inspectors, then just remember old Gary Snapper helped you out when you needed it, yeah?"

Toby offered a spirited thumbs-up, even though Gary now had his back to him. "Uhm, yes. Of course. Thanks, Mr Snapper. We'll be sure to make a note of your cooperation," he said, easily slipping into his new role as an enforcer of TV licences.

With Gary soon safely inside, Toby took a deep breath, almost afraid to say what he was about to say next. "Okay, so about the HMS *Ding-a-Ling*," he said to Quinn, in reference to her earlier, somewhat delayed boat explanation. "I'm sort of intrigued and invested in your story, but can we maybe fast-forward and skip to the conclusion?"

Quinn, always happy to oblige, did as requested and cut to the chase. "Well, the owner or captain that I'd stopped to speak with was thoroughly fed up with having his boat constantly vandalised. So his son installed a couple of those video doorbell thingies in the wheelhouse, hoping to capture the culprit in the act."

"A-ha! I think I see!" said Toby, suddenly very interested. "And one of these cameras might just have captured some video of the beach on the day Vincent Goodacre was murdered...?" he asked, putting two and two together in what might have been the most protracted story he'd listened to all year.

"That's the hope. The captain first needs to check with his son who'd rigged up the cameras for him. So he promised he'd give me a call later. But..."

"But?"

"If he helps us, then he wants a favour in return."

Toby wondered what help he could possibly be to a fisherman and wasn't sure he liked the sound of this. "Look, I get seasick," he was quick to point out. "So don't be thinking I'm going out on the water to catch fish, or lobsters, or something."

"Eh? Don't be daft, Toby. I remember you telling me you got violently ill going on that little bumper boat ride at Thorpe Park over in Surrey thirty-some-odd years ago. Although why you felt the need to keep reminding me of it during each and every one of our assignments, I have no idea."

"The wound is still fresh, even now," Toby complained. "Other children were laughing at me, the rotten little devils."

"Anyway, knowing your history, Toby, I wasn't about to offer up your services on some sea-faring vessel, now was I?" Quinn answered. "Toby...? Toby, are you listening...?"

"What? Oh, sorry, I was still thinking about the other children laughing at me while I was spewing my guts out. Evil bastards. Sorry, go ahead. You were saying?"

"Right. I'd mentioned to the skipper during our conversation that I was a private investigator," Quinn went on. "So, naturally, he asked for our help in finding out who's been desecrating his vessel, in return for aiding us if he can. Assuming the cameras set up by his son didn't already capture the culprits in the act."

But before Toby could bestow praise on Quinn's investigative genius, as it looked like she was waiting for, a wooden window frame in the nearby flat creaked open, diverting their attention. And a short moment later, a plume of acrid smoke billowed forth like a steam train emerging from a tunnel.

Quinn took a slight step away from the entrance and glanced over to the side, where she saw a woman's head partially appear through the open window with a fag hanging out of her lips. The flat's occupant, a young lady with bright auburn hair, rested her elbows on the window ledge, sucking the life out of her cigarette like it was the only thing keeping her alive.

Eager to seize the moment and strike while the iron was hot, Quinn moved over a bit so she could clearly see, and could clearly be seen by, the young woman she assumed must be Cindy.

"Oh, yes. Hello," Quinn said, raising a hand and waving as if greeting an old friend. "Hiya. Are you Cindy, by any chance?"

The young lady with her head poking out glared back, looking at Quinn root to branch, so to speak, and regarding her like a lumberjack surveying a tree they were about to tackle with their chainsaw or axe. She sucked in a lungful of smoke before releasing a slow and steady stream that partially shrouded her from view like London fog. "It depends," came the surly response, just as the poisonous cloud wafted skyward, possibly towards Gary Snapper's flat for his continued appreciation. "Look," Cindy then added, sounding as if she was now very much about to go on the defensive. "If you're Tyson's wife, then you should know that he told me he wasn't married, right? So if you've got a problem then you should take it up with—"

Quinn cautiously moved a tad closer to the opened window, holding out both hands as if this would in some way demonstrate that she wasn't a jilted wife intent on exacting some kind of revenge for her gallivanting husband's unfaithful ways. "I'm not Tyson's wife," Quinn said calmly, maintaining a respectful distance, both from Cindy and the carpet of fag butts scattered beneath her window. "My name's Quinn," she advised. "And the gentleman over there is my partner, Toby."

This formal introduction served only to irritate Cindy, who now reared up—as much as the confines of the opened window frame would allow, at least—deftly dispatching the remainder of her ciggy with an impressive flick of her middle finger against the tip of her thumb, the fag butt landing next to its comrades on the grass who had already made their ultimate sacrifice. "I've already spoken to the police," Cindy insisted, retreating from the window a bit and folding her arms in front of her, utilising her pink fluffy dressing gown as a sort of protective shield. "And like I already said, I only worked for the Major for a few weeks, and I don't know nuffin' about nuffin', alright?"

Quinn raised a palm in the air, swirling her hand around in little circles, as if she were a snake charmer trying to mesmerise a snake. "Cindy, relax. We're not the police," she said, calmly and gently.

Cindy gave the impression that she was somebody who liked to jump to conclusions without knowing all the available facts, Quinn observed. A personality attribute that repeated itself just a very short moment later, in fact.

A CASE OF MAJOR MURDER

"Well if you're working for the landlord, then you can tell that greedy sod I'll pay him his outstanding rent when he replaces the living room carpet, yeah? It's that riddled with fag burns it looks like somebody's opened fire on it with a bleedin' machine gun," Cindy growled. "And I swear it was like that when I moved in!" she quickly added.

Quinn suddenly felt a great deal of sympathy. Not for Cindy, that is, but for Cindy's landlord, as well as her neighbours.

"No," Quinn said, softly but firmly. "No, if you'd let me finish, Cindy. My colleague Toby and myself are private investigators. We hoped to simply ask you a few questions about your time working for Mr Goodacre. Could we perhaps come in and speak with you for a few minutes...?"

Cindy uncrossed her arms and pointed a rigid finger through the opened window. "No, I've a far better idea. Why don't the pair of you go ahead and just piss right off," she said, admonishing Quinn, in addition to poor Toby, who hadn't even as yet opened his mouth. "I've got nothing to say to Tyson's wife, the police, or to you two shady characters. Understood?"

Toby, for his part, could be forgiven for thinking that Cindy wasn't the forthcoming type. So before she had the opportunity to slam the window shut, he leapt forward, holding it open from his spot outside. "Sure, Cindy, we'll be happy to bugger off for you as you've requested," he told her. "But before we do that..." he said, accompanied by his most charming of grins, as if he was chatting up a pretty girl in a nightclub. "Rather than play games and dance around the reason we're standing here outside, how about if I just come out and tell you something...?"

"Tell me *what?*" she said, her eyes shooting daggers at Toby's hand for holding her window open when she wanted very much to close it just now.

"The something in question is that I know you were stealing money from a man who later turned up murdered on Port Erin Beach. How does *that* sound...?" Toby put forth. He then held his breath for a second or two, just long enough for Cindy to register what he'd said, before he continued.

"Oh, and if you've spoken to the police, Cindy, do they know about the thefts? Because if they don't, then I'm certain they'll find it to be very, *very* interesting."

With the fight leaving Cindy faster than air escaping from a squashed whoopee cushion, her head fell to one side, shoulders sagging in defeat. "Fine. Go and wait over by the front door," she told them. "I'll let you both in..."

Chapter Ten

The Bay View Garden Centre, positioned equidistant between the villages of Port Erin and Port St Mary, provided a mecca for those green-fingered Isle of Man residents eager to scratch their horticultural itch. And like many similar establishments on the isle, it also attracted and maintained an additional client base thanks to its onsite tearoom, renowned for serving up an enticing array of home-baked treats both sweet and savoury. Quite how the business ended up with its idyllic-sounding name was something of a mystery, as it appeared to be a slight embellishment of the truth. Because, as far as its clientele could see, there wasn't a view of the bay to be enjoyed from within any square inch of its botanical walled gardens.

Still, such minor details didn't seem to be playing too heavily on the minds of those filling up their assorted shopping baskets and trolleys with an array of flora and other items, if their jolly demeanours were any yardstick.

All jolly, at least, until a sour-faced Cindy Shuttleworth peeked out from her position of cover behind the large feathery plumes of a flourishing pampas grass plant. It'd been nearly twenty-four hours since she'd been doorstepped by the pair of investigators, Quinn and Toby, but she was still intensely displeased at being subjected to such an accusatory line of questioning in her own home. (Well, her home until the landlord could evict her for not actually paying rent for the pleasure of living there.)

Cindy wasn't exactly inconspicuous at the present moment, on account of her flamingo pink tracksuit and lime green trainers. But on the basis she'd not yet been observed by those she was trailing, it suggested she was doing something right, one might argue. Indeed, one might further suggest that being surrounded by such vibrant and vivid blooms as she was, her sartorial explosion of colour was the ideal outfit with which to blend in.

Cindy paused, standing beneath an ivy-covered wooden arch, watching on intently like a lioness stalking a Serengeti watering hole and waiting for the perfect time to strike. Her unsuspecting victim, up ahead, with her nose pressed up to a potted geranium was Primrose Ellis, presently harbouring notions of refreshing her extensive hanging basket collection at home. Primrose, the social secretary and lady's team captain at the bowling club, was dressed in cream-coloured shorts and a yellow sleeveless collared shirt, appearing ready for a round of golf, perhaps, rather than a wander around the garden centre.

The very instant Primrose's husband finally left her side, leaving her vulnerable and exposed, Cindy approached her quarry, replacing her frustrated scowl with a friendly smile. "Oh, hiya! Fancy meeting you here, Primrose," she said casually, sounding as if their meeting was entirely coincidental and she absolutely hadn't been shadowing the woman and her husband all morning. Which she absolutely had.

Primrose removed her sniffer from the floral petals, looking Cindy up and down, and then up and down again. It was evident from the look on her face that Primrose had precisely zero idea who the polychromatic creature standing in front of her actually was, much less addressing her on a first-name basis. "Erm, yes. So good to see you," Primrose eventually offered, although it was anything but sincere.

Conscious that Primrose's husband could return at any given moment, Cindy didn't have the luxury of time to engage in too many pleasantries. "It's me, Cindy," she said, deciding it best not to beat around the bush too much. "Cindy, the barmaid from the bowling club."

Primrose appeared thoroughly inconvenienced by this interruption to her activities. "Ah, yes. Always a pleasure, Cindy," she replied, before placing the geranium she'd been looking at into her shopping carriage. However, when the barmaid in the gaudy outfit didn't continue on her way, Primrose felt the unfortunate pressure to exchange small talk. Something she detested. "Are you here to buy something for the garden?" she offered, sounding completely disinterested in the response before it had even arrived.

Cindy laughed. "Me? Oh, no. I live in a poxy ground-floor flat. Besides, I'd probably only kill the thing."

Primrose offered an uncomfortable smile. "Well, don't let me keep you, Cindy..." she suggested.

Cindy glanced over her shoulder, making sure they were still alone, before taking two short steps closer so that their feet were almost touching. Then, in a whispered voice, she leaned in and said, "I know all about you and Derek," referring, of course, to the conversation she had overheard at the bowling club. With that stark revelation thus delivered, she took a step back, watching as Primrose's pupils dilated.

"What are you prattling on about, girl?"

However, Cindy didn't have the time or the inclination to skirt around the particular issue. "Look, Primrose. We can either talk now, just me and you. Or we can wait until your loving husband returns, yeah? But the fact of the matter is that I know exactly what you and Derek Ogilvy-Pratt have been up to."

Cindy's heart was bouncing against her ribcage, unsure if she was about to have a potted plant smashed over her head. "I also know about the letter you received from Major Goodacre," she then added. "So it's pretty convenient the old duffer ended up dead before he could tell your husband, isn't it?"

"Poppycock. You're talking rubbish, girl. Now get out of my way before I—"

But Cindy wasn't for moving, with her now on a roll and eager to unburden herself entirely of what was on her mind. "As well as your husband, I'd reckon the police would also be very interested in your affair, Primrose," Cindy was happy to point out. "Well, the part about you receiving a threatening sort of letter from a man later found dead. Now, I'm no legal expert, Primrose. But I'd imagine that's the sort of information the police would be grateful for. Whaddaya think?"

Primrose noticed that her husband was now walking past the small potted apple trees and would be returning to her location momentarily. As such, her bluster rapidly evaporated. "What do you want, girl? And make it quick!"

Cindy resisted the urge to rub her hands together in delight. "I need a bit of cash," she said. Although considering that money was often the primary reason for extortion, this should've likely come as little surprise. "You see, I'll need to leave the island for a while," Cindy added, figuring an indefinite vacation would be just the ticket following the allegations of theft the two troublesome investigators had levelled against her the previous afternoon. "So, thirty grand up front and then two thousand a month thereafter should do it," she stated.

"You've got bats in your belfry if you think I'm paying you any of that, you cretinous trollop," came the response.

Cindy wasn't sure what that meant, but she was fairly certain it wasn't complimentary. "Fine. In that case, I'm sure your exceptionally wealthy husband would like to know what his darling wife has been up to. As would the police, no doubt." Cindy then began to turn her back, giving the impression that she was about to intercept the advancing Oscar Ellis, Primrose's unsuspecting husband. "You know," Cindy added, as an apparent afterthought, "I may even stop by the offices of the local newspaper on my way home..."

Primrose lurched forward, placing a taloned hand on Cindy's shoulder. "Okay, I'll pay you. But keep your filthy mouth shut, all right?"

Just then, Oscar returned from wherever he had been previously, carrying a Venus flytrap in his hand. "Look what I found, Primrose," he said to his wife, offering Cindy a cordial nod of the head. "I always wanted one of these to keep the pesky flies at bay in the orangery."

Primrose removed her claws from Cindy's shoulder. "Darling. This is Cindy. Cindy from my bowling club. We were just talking about... erm..."

"My goodness, you're like an explosion in a paint factory, my dear!" Oscar approvingly declared, admiring Cindy's colourful attire, as well as her bright auburn hair. "And I'm charmed to make your acquaintance."

Cindy sensed her work here was done, and that it was time to make a strategic exit. "Erm... ditto," she said. And then, turning to address Primrose, "I'll be in touch very soon," she added. "We can arrange for you to drop around that... uhm... that *recipe* we discussed. Anyway, I'll leave you to your plants. Toodle pip."

***

"For a girl so eager to get healthier and shed some of her extra poundage, having a temporary office located in the corner of an ice cream shop isn't ideal," Quinn remarked, in reference to herself, while using her spoon to scrape out the last remaining bit of goodness from the little plastic serving tub in her hand.

Toby glanced up from his laptop screen. "You know, they also sell fruit smoothies, Quinn. So there's a decent variety of fresh fruit you could have introduced into your diet, instead of simply opting for ice cream again?"

Quinn looked at him as if he'd taken leave of his senses. "Have you gone mad...?" she said. "That's like going to a steakhouse and ordering yourself a salad, Toby. Complete madness."

But with snack time concluded and returning to business, Quinn shifted her focus to the pile of documents she had been diligently sifting through for much of the morning. This included a thick stack of (not-quite-legally-obtained) bank statements for Vincent Goodacre and several other individuals that Quinn and Toby considered to be of interest and pertinent to the case. But Quinn wasn't entirely sure what she was looking for, exactly, instead just ploughing through and hoping something of relevance or importance might perhaps catch her eye. It was rather like trying to complete a jigsaw puzzle when you didn't have the benefit of viewing the finished picture on the front of the box, as she'd earlier remarked to Toby.

However, still lingering in Quinn's mind and slightly distracting her efforts was their meeting with Cindy the previous afternoon. During their limited interaction, Cindy had initially presented herself as a bit of a harmless scatterbrain, making light of her involvement—and the evidence presented against her—as being nothing more than an innocent coincidence. Indeed, between her garish dress sense and her potty mouth, some would no doubt have suspected her of being a bit of a scallywag and nothing more. Still, Quinn couldn't help but suspect there was a highly intelligent, conniving and calculated individual lurking beneath her thick, carefully applied makeup.

Not for a moment did Quinn ever imagine that Cindy would simply roll over and confess to being a cold-hearted murderer when presented with their evidence about Vincent Goodacre's misappropriated funds. But her immediate and casual explanation for how multiple debits went out of Mr Goodacre's account and subsequently ended up in hers took Quinn by surprise.

"Oh, *that*," Cindy had remarked at the time, appearing entirely unconcerned about any allegations being directed her way. "The Major liked pretty girls, if you see what I'm saying," Cindy had offered dismissively. "And if I happened to be wearing a particularly short skirt or figure-hugging top when I went around to clean his house... well, let's just say that he was especially generous when it came along to payday."

Quinn knew—or at least strongly suspected—that this was a boatload of rubbish, providing an unlikely and dubious explanation for the numerous credits appearing in her bank account at such strange, suspicious intervals. But with the only person able to discredit her story lying in a morgue on a cold slab, there was no other option but to take her story at face value. For the time being, at any rate. Therefore, with no crime to speak of—or none that could be currently proven, at least—Cindy was anxious to point out that there was no motive at all for her to want to "bump off" her regular provider of paycheques that was the Major.

At the conclusion of their meeting in Cindy's flat, Quinn had been frustrated and disappointed, suspecting she'd just listened to a complete pack of lies from a practised and quick-thinking storyteller. But being able to actually prove that suspicion was something else again. After all, what went on between an exhibitionist cleaner and a potentially frisky old geezer was known only between the two of them.

Later that morning on the present day, while beavering away at their ice cream shop HQ, Quinn began tapping her pen down on the tabletop as she slowly drowned in a sea of paperwork—with the incessant tapping almost sounding as if she was trying to send out some kind of message in Morse code.

Toby, troubled by the repetitive racket, attempted to drop a subtle hint to bring this impromptu performance to conclusion. "I don't have an Enigma machine to be able to crack that code. What is it you're trying to say, partner?"

Quinn, nibbling down on her bottom lip, was staring off into the distance as she ran something through her mind. "I was just thinking about Mr Goodacre's bank statement," she said after a moment or two. "He received two large payments from a Swiss-registered company last year, correct?"

"Yes, that's right. Two whopping payments of a hundred thousand pounds each. However, with it being Swiss-domiciled and owing to their draconian secrecy laws, I've not yet been able to determine who owns that particular company."

Quinn chewed this over for a bit. "What do we know about his business interests...?" she asked rhetorically, now using her pen as a pointer, running it down a list of the Major's known assets. "He received regular rental income from three residential properties he owned, a generous pension from his time in the British Army, and a modest annual payment from the bowling club for use of the clubhouse."

"The Major owned the bowling clubhouse?" Toby asked.

Quinn scanned her notes again to make sure she had her facts correct, which she did. "Mm-hmm, and the land it sits on. From reading through the public records, it revealed how he inherited a great swathe of land from his uncle twenty or so years ago." Quinn peered at the map she'd downloaded from the Land Registry and printed out. "According to this, he inherited the land on which the bowling club resides and also a huge chunk of the surrounding area," she said. Then, reaching over to another stack of documents, she sifted through the pages, glancing over and cross-referencing the information with the printed map. "Hmm, it looks like he then subsequently sold off most of the neighbouring land but chose to retain the parcel on which the bowling club rests. I suppose he must have really liked crown green bowling."

"So, we know the Major wasn't short a bob or two, but there's nothing on his list of assets that would warrant the payment of two hundred large?"

"Nope. Nothing that I can find."

Toby flicked his arm forward, glancing down at his watch. "Right. We should go, Quinn. We've got an appointment with the chairman of the bowling club in twenty minutes. A Mister Derek Ogilvy-Pratt."

Quinn couldn't help but smirk as she collected her papers into a neat pile.

"You're grinning about his ridiculous name?"

"No," Quinn replied. "It's just that there's a little girl on the next table who hasn't stopped gawping at your sunburnt head since she sat down."

Toby looked over his left shoulder, pulling a funny face for the benefit of the wee girl who was waiting patiently for her mum to return to their table with her promised ice cream. "When your mum tells you to put your suncream on, make sure you always do it, yeah?" Toby cautioned. "Otherwise, you'll end up with a bright red bonce. Like me!"

The little girl gave a big smile, highlighting the fact that one of her front teeth was missing. "Does it hurt?" she asked.

"Nah, it's not so bad right now. Besides, the doctor told me I ought to eat ice cream all day in order to cool it down. Which is why I'm in *here*," Toby said with a wink.

The little girl's eyes widened at this wondrous prospect. "If I get sunburned then I get to eat ice cream all day?" she asked, just as her mum returned to their table wondering why this stranger was telling her little cherub to get too much sun exposure.

Toby quickly realised his woeful attempt at humour might have some unintended negative consequences. "What? Did I say that...? Absolutely not!" he insisted, pushing his chair back, now keen to make a sharp exit. "Not only is getting sunburned bad for your health," he advised, looking first at the girl and then at

A CASE OF MAJOR MURDER

her mum, hoping to demonstrate what a responsible citizen he was. "But you'll also look like a bit of a plonker if you do!"

"Like you, mister?" the cheeky little monkey ventured, while accepting the ice cream cone her mum handed her.

"Exactly," Toby was happy to agree. "And always remember to wear a hat!"

***

In any ongoing case, one of the most valuable commodities for any seasoned investigator is first-hand information. Any details learned, no matter how trivial or inconsequential they might appear at the time, could ultimately mean the difference between a successful result or an abject failure. But with no family members living locally, Quinn and Toby were solely reliant on other sources to get to know the man that was Major Vincent Goodacre. Though without a police warrant card, getting any facetime with potential witnesses and such was due only to the goodwill of those they hoped to speak with.

One of those people they desperately wanted to talk to—as both a longtime colleague and the current chairman of the crown green bowling club—was Derek Ogilvy-Pratt, a fellow that Quinn hoped could provide answers to many of the questions on her mind. Most fortunately, Mr Ogilvy-Pratt had seemed amenable to such a discussion, and the agreed rendezvous point, at his suggestion, was the HQ of the Castle Rushen Bowling Club. A destination that Quinn and Toby were presently arriving at...

Quinn pressed down on the car's indicator lever, manoeuvring off the main road and into the bowling club car park. "So you never fancied giving it a go?" she asked her colleague, over in the passenger seat.

"This particular type of bowling? Dunno, really," Toby replied. "Well, there was a bowling green in our local area when I was a kid," he recalled. "But it always appeared to be packed with old people wearing white trousers and those silly sun visor hats."

"And that's put you off bowling for life?" Quinn asked.

Toby cast an admiring eye over the substantial clubhouse—a charming, ivory-coloured wooden structure, boasting an imposing veranda area along the length of the front facade—and then across the pristine playing surface where hardly a blade of grass dared to be out of position. "Hmm, on reflection... I suppose an afternoon in the sunshine rolling a ball about, followed by a few cocktails in the clubhouse, does hold a certain appeal. Maybe we should give it a go once this investigation is concluded?"

"I'll be sure to buy you one of those silly sun visor hats," Quinn suggested, spotting a figure appearing through the patio doors at the side entrance of the building. "Mister Ogilvy-Pratt appears eager to greet us," she advised.

"And he looks like he's made an effort," Toby commented.

Once they'd climbed out of the car, Quinn and Toby walked across the gravel car park where Derek—wearing a navy blazer with polished gold buttons, and beige slacks boasting a razor-sharp crease down the front of each leg—waved them over like old friends.

"Thanks for agreeing to meet with us today, sir," Quinn said, once they were standing before him. "It's much appreciated."

"Please, call me Derek," said Derek, removing his Panama hat before flashing them a broad smile and extending his arm towards the clubhouse. "And it's a pleasure, my dear. As I assured the police earlier in the week, anything I can do to expedite the capture of the wicked killer of our wonderful and dear friend is the least I can do."

Derek gave the impression of being a cordial and willing host, escorting them both inside and inviting them to take a seat at a table where a pot of tea and a side plate full of lovely shortbread biscuits awaited them. Once sat down and the tea poured, they all enjoyed a good several minutes of pleasant small talk, during which Derek regaled them with the proud and noble heritage of the bowling club.

But with time of the essence and not wanting to outstay their welcome, Toby sought to carefully move the conversation along to the purpose of their visit. Wishing to keep their host at ease, Toby first posed two or three open questions about the Major's personality before then moving on to a few more delicate queries about who might possibly have harboured any bad feelings or ill will towards the man.

All the while, quietly observing for now, Quinn watched on intently, running her eyes over Derek discreetly as he answered any questions asked of him. He was impeccably presented, she considered—relaxed yet smart, like he'd just stepped off a yacht on the French Riviera. With his well-spoken manner, he came across as an educated man. While Quinn was listening to every word spoken, she was equally focused on Derek's body language. With years of experience working on complex insurance fraud cases under her belt, Quinn prided herself on knowing if and when somebody was being a fair bit liberal with the truth—her "bullshit detector," as she liked to refer to it. Usually, from what she had previously observed, it might be a nervous, overly loud laugh, maybe a simple glance up and to their left when answering a challenging question, excessive fidgeting with something, or perhaps some undue perspiration. But as far as she could discern with Derek Ogilvy-Pratt, there was nothing obvious going on. He spoke in a confident, assured tone and portrayed himself as a man both shocked and saddened by the brutal murder of a man he considered a friend.

"Okay, Mr Ogilvy-Pratt. Or Derek, that is," Toby said, drawing his questioning to a close after going through all the points he'd prepared on his notepad beforehand. "I don't think I've anything else." With that, he glanced across to Quinn, sitting next to him. "Unless you've got anything further...?" he asked.

Quinn, who'd remained passive throughout the proceedings, shook her head. "No, nothing from me," she said, before draining the remaining contents of her China teacup.

Derek clapped his hands together in a that-takes-care-of-that sort of manner, rising from his chair in order to show his guests out. "Please make sure either you or the police catch that awful lunatic," he said, returning his hat to its rightful home atop his head and giving it a few quick pats to settle it into place.

Quinn and Toby followed Derek towards the exit at the side of the clubhouse. But just as they were about to reach the patio doors through which they'd come in, Quinn raised a finger in the air like a sudden thought had only just that very moment presented itself to her.

"What is it?" Derek asked, noting that Quinn had also drawn to an abrupt halt.

Quinn tilted her head to one side, almost as if the thought that had recently arrived in her head was perhaps a bit too heavy for her neck to properly support. "There was one further thing, Derek. That is, if you don't mind...?"

Derek offered her a flourish of his hand by way of encouragement. "Anything, young lady. I'm happy to oblige."

"Well, it's just that we've spoken with a few members of the bowling club," Quinn stated. Although this information, on its own, wouldn't have come as any surprise in the circumstances. "And there were some among them who suggested to us that you and Major Goodacre's relationship wasn't quite as amicable as you've portrayed," she then added.

This frank submission caught Derek off-guard, if the narrowing of his eyes was anything to go by. "What? Preposterous!" he said. "Who have you been speaking to?" he demanded, his friendly demeanour immediately replaced by a furious frown.

But Quinn wasn't about to elaborate on the identity of her source as Derek was requesting. Instead, she was observing with satisfaction the reddening capillaries in their current subject's cheeks. "Indeed, there was one person we interviewed who suggested that Major Vincent Goodacre didn't much care for you at all," Quinn calmly put forth, sensing she had Derek on the ropes. "According to our interviewee," Quinn went on, "the good Major even referred to you as 'a bad egg' during one exchange that was described to us. In fact, this same source went on to reveal how they believed Mr Goodacre was preparing to contest your reappointment as chairman at the club's next annual meeting."

Derek was now angry and furiously fidgeting with his tie as if the knot was too tight and suddenly restricting circulation to his head. "I've shown you both nothing but courtesy and kindness, and *this* is the nonsense you come up with?" he said, before motioning firmly towards the door. "Now, if you please. I have another appointment I'll need to prepare for."

However, Quinn wasn't quite finished, as it should happen. "Derek, there was just one more—"

"That's *Mister Ogilvy-Pratt* to you now! And you've exceeded your welcome!" Derek shot back, cutting Quinn off midsentence. And then, "I don't know why I've even wasted my time talking to the pair of you!" he barked, darting his bulging eyes between the two of them. "After all, what are you? A couple of budget, part-time private detectives? In fact, when I attempted to look you up on the internet, I struggled to find any mention of you at all! Do you even have a business on this island?!"

Toby wiped away a droplet of spittle from his cheek that had been expelled by Derek during his furious rant. "Yes, of course," Toby replied. "We're working out of the ice cream shop near Port Erin Beach," he informed Derek, though uncertain as he said it if this would offer their services any credibility or not.

But Toby immediately received the answer to his uncertainty when Derek sneered, delivering a sarcastic laugh. "What? Do you mean Chester *Flitcroft's* shop? As in Chester Flitcroft, the prime suspect in this *murder* case? Are you two even qualified investigators, or is this whole thing some sort of practical joke?"

Quinn didn't allow herself any kind of reaction. At no point during their meeting had she given her surname, meaning that Derek wouldn't have had any idea that she was Chester's daughter. She felt this to be an important consideration in advance, not wishing this very minor detail to impact or potentially derail her investigation.

"Mr Ogilvy-Pratt, I can assure you this is no practical joke," Quinn stated. "Not only am I a former police officer on the isle, but my colleague and I are two of the most experienced private investigators in Great Britain."

Derek let out another sarcastic laugh, this time even louder than previously. "What? And your headquarters are at a seaside *ice cream* shop?! Don't tell me the name of the place, it's on the tip of my tongue... Oh, yes, now I remember. It's The Bucket 'n' Spade, isn't it?" he said. "So what do you call yourselves? Bucket 'n' Spade Private Eyes?" Derek added with a sneer. "Tell me, then. Which one of you chancers is Bucket, and which one Spade?"

"Thank you for your time, Mr Ogilvy-Pratt," Quinn offered politely, leaving their host's mocking questions unanswered, as she had no interest in taking his bait. "And we'll be sure to pass on our findings and witness statements to the police."

"Thank you very much for the shortbread biscuits. They were lovely," Toby added. He wanted to ask which kind they were, but he decided it best not to.

Soon outside in the fresh air and walking across the car park, Toby glanced over his shoulder, ensuring no one had followed them out with any sort of weaponry, which they hadn't. "Bloody hell, that Pratt is a prat," he remarked, talking through the side of his mouth as they approached their vehicle. "I thought he was about to have a bloody aneurysm in there, did you see the vein throbbing in his neck?" he asked. But instead of waiting for an answer, Toby had a different question to ask. "Wait, hang on," he said, having given what Quinn had just been talking about a brief moment of thought. "Who did we interview that said the Major was trying to oust Derek as chairman...?"

Quinn removed the car keys from her pocket. "We didn't," she said with a smirk. "There was no such person. But Derek's whole act he was playing in there didn't sit right with me. So I decided to throw him a curveball and see if he might take a swing at it. Which he did."

Toby was highly impressed. "Ah! Bravo!" he said, resisting the urge to offer her applause, as he was unsure if their departure was being observed. "Well, your little ruse certainly revealed two quite different sides to Mr Ogilvy-Pratt's personality, that's for sure. You think we have another suspect to add to our list?"

"Oh, yes. I most definitely think we have another confirmed suspect to add to our list," Quinn answered.

Back inside the clubhouse, muttering curse words to himself and repeatedly punching a clenched fist into the open palm of his other hand, Derek was apoplectic. However, his furious bit of self-flagellation was interrupted at the same time he heard the car tyres of his recent guests kicking up the loose gravel out in the car park.

A CASE OF MAJOR MURDER

"*Leave it to me, Primrose,*" said a voice dripping with sarcasm, with the owner of the voice partially emerging from behind the door where they'd remained hidden throughout the proceeding. "*Oh, trust me, Primrose. They're a couple of backwater investigators who couldn't find their way out of a telephone box, Primrose.*" Then, appearing fully into view with a look of scorn etched on her face, "So, Derek, how did it go?" Primrose asked rhetorically. "Because from where I was standing, it certainly sounded like a complete and utter trainwreck!"

Derek didn't need this right now, and was grinding his knuckles into the palm of his hand like he was pulverising spices with a mortar and pestle. "Dammit, Primrose, I need time to think!"

Primrose, now standing before Derek with her hands pressed firmly onto her hips, continued, "You assured me that you'd get rid of these two like you did the police, Derek. Something about *turning on the old Ogilvy-Pratt charm,* as you put it. However, after that little outburst of yours, I wouldn't be surprised if you were now ranked number one on their prime suspect list. And if so, how long will it be before they come knocking on *my* door...?"

"We need to come clean," Derek advised in an apparent moment of clarity, unclenching his fist and relaxing his hands. "We need to admit to our affair and then tell the police all about how the Major was attempting to blackmail us," he insisted.

"Derek, my dear Derek, I thought you were an educated man? If we come clean about our affair and the subsequent extortion attempt, the police will be convinced that *we* killed the Major to shut him up. But let's just assume, by some miracle, the police don't believe either of us had anything to do with it. Then what about me? What do you think *Oscar* will say? Because he won't be kept in the dark about our affair for very long, will he?"

"He'll divorce you...?" Derek ventured.

Primrose softened her confrontational posture, removing a hand from her hip and placing it on Derek's upper arm. "My love, as it stands, the only person who knows about the two of us is that wretched girl who pulls pints behind the bar, yes?"

Derek nodded.

"So as it stands," Primrose continued, "the only negative thing linking you to the Major was the possibility, according to that private investigator, that he was trying to block your reappointment as chairman of the bowling club. Not ideal. But on its own, not in any way a motive for you to want to *kill* the man."

Derek gritted his expensive veneers together at what was being presented to him. "Oh, why on earth did I react like that?" he admonished himself. "If I'd only smiled politely and brushed it off as ridiculous hearsay, I'd be—"

"It's fine, Derek," Primrose assured him, speaking in soothing tones, concerned about his blood pressure and the effect that all this drama might be having on it. "There's only one person who can positively link us to all of this unfortunate mess. And that's Cindy Shuttlecock."

"Shuttleworth," Derek gently corrected her. Then, "So what do we do about it? About Cindy, I mean."

Primrose briefly glanced down at her Gucci shoes. "We both know what we need to do," she said, raising her head slowly back up until she was looking Derek directly in the eyes again. "We need to make sure Cindy Bigglesworth keeps her filthy mouth shut. Permanently!"

Chapter Eleven

There was a palpable sense of unease around the Isle of Man, and in particular the village of Port Erin, as the police still hadn't formally announced that they'd identified a suspect in the murder of Major Vincent Goodacre. However, as the police would be keen to point out, they had their hands tied to a certain extent, constrained as to what they could or could not reveal for fear of jeopardising their ongoing investigation.

But what this 'radio silence' from the authorities meant in practical terms was that, with the limited information available to them, the good people of the isle were busy jumping to their own conclusions, listening to whispers at the post office, for instance, or sharing gossip over a pint while down at the local pub. Of course the Manx people weren't daft, though, with word that Chester Flitcroft was "helping the police with their enquiries," as the coppers liked to phrase it, spreading like wildfire.

Fortunately for Chester, he at least remained insulated from most of the unkind comments currently being said about him, as he was still presently holed up in his upstairs flat convalescing from his tumble down the stairs. But there was one thing Quinn couldn't prevent her dad from finding out about, and that was the dismal sales figures from his beloved ice cream shop below, as a simple look outside his living room window would no doubt make obvious to him.

Standing opposite The Bucket 'n' Spade on the beach side of the promenade, Quinn and Toby quietly observed those people passing by. Normally, on a sunny day such as this, with the beach packed like a tin of sardines or lovely, locally produced kippers, there would be a steady and constant queue outside the shop. But not today. Nor yesterday, for that matter, or the day previous. It would appear, Quinn could only surmise, that people didn't like frequenting a shop where a wanton killer was apparently hiding out on the premises (and so near to where the victim's body had been found, no less). Because other shops in the vicinity, such as the Bridge Bookshop a bit further down the road, were still doing a roaring trade plying their quality wares, she noted.

"Oh, this is ridiculous," Quinn commented, watching on as another family slowed up and had a quick peek through the shop window, only to then proceed along the way once they'd had their gander. "The place is becoming some sort of morbid curiosity, Toby, and a business my dad has spent the better part of his lifetime building is in danger of imploding in a matter of days if we don't find the real killer. Honestly, if the police aren't going to formally charge him, then they need to release a statement saying he had nothing to do with the murder. Otherwise, it won't be long before we're shuttering all the windows and closing up the shop for good."

"Speak of the devil," Toby said, raising a hand to shield the sun from his eyes as he spotted something or someone nearby.

Quinn followed Toby's line of sight, and sure enough, climbing out of a marked vehicle were two officers of the law. "Oh, how perfect," Quinn remarked. "A police presence is *just* what we need to help drum up business."

However, the two officers—one of which was now visible as being Sergeant Megan Stonehouse, Quinn's former colleague—didn't appear particularly concerned at the moment about possibly persuading or dissuading people in entering the ice cream shop. "Erm, they're coming straight towards us," Toby pointed out, a fact that had now become obvious to Quinn as well.

"Marvellous, *now* what?" Quinn muttered to herself. And then, once the police were in front of them, "Ah, Megan, it's so good to see you again," she lied. "May I introduce you to my friend and colleague, Toby Haddock?" she said.

Megan offered them a polite nod. "And this is my associate, PC Hendricks," she responded, courteously introducing her own colleague in return.

"Are you both here to arrest my father? Perhaps for the kidnapping of Lord Lucan, or the theft of the Hope Diamond?" came the snarky response, with Quinn's manners slipping a tad.

Megan didn't seem to allow Quinn's bit of moderate sarcasm to ruffle her feathers, however. "Quinn, I understand that you're upset about all of this," she said. "But it's about the ongoing investigations that we need to speak with you. Well, to you both, as it happens."

Quinn panicked, wondering in which direction this conversation was heading, exactly, and if it was perhaps some unhappy news in relation to her father. "Oh. How can we help?" she asked, making it a point to adjust her tone to something less combative.

Megan glanced down at her polished boots briefly, giving the impression that she was thinking how best to word what she was about to relate. "Quinn, there's no easy way to say this, but we've received a complaint about you both harassing members of the public," she said. "Specifically, pressuring them to speak to you about the murder victim and their relationship with him."

Quinn looked over at Toby, incredulous and with mouth agape. "What...? You're being serious?" she asked, returning her attention to Sergeant Megan. "All we've done is spoken to friends and colleagues of Vincent Goodacre, who were perfectly willing to talk to us."

"That's right," Toby agreed. "We didn't twist anyone's arm or administer thumbscrews. There weren't any pressurising tactics or anything like that."

Megan now adopted the haughty appearance of a school hall monitor who'd just caught a pupil cutting class. "Quinn, need I remind you that you're no longer a serving police officer?" she advised. "And if it wasn't for me having a word with the Inspector, then we'd be having this conversation back at the station."

"We'd be grateful if you could leave matters to the police, Miss Flitcroft," PC Hendricks added. "We're devoting all of our available resources to this case and don't need private citizens trampling around and muddying up our investigation."

Quinn could feel the anger boiling up inside her. "Oh, and just how is that investigation going, PC Hendricks? Close to making an arrest, are we...? Someone *besides* my father, I mean. Because he's *also* a victim here, in case you didn't realise."

"Please just remember that you're no longer a serving police officer, Quinn. You need to leave the case to the professionals," Megan reiterated, after which she turned to her partner, tipping her head towards their patrol car. "We should go," she said.

Quinn resisted the overwhelming urge to further shoot her mouth off, knowing it would serve no purpose and only land her in a heap of trouble. "Of course, Megan. Have an enjoyable day," she said instead.

Toby wondered who had lodged a complaint against them as he viewed the two officers returning to their vehicle. "You reckon it was that Ogilvy-Pratt fellow who must have said something?" he asked Quinn, talking out of the side of his mouth.

"Uh-huh. One hundred percent," she replied.

"And I take it we're not standing down?" Toby asked.

"Not on your nelly, Mr Haddock," Quinn responded, although at the same time distracted by her phone ringing in her pocket. "Let me grab this and we'll plan out our next steps."

Toby moved several paces away, giving Quinn some privacy to accept her call, and shifted his attention towards the bustling beach—an enviable sight he suspected he'd never tire of. Indeed, after living the hectic city life for what seemed like forever, waking up with the option of seaside views before him and sweeping countryside vistas in the other direction was something he could quite easily get used to, he considered. Further, the thought of soon returning to the UK, and having to spend hours commuting between cities, was becoming less appealing by the minute.

"That was the skipper!" Quinn said a minute or so later, snapping Toby out of his moment of quiet reflection.

"Eh? The skipper?"

Quinn's excited manner suggested that she'd moved on from the frustration of the recent police rebuke. "Yes! The captain of the boat with the big you-know-what painted on the side."

"Oh. Did his doorbell cam reveal who the talented artist was?" Toby asked.

Quinn shook her head. "No, sadly not," she advised. *"But...* there was a brief glimpse of Major Goodacre very near to the beach on the evening of the murder!"

"No way!"

"Yes, way! Apparently, it was only for a few seconds, and from a bit of a distance away. But the captain has met Vincent plenty of times in the past and knows well what he looks like, he tells me, and he was confident that it was him in the video footage."

"Interesting," Toby said. "So we can now be fairly certain that Mr Goodacre made his way to the beach under his own speed rather than being murdered elsewhere and the body placed on the sand afterwards?"

"Indeed. But that's not the best bit..." Quinn said, pausing dramatically ahead of the reveal.

"Quinn, now's not the time to keep me in suspense like this. Out with it!" Toby insisted.

As they were talking openly in public about a recent murder, with carefree families cavorting only yards away on the beach, Quinn first glanced about to make sure nobody was within easy listening range. "Okay, so the skipper told me that Vincent was speaking to somebody for several seconds before moving outside camera range," Quinn continued, her voice slightly lowered this time. "He said the other person was wearing a dark jacket with a sparkly design of some sort on the back."

Toby gasped in anticipation, pressing his palms together like he was offering up a little prayer. "Please tell me we can see who the other person is...?"

"Toby, is life ever that simple? Sadly, this other person wasn't facing in the direction of the camera, plus they had a hood pulled up over their head as well, according to the skipper."

"Damn! If they were the last one known to talk to the Major before his murder, it would definitely go a long way in proving your father's innocence if we could properly identify them," Toby remarked, before crouching down to retrieve an inflatable beach ball that had landed by his feet. Then, spotting a small boy jumping up and down on the sand nearby and waving furiously, Toby deftly launched it back, reuniting the beach ball with its grateful owner. "But if we can't see their face, then unfortunately there's no way of confirming that it wasn't your dad," Toby added, while offering the young lad a friendly wave.

But this reality check didn't appear to dampen Quinn's spirits any. "Oh, I can safely say the person talking to Vincent Goodacre *wasn't* my father, Toby," she said with a distinct air of confidence. "This I know, because the person in that footage was a woman."

Toby considered this point for a moment, wondering whether he had somehow missed a crucial detail during the conversation, perhaps when playing with the ball just now. "But if their face or hair wasn't visible, then how do we know it was a woman...?"

"Because they were wearing a skirt, my dear Watson! Granted, that's no guarantee of anything these days. Plus, I suppose it also could've been a Scotsman wearing a kilt, perhaps. Still, I'm operating under the far more reasonable presumption that the last person the victim spoke to on the night he died was a woman," Quinn explained. "Now, come on. The skipper's working down by the harbour and said we could come aboard and he'd show us the video for ourselves."

Toby held a hand aloft. "Wait! What about the police, Quinn? We've literally only just had a bollocking from them, and if you keep this key bit of information from them..."

Quinn shrugged off his concerns. "I'm not going to keep this piece of information from the police, Toby. I'm not that stupid."

"So we're going to phone them?"

"Of course I'm going to phone them. *Eventually.* Now come on. Oh, and get your notebook ready also, as I've just been reminded that Bucket 'n' Spade Private Eyes have officially just taken on an additional case."

Toby appeared unconvinced about the name of their fledgling enterprise—a business name conceived by Derek Ogilvy-Pratt's dismissive remark. "That would be in accepting to look for the local graffiti artist, I suppose?"

"Spot on, Toby. I always knew you had a brilliant investigative mind."

A CASE OF MAJOR MURDER

Toby, deep in thought, though, remained rooted to the spot as Quinn began heading in the general area of where the skipper's defiled boat was still drydocking. "Quinn!" he called after her a few seconds later, breaking into a jog to catch his partner up.

Quinn turned slightly, anxious to get a wriggle on and watch the video footage for herself. "Yes? What is it...?" she asked. But then, after looking at Toby's face for a moment and studying it like a mind reader, "Ah! I think I know just what you want," she said. "Are you wondering, perhaps, which one of us is going to be called Bucket and which one Spade?" she asked. "Because I have a few thoughts about that."

"Well, I wasn't wondering that," Toby answered. "Although I am now. But, no, what I was going to ask, if you don't mind, is why you ever left the Isle of Man Constabulary? I mean, it's a job you clearly enjoyed, as you've told me previously. But you never mentioned why it was that you walked away from it, as far as I can recall."

Quinn resumed her previous pace, hoofing it along Port Erin's seafront with a renewed sense that they'd soon be able to prove her dad had nothing at all to do with the awful crime of which he'd been accused.

"Well?" Toby pressed, while travelling alongside her, after no response to his recent question was forthcoming.

"Hmm, I *could* tell you, Toby... But then I reckon I'd have to kill you, and I don't think I fancy having to deal with *another* crime scene," Quinn answered. "Now don't dawdle, because we need to locate a potential murderer last seen wearing a skirt!"

Chapter Twelve

For many people, starting your day off with a lovely pint of Guinness and a tot or two of rum wasn't exactly the typical breakfast of champions to be enjoyed. Especially for those who had the inconvenience of a job to get to. But for Gary Snapper, the luxury of heading to The Shore Hotel at ten o'clock on the dot each morning was just one of the many blessed perks of retired life, he reckoned.

Sure, there were those passersby who might cast a disapproving frown at a hotel pub full of men enjoying an alcoholic tipple at a time when most would've only finished their morning porridge not too terribly long before. But these were a hardworking bunch to be found at the pub, more often than not, with many of the early morning drinkers on their way home from work following a nightshift. Or like Gary, they were retired folk who were no longer dictated to by the hour hand on a watch.

As a former professional baker, Gary was well used to having already put in a solid shift by the time others had rolled over to press the snooze button on their alarms. But after a forty-year career of rising in the wee hours, he'd served his time, had Gary. And if he now wanted to while away the morning in a seafront tavern that catered to a certain crowd then he'd do exactly that.

On this particular fine morning, Gary's normal drinking routine had been extended by an extra round or three on account of bumping into Norman Aldershot, a former player on the local darts team who he'd not seen for at least a year. No matter, Gary Snapper was the adaptable type and he would happily push back the start of his regular afternoon nap, he'd decided, to accommodate this not unpleasant adjustment to his schedule.

So, with the last of the tasty dark liquid eventually drained from his pint glass, Gary bade a fond farewell to the barkeep and his fellow boozers, armed himself with both his walking stick and his trusty bag of shopping to help him maintain his balance, and commenced the journey back to his flat. His overall mobility wasn't as it once was, he'd be the first to admit. But his regular morning outing, to and from the centre of Port Erin at the coast, was the highlight of his day—even if it did take him considerably longer than it once had.

As a lifelong resident of the village, and also a sociable chap who liked to natter, the return journey to his flat was often further delayed by familiar faces eager to check in on their friend and favourite former baker. And no matter the weather that day, be it sunshine, rain, wind, or hail, he'd always take the time for a relaxing pitstop on one of the benches partway up the headland. Because over the years he'd never once tired of drinking in the panoramic view of the golden beach below and the surrounding area. Perhaps, as he'd often remark to anybody willing to listen, his daily dose of the fresh salty breeze whipped in from the Irish Sea was the key to a long, healthy life. Well, that and a few pints of the famous black stuff, as he'd often remark—a quip usually accompanied by an infectious, worldly-wise smile.

Gary, with his walking stick in one hand and his shopping bag in the other, ultimately reached the final part of the return leg, ambling up the concrete path to the block of flats he had called home for nigh on thirty years. Drawing to a halt partway up the path, he rested his walking stick up against his hip, freeing up a hand to rummage through the pocket of his lightweight waterproof harbour jacket in an effort to locate his key. "Where are you...?" he said, digging his fingers amongst the loose change, a well-used handkerchief, and a sticky boiled sweet that'd somehow managed to unwrap itself.

"Eww, yuck," Gary complained, as the tips of his fingers made contact with the melted sweet. Well, he hoped it was a rogue, melted sweet, at any rate, because if that dense, gooey substance he'd just felt was the contents of his handkerchief, then his next mission of the day was to phone the emergency doctor, because

A CASE OF MAJOR MURDER

that would be the more worrying variety of phlegm they always tended to warn you about.

Despite his best efforts, the key continued to elude his wandering grasp despite the fairly modest size of his jacket pocket. "Bloody thing," he moaned, wondering if he'd need to extend the search to his other pocket as well.

However, with his attention taken by the missing key, Gary failed to notice the person sprinting out of the front door of his apartment block until they were almost upon him. But hearing the thumping sound of swiftly approaching footsteps, a startled Gary finally looked up, though only catching a fleeting glimpse of a figure dressed in dark-coloured clothing as they bundled hastily past him with little regard if he was sent crashing to the ground as a result of their carelessness.

"Oi, watch where you're bloody going!" Gary shouted, pivoting around to administer a fierce and, he felt, well-deserved tongue-lashing. But it was too late, as the impatient creature was halfway down the street by now and very unlikely to hear his indignant outburst.

Fortunately, after a bit more rummaging, his key presented itself a moment later without any trace of boiled sweet residue—or thick snot, as the case may be—sticking to it. With his key and walking stick secured in the same hand, Gary began to step forward, only now discovering that the front door hadn't been fully closed behind the previous visitor. A clear breach of security protocols, and one that Gary took a mental note to bring up with the other residents in his block at the earliest opportunity. Perhaps he might suggest to management, as well, that one of those automatic door-closing device thingies should be installed. It was also about this time that he also noticed the unsightly collection of discarded cigarette butts lying on the grass outside the window of the flat positioned directly below his, off to the side of the building's entrance. "The state of that!" he grumbled, with a disgusted shake of his head.

Still frustrated about being unceremoniously barged out of the way, Gary stepped inside the communal area, making sure the main entrance door was securely closed behind him before he pressed on towards the set of stairs leading up to his upper-floor flat. But he'd not progressed more than two steps towards the direction of the stairway when he spotted what appeared to be a fluffy pink roll of carpet dumped into the far corner of the communal hallway. "Oh, for the love of Pete..." he said, ready to include the improper disposal of refuse to his list of things to be discussed with his fellow residents and/or management.

But as his eyes adjusted from the bright natural sunlight outside to the more dimly lit communal area indoors, Gary froze, noting that the fluffy pink roll of carpet had feet attached at one end and a tangle of auburn hair at the other. Although he could only see the back of the figure before him, he suspected he recognised the person as the very same downstairs neighbour he'd just been thinking about. "Yes, hello," he said, unable to immediately recall the name of the girl who smoked so much and was the source of the horrid mess of cigarette ends outside. Taking a step over in her direction, he gave a further shake of the head, as sleeping in the hallway after a late night out obviously wouldn't do. "Here, did you misplace your keys?" he asked. "I nearly did the same thing just now, so I suppose I can sympathise to some degree. Still, young lady, you really oughtn't be..."

With no response, either verbal or physical, Gary approached with caution, uncertain if he should prod the recumbent figure with his walking stick. "Oi, I said that you really oughtn't be..."

But now, as he was standing over her with eyes fully adjusted to the light, Gary caught sight of a pool of dark liquid that was forming at the base of her skull. And unfortunately, it was in no way the good sort of dark liquid one might enjoy, like the lovely pints of Guinness he'd had earlier. No. This was most definitely of the *bad* variety.

"Oh, blimey..." Gary said, letting his bag of shopping drop to the floor, unconcerned about breaking the eggs he'd purchased for tomorrow's breakfast.

"Help!" he said in a state of panic, hoping to attract the attention of one of his fellow residents. "Help me! Please, help me...! It's the girl from Flat One! I think– I think she's dead...!"

A CASE OF MAJOR MURDER

***

Even within the confines of the good-sized garden at his plush, mock Georgian house, Derek Ogilvy-Pratt was rarely to be found in casual attire. Indeed, some of his neighbours had jovially remarked during a recent soirée at the Ogilvy-Pratt residence that he likely retired before bed each evening wearing a velvet smoking jacket and silk cravat. So it would likely come as no surprise to those neighbours that Derek retained the same level of sartorial elegance when it came to attending to relatively mundane tasks, such as mowing the lawn.

Wearing a linen suit with a pale blue shirt and accompanying tonal tie, the casual passerby might be forgiven for thinking that Derek was on his way to Lord's Cricket Ground to view the test match rather than ensuring the height of his grass was at an optimum level and only so many millimetres in length.

However, this wasn't just any lawn, Derek would be eager to stress to anybody who might be interested. Because the expanse of grass in the front of his property was fastidiously maintained, with no expense spared, by Clarence—the same talented fellow tasked with caring for the immaculate playing field over at the crown green bowling club. Although every so often, like at present, Derek would proudly push his Allett Stirling mower around his flawless lawn, giving the happy impression that this triumph of healthy greenery was down to him and him alone (as opposed to Clarence, who actually did almost all of the work).

Finished with the grass for today, Derek removed his favourite Panama hat, wafting it so the breeze it created caressed his forehead, preventing any sweat from forming as he surveyed the fruits of his labour, as a gentleman, of course, never perspired. Not that there would've been any danger of that anyway, as there hadn't really been any labour to speak of, currently, with Clarence having already mowed the lawn to perfection two days before.

"Would you like a refreshing glass of Pimm's, dear?" Virginia, Derek's wife, called over from the porch. "And I've just baked a fresh batch of scones as well, if you're peckish after all your hard work."

Derek offered a firm nod in response. "That sounds marvellous, Virginia!" he called over, returning his hat to its rightful spot on his head. "Just let me put the old girl back in the shed," he advised, affectionately tapping the handle of his mower. "And then I'll be straight up."

Derek tilted his head back, enjoying the scent of freshly cut grass, as well as the enticing aroma of straight-out-of-the-oven scones that was being carried on the wind from the direction of the open kitchen window of his house. With a contented grin, he began pushing the Allett Stirling mower in the direction of the shed—a handcrafted outbuilding, as opposed to the sort you'd buy prefabricated from your local garden centre, that recently cost him a small fortune to have constructed. But he liked a touch of quality, did Derek, happy to shell out on the finer things in life such as a shed with a larger square footage than probably that of his first rented flat.

However, before he'd managed to tuck the 'old girl' away until her next outing, the sound of a screaming car engine shattered the peace of the tranquil afternoon. "What the devil is that...?" he demanded, tipping the brim of his hat.

Furious, he spun around, looking up the length of his street, suspecting his annoyingly flash neighbour Peter—or Pompous Pete, as Derek had unofficially christened him—was letting his right foot get a little too heavy in his new Aston Martin again. After all, Derek valued the peace and quiet of this upmarket and usually sedate neighbourhood. Which may have been somewhat ironic, given that his own throaty lawnmower had been disturbing that tranquillity for others over the last half hour.

Derek marched towards his perimeter boundary, a glare at the ready for when Pompous Pete should come roaring by. However, as quickly became evident to him, the source of the racket wasn't an Aston Martin, but rather a seemingly unremarkable modest blue hatchback tearing up the street towards his house.

"Bloody yobs!" Derek yelled with an angry raised fist, suspecting the occupants to be aimless young lads out causing mischief and mayhem. "You don't behave like that in an area such as this!" he added.

But his bravado ebbed the moment the speeding car veered distinctly in his direction before abruptly slowing under heavy braking and mounting the pavement in front of him, with some of its wheels coming to a stop on the pavement and the others scraping to a halt on his magnificent lawn.

Derek wasn't sure what to do next. He was of course furious about the deep skid marks on his prized turf, but he didn't know if the occupants of the car were about to do something far worse, like possibly cause him serious bodily harm. Short seconds later, another vehicle arrived in a similarly frightful manner, leaving Derek, fearing the very worst, to wonder if he was on the brink of being abducted, beaten senseless, or perhaps both.

The uniformed driver of the first car—with that car's distinctive markings now becoming more evident to Derek—was the first to leap out, brandishing both a firm, resolute expression and a warrant card. "Derek Ogilvy-Pratt?" she asked, although already appearing to know precisely with whom she was speaking. "My name is Detective Sergeant Julie Maddocks from the Port Erin Police," she announced, as her colleague, who'd now joined her, took hold of Derek's right arm while poised and ready with a pair of handcuffs.

Of course Derek was relieved he wasn't about to be kidnapped by criminals and stuffed into the boot of a car. But still in a state of shock because of what was happening, the next few words the Detective Sergeant uttered to him didn't immediately register as his hands were being secured behind his back.

"*What?* What do you *mean*...?" Derek said as he was stuffed into the back of one of the two cars. "Did you say *murder*...? What do you mean I'm being arrested for *murder*...?" he pleaded as the car door slammed shut.

Watching on in apparent horror, Virginia Ogilvy-Pratt staggered down the garden path in her fur-lined slippers, crying out in anguish. "What are you doing with my husband?" she shouted. "Derek? Derek, what are they doing to you!" she yelled, frantically slapping her hand against the rear window of the police vehicle upon arrival.

"You let my husband go this instant! Do you hear me? Derek! Derek! Officers, you can't! I've just buttered him a freshly baked scone...! Derek! You let him out of that car immediately! Derek! Derek...!"

Chapter Thirteen

Quinn Flitcroft felt conflicted. Why? Because for purely selfish reasons, she was very relieved to learn there had been another murder on the Isle of Man.

Of course she was devastated for the victim and the victim's family, which went without saying. But the horrible news of another vicious attack on the island meant that the 'heat' on her father was now extinguished as a result.

At this stage of the investigation, the police were working under the theory that the two murders must be linked on account of the victims sharing identical injuries—both having suffered blunt force trauma to the head. And because the suspect in the *previous* murder, Quinn's dad, was physically out of commission and presently immobile (and very likely under regular police observation as well, Quinn suspected), it was virtually impossible that he could've been involved in this latest unfortunate affair. As such, the constabulary had formally advised Chester Flitcroft that he was thankfully no longer considered a suspect.

Welcome news, of course. But both Quinn and her dad knew that while they were finally able to breathe a little easier, somewhere a family was mourning the loss of a loved one and an evil killer remained at large.

The murder of Cindy Shuttleworth in such a cold and vicious manner—bludgeoned to death outside her own flat—had quite rightly sent waves of shock crashing across every square inch of the isle like a tsunami. The collective sense of worry and dread from one unsolved murder had already been palpable. But now, with another homicide in such a short space of time, it was nothing short of panic-inducing.

The police, for their part, had remained initially tight-lipped during their investigation into the untimely demise of Major Vincent Goodacre. But with so much fear and anxiety running rampant in the community, this was a risky tactic they couldn't afford to continue. The people of the island needed reassurance from the authorities that it was safe to walk the streets of the ordinarily tranquil place they called home.

And what better way for the constabulary to reassure the populace of their positive action than by announcing the arrest of not one, but *two* suspects in the brutal killings?

As yet, the police had not formally revealed the names of the two individuals they were currently holding in custody. But once again, the Isle of Man grapevine was working in overdrive, as it often did, with the culprits understood to be the chairman of the Castle Rushen Bowling Club, Derek Ogilvy-Pratt, and the social secretary of the same club, Primrose Ellis.

And with the two prime suspects presently behind bars, nice and secure, the good folk of the Isle of Man could certainly rest easy once more.

Well... not all of them, precisely. Because just now, stomping along one of the rugged, winding sections of the *Raad ny Foillan* footpath which leads up to the summit of Bradda Head, Quinn Flitcroft was deep in thought while paying little heed to the stiff, briny sea breeze doing its best to impede her further progress. She paused for a moment, allowing Toby, who had fallen behind yet again, the opportunity to catch back up to her.

"Sorry about that," Toby said upon reaching her position. "My legs haven't grown accustomed to this yet, like yours have."

"It's probably because I'm so used to this climb from when I was younger," Quinn advised.

"Yeah, I figured as much," Toby responded. "Anyway, what's the name of this tower we're heading to?" he asked, in reference to the summit which was, right now, feeling like there was still a fair way to go. "Millicent's Tower? It better be worth it."

Milner's Tower, rather than Millicent's Tower, built in the shape of a lock and key, was a memorial to William Milner—a once-renowned manufacturer of fire-resistant safes, and local philanthropist—and had stood proudly atop Bradda Head since its construction in 1871.

While challenging in parts, the walk up Bradda Head, which shelters Port Erin Bay from the northern elements, has afforded those plucky adventurers willing to engage in the hike over the generations an impressive eagle-eye view down onto the seaside village, as well as the much wider scenic and panoramic view. To the south, for instance, half a mile off the coast, was the Calf of Man, a lovely island known as an ornithologist's delight, and also a haven for grey seals. And while relatively small in size, the Calf and its little surrounding islets boasted no less than four lighthouses! And then, over in the distance to the west across the Irish Sea, one could make out, if the visibility was good that day, the outline of the Mourne Mountains of Northern Ireland towering against the horizon, their massive, irregular profile bringing to mind a great prehistoric reptile snoozing in the water.

With the both of them now paused about three-quarters of the way to the summit, Toby looked at Quinn, waiting for an answer to his question about the tower they were about to visit. But when a response didn't show any indication of arriving, he waved a hand in front of his partner's face. "Erm... Earth to Quinn? Is there anybody home?"

"What? Oh, sorry, Toby. It's just that I can't get my mind off of these murder cases. You see, I was—"

Toby held up a rigid finger, interrupting her mid-flow. "Ah! Need I remind you as to what you said to me only last night, Ms Flitcroft?" he asked. And then, proceeding to remind her of what she'd said only last night, and mimicking her voice as best as he could, *"The important thing is that my dad is no longer in the frame, Toby. We should step back and leave the ongoing investigation to the police,"* he said. "Your exact words," he advised with a smile.

The problem for Quinn, however, was that she was completely immersed in this investigation and was unable or unwilling to let it go completely. Which directly contradicted what she'd said to her partner the previous evening. There was just something about it gnawing away at the back of her head like a parasitic brain worm. Although what that something was, precisely, she couldn't say.

Utilising her established police contacts, and by now perhaps exhausting what remained of a small handful of overdue favours, Quinn had managed to confirm that the two suspects being held in custody were indeed Derek Ogilvy-Pratt and Primrose Ellis, as first reported via the Isle of Man rumour mill.

Further, from the details she was able to glean, the authorities had spoken with one of Cindy's closest friends. It was that friend who revealed the details of her mate's barmy scheme to blackmail one of the two people now in police custody. And it was also thanks to Cindy's talkative friend that the police were now also aware that Derek and Primrose had been further blackmailed by Vincent Goodacre before *his* unfortunate demise—with Cindy having divulged to her friend everything about the conversation that'd been eavesdropped and overheard at the bowling club.

So, two solid motives to commit murder, then. And, most fortunately for Quinn's father, those solid motives were the reason her dad was no longer wearing the cloak of suspicion.

For the sake of complete transparency, as well as repayment for the favours she'd been calling in, Quinn had also shared the evidence they gathered about Cindy and her subsequent, strenuous (though entirely dubious) denials about it. That evidence, of course, indicating that Cindy was very likely culpable in multiple instances of theft from Major Vincent Goodacre. However, as both parties were now deceased, there was perhaps no further action to be taken in that precise regard. But at least the police were aware and could choose to proceed as they deemed fit.

On the windswept hillside, Quinn couldn't resist a friendly smirk in response to Toby's finest impression of her from just a moment ago. "Oi, do I really sound like that? I mean, that nasally, whining tone...?"

Toby nodded. "Yes. Yes, you do," he added, conscious his heart rate was now dropping to pre-exercise levels. "Anyway, shall we press onward to A A Milne's Tower, or whatever it's called?" he suggested, before proceeding to do just that.

But rather than press on with gusto as before, it was Quinn's turn to temporarily trudge a pace or two behind this time, still consumed in her own thoughts as she was. "Wait up!" she said a few moments later, eager to share what was on her mind. "I just don't get it, Toby," she said once beside him. "Vincent Goodacre, as we know from his financial records, wasn't exactly short of a few quid, yeah?"

"Sure. I agree," Toby answered. "Why?"

"If, as we know, the Major didn't need the money," Quinn continued, thinking aloud to Toby as they walked along. "Then why would he try to extort Primrose, and also, perhaps by extension, Derek? It doesn't make sense, does it? And as for Cindy..."

"Ah! But in Cindy's case, we know that she *did* need the cash," Toby was happy to point out. "And especially so, as we learned from your police contact, because Cindy was planning to get out of town as soon as possible from fear of being implicated in the Major's murder. Or I suppose she could have been worried about being sent to jail for stealing from him as well, after being presented with our evidence against her in that regard. Either way, both exceptionally good reasons to want to leave the island for a while, and also something you'd need a decent amount of money set aside to accomplish."

Quinn puffed out her cheeks in frustration before expelling a steady stream of air. "Maybe I'm just overthinking things," she replied. "Seeing patterns that simply aren't there."

"It's the investigator in you," Toby offered. "Always digging, leaving no stone unturned, moving heaven and earth, pulling out all the stops, and so on and so forth. But your father is in the clear, yes? And the prime suspects are now behind bars. Surely that wraps things up rather nicely?"

Quinn couldn't argue with Toby's logic. But there remained a niggling doubt both in the back of her mind and the pit of her stomach, like somehow they were perhaps overlooking something obvious. "You're most likely correct," she conceded. Until a further thought presented itself to her, at least. "Yes, but what about that handwritten note placed inside Vincent's pocket...?" she said.

"The one suggesting your father owed Major Goodacre seven thousand quid?" Toby asked.

"Exactly! Somebody must've fabricated that note, as my dad most certainly didn't lose that sort of money gambling. And if it was either Derek or Primrose, did they also then break into dad's flat and try to kill him? If so, why would they do that...? I mean, it just doesn't make any sense to me at all. Any of it," Quinn said. "*Argh*... my head feels like it's about to explode."

"We both know how the police work. And if they've got the scent of blood, so to speak, then I'm sure they'll gladly tag on the attempted murder of your father to the charge sheet if they can," Toby assured her. But he could see she was still a little troubled. "Quinn, the main thing is that with two people being arrested, your dad is no longer a suspect. He's free and clear," he told her. "Plus, I couldn't help but notice that there's a healthy queue outside The Bucket 'n' Spade once more, yeah? So business appears to be booming again."

Quinn appreciated Toby's kind words, as he always seemed to know just how to raise her spirits whenever she needed it. "Right. Well we're never going to reach the summit this way if we keep doing more chattering than walking," she advised. "And, if you're very lucky, I just might have packed us a few bottles of local beer as a reward for when we reach the top."

Toby allowed Quinn to take the lead again, travelling behind in her wake like a duckling chasing after its mum, eager as he was to crack open one of those lovely beers he'd just heard mention of. "You know," he said, struggling to stay close, "I reckon I understand why you're so keen to keep this investigation alive."

"Oh? You do, do you?"

Toby's little legs were now going like the clappers in an effort to keep up. "Sure I do!" he said confidently. "And that's because once our case is officially closed, then I'll be heading back home. And you're enjoying working with your old partner so much that you don't want that to happen. Eh...? That's the reason... right?"

In truth, this was an outcome Quinn hadn't even considered, really, as with all that had been going on, her thoughts had very naturally been elsewhere. But this realisation served to slightly dampen her spirits that'd now only just been lifted. Because she enjoyed working with Toby, and would genuinely be gutted when he returned to his regular job across the Irish Sea, over to the east. "You're not going immediately, are you?" she asked.

Toby looked skyward as a pair of Manx shearwaters—a type of seabird in the same family as petrels—glided effortlessly overhead, with Toby giving the impression that he was considering the various options open to him. "Nah. I thought I might hang about for a little while longer, at least, and allow you to continue showing me around this pretty little isle of yours," he replied.

"And help dish up some ice creams in the shop?"

Toby, who'd rolled up his sleeves to lend a hand serving customers several times already during the course of his temporary stay, didn't appear averse to putting in an additional shift or two. "Hmm, Bucket 'n' Spade Private Eyes working behind the counter of The Bucket 'n' Spade?" Toby said with a cheerful grin. "That sounds like a plan to me. But only if I get to routinely sample the merchandise in lieu of cash wages!" he proposed.

"Deal!" said Quinn, as she broke into a trot, the close proximity of Milner's Tower spurring her on. "And hurry up, will you? Otherwise, I'll have polished off all the beers by the time you get to the summit!"

Not wanting to be outdone, Toby set off in hot pursuit. "Oi, I was saving up my energy for the final push, that's all!" he offered as explanation for lagging behind. And then, a thought occurring to him, "I hope you've remembered to bring a bottle opener for this beer you promised...?"

But a passing flock of lively gulls, all of them squawking at full volume, had drowned out Toby's words.

"Quinn, I said before we go too much higher, you *do* have a bottle opener with you, I hope...? Quinn...?"

Chapter Fourteen

Day by day, Chester's strength was starting to return, as was the healthy, ruddy tinge to his jolly cheeks. Perhaps it was an indication that his body was working through the healing process, or it could have also been down to the fact that he was no longer considered a murder suspect by the Isle of Man police, with the weight of living with such a burden now removed from his shoulders.

But for such an ordinarily social creature, the torture of being confined to his upper-storey flat, no matter how charming the seaside view from the front window, was by his own admission starting to drive him a bit stir-crazy. He did have his wheelchair to propel himself around the flat, of course. But with his left arm largely unusable, anytime he attempted to move forward using only his right arm, he usually ended up spinning round in circles rather than travelling in the direction he'd intended.

He had Quinn and Toby on hand with the both of them happy to help out as and when required, as were the friends and well-wishers who would occasionally pop in to check up on him. But with cabin fever beginning to take hold, and Chester starting to tear what remained of his thinning hair out, it was decided that he needed a change of scenery.

As such, Quinn was determined to take her father outside for some fresh air and to enjoy the charms of the lovely village he called home. The challenge, however, was the fact that Chester lived in a residence that was linked to ground level by a relatively steep staircase. Although, with a large degree of assistance from both Quinn and Toby, plus the gradually improving mobility in his hip, Chester had eventually been able to make his way down the staircase without incurring any additional injuries and with only a small handful of curse words expelled.

The moment he had been successfully extricated and sitting comfortably in his wheelchair again once outside the street-level front door, Chester breathed the sort of liberated breath that a recently paroled convict might enjoy when stepping beyond the prison gates. Sure, he had only been confined indoors for a little over a week and a half, but the horrendous prospect of possibly spending the next thirty years or so in a six-foot-by-eight cell—for a crime he didn't even commit, no less—certainly gave him a renewed and pronounced appreciation for the outdoors.

Quinn waited patiently while a visiting coach full of tourists drove by, then gingerly pushed her dad across the road towards the walkway on the opposite side. "How about a nice journey up the length of the promenade?" she suggested. "Then we can park you up and crack open the flask of tea I've brought along?"

Chester gave her a nod of approval. "Lead on," he agreed. "And don't spare the horses."

The moment the wheels started turning, Chester looked over his left shoulder with a shifty expression about him, something evidently on his mind. "I was just thinking about Toby..."

"He was supposed to be joining us, but Doreen collared him as soon as we got down the stairs, asking him to help out behind the counter," Quinn replied. "Probably just as well, too, considering a busload of tourists are hopefully about to descend on the shop," she added. "Anyway, what about him?"

"I really do like him. He's a nice lad."

From previous experience, Quinn knew in exactly which direction her dad was heading with his sudden declaration of approval about a particular man who happened to be in her life. So, not really biting on this occasion, she replied simply, "Yes. He's a decent bloke," and deciding it best to leave it at that.

However, her father wasn't quite finished scratching this particular itch, it would appear. "Good-looking lad with a cracking sense of humour, too," he put forth.

Quinn guided the wheelchair around a young toddler who'd decided that the middle of the walkway would be the ideal spot on which to plant herself down and take a short rest.

"*Dad...*" Quinn then answered, in response to her father's comment, "Toby is a valued colleague and a good friend, *alright?*" And she said this in the same sort of tone you might use to address a pesky double-glazing salesperson who didn't like to take no for an answer. "And I'll thank you for not muddying those particular waters!" she added firmly, along with a partially disguised smile, suspecting that she'd better nip this little topic of conversation in the bud before it had a chance to bloom.

"Okay, okay," Chester protested. "It's just, you know, you're not getting any younger, and Toby is quite a—"

Quinn playfully swatted her father's good arm. "Oi! Not getting any younger? I'll have you know I'm still in my prime!" she insisted. "And you'd do well to remember that I'm piloting your wheelchair and could quite easily pitch you into the harbour if the mood took," she cheekily advised.

But when her dad didn't immediately reply and lowered his head like a naughty child caught by Mum stealing sweets from the kitchen counter, Quinn panicked, worried her father might have taken her rebuke more seriously than she'd intended. "Dad, I do appreciate your concern for me," she said, gently caressing the same shoulder she'd just playfully slapped. "And I *promise* you I won't chuck you into the sea, if that's why you've gone quiet all of a sudden?"

Chester reached up with his good arm, placing his hand atop hers. "I was just thinking about you, is all," he said as explanation. And yet despite the warmth of his words, he was sounding more despondent than anything else, almost as if he were contemplating a trip to the dentist for root canal treatment rather than advising a daughter he clearly adored.

"Then why so glum...?" Quinn asked, unsure if she should be worried just now.

"Ah, sorry," Chester answered. "I was just reflecting on how much I've enjoyed having you back home. And how it'll be tough when you need to move away again."

"Well, you needn't worry about that," Quinn assured him. "At least not yet. Because I'll be going nowhere until you're up and about, sprinting along this promenade like Usain Bolt, okay?"

"So you're not heading back anytime soon?"

"Nossir!" Quinn was pleased to report. "Assuming you're willing to put up with me, that is?"

"You stay as long as you like, kiddo. The longer the better."

Progress along the promenade was a leisurely affair, designed to blow away the cobwebs and, additionally, to allow Chester to finally show his face in public again and proudly hold his head up. Because less than twenty-four hours ago, he had been public enemy № 1, accused in the vicious murder of a decorated military veteran. Fortunately, however, the same rumour mill that'd so efficiently spread word of his suspected guilt was now working in his favour. Indeed, a fair number of people were stopping them during their outing, eager to convey just how pleased they were that Chester was no longer in the frame. Not that they ever doubted his innocence for a moment, they were also terribly keen to stress. Quinn, not entirely convinced of their sincerity on this last point, smiled politely nevertheless.

Chester didn't hold any ill will over much of it, though. After all, he was certainly able to understand why people might have wanted to maintain their distance from him with such a serious allegation hanging over his head.

What did frustrate Chester more than anything else, however, was the fact that he still had no recollection to speak of from the evening of the murder. Indeed, his last memory of that fateful day, as he'd previously told the police, was standing by his front window enjoying a view of the sunset when he'd walked over to investigate a noise at the top of his stairs. He felt an unexpected shove to his back, and the next thing he knew, he was waking up in a hospital bed with very little idea how he got there.

And with Port Erin being such a small, friendly, close-knit community, most people knew everybody else well enough to at least say hello when running into each other. Certainly this was the case for Chester with Derek Ogilvy-Pratt and Primrose Ellis, each of whom he'd known for many years, bumping into either of them often enough in this place or that. Granted, he wasn't close friends with them or anything like that. But he'd certainly been in their company on any good number of occasions. So the realisation that he could have very easily been a *third* murder victim—at the hands of people from his local community that he personally *knew*—was harrowing to say the least. Not to mention it seemed like they'd apparently tried to frame him for the Major's murder on top of it!

Nearing the end of the Port Erin promenade on the outward leg of their journey, Quinn couldn't help but smile as she clapped eyes on a small group of school-aged kids who were doubled over from a fit of the giggles while standing beside a fishing boat at the marina on nearby Raglan Pier. "I think I know what that's all about," she told her father. "Wait until you see what's painted on the side of the hull..." she advised ahead of their arrival.

Chester could soon see the oversized organ for himself as they came upon the scene, and being a big child at heart, he let out a guffaw, loudly snorting through his nose at the sight of it. "Oh, dear," he commented. "And that's the boat you mentioned to me before? The one the boat's skipper placed a video camera in?" he asked, in reference to the footage Quinn had filled him in about which featured the Major talking with a skirt-wearing, hooded woman on the day of his murder.

"Yep. It's the very same boat," Quinn confirmed. "Though I'm surprised he hasn't yet had the artist's questionable handiwork painted over again."

"Aye, Banksy, he's not," Chester observed. "Still, this vandal's artwork may have a certain appeal to it...?"

"Well, it appears to be keeping both you and the local children entertained, so maybe the captain decided to keep it there as a tourist attraction?" Quinn proposed with a laugh.

Continuing along, and after a bit of erratic driving on which Quinn blamed a wonky wheel, they were soon nearing the end of the available way, at a point in which the section of lane they were travelling on had turned into Breakwater Road, where the official Lifeboat Station resided. And directly after that were the mostly demolished remains of the Port Erin Marine Biological Station, an iconic Manx landmark building that had been situated for a good number of years on the southwestern tip of Port Erin Bay. From here, you were gifted with a sweeping view of the entire area, with the sandy beach over to the right, and across the open water past the other end of the crescent-shaped coast was a grand view straight towards Bradda Head and Milner's Tower—where Quinn and Toby had previously enjoyed a couple of well-earned beers. And because the bulk of the tourists had flocked to the beach, the place very near the end of the road where Quinn eventually parked her dad's wheelchair remained relatively quiet, with their spot largely to themselves save for a few campervans parked in the designated parking area nearby, no doubt enjoying a rather pleasant backdrop for the afternoon.

Quinn planted her backside onto the edge of the wall that ran along this section of the road, behind which was a short plunge down to the sea. Sitting comfortably now, she looked directly at her dad, positioned no more than an arm's length in front of her. "How are you holding up, Dad?" she asked, tilting her head as she considered her father's well-being, both physically and mentally. After all, it hadn't been so long ago that he lost his beloved wife, Quinn's dear mum, and here he was now, sitting in a wheelchair, and recently implicated in a murder as well.

Chester smiled back at his daughter. "I'm fine, I promise," he said. "And getting out in the fresh air was just the tonic I needed, so thanks for this," he added. He smiled further, reflecting on what must've been a surreal couple of weeks he couldn't have imagined happening in ten lifetimes. "You know," he said brightly, "I suppose this whole thing is a tale to tell the grandkids about." And then, realising his faux pas, "Uhm... I meant *eventually*. Not that there should be grandkids right away, of course. I mean, I'm not expecting... erm, I'm not expecting you to be expecting. That is, I'm not saying you should immediately... or, you know..."

Quinn enjoyed the spectacle of seeing her dad squirm for a few long moments, tying himself in knots while trying not to say the wrong thing. Then, deciding to put her poor father out of his misery, so to speak, Quinn unzipped her backpack and retrieved the flask she had made certain to bring along. "Should we have our cuppa here instead of the beach?" she suggested. "It's a lovely spot with a gorgeous view." Receiving a nod in confirmation, she poured the steaming hot tea into two plastic mugs.

"You know who else I feel sorry for in all of this awful mess?" Chester asked, recent tragic events still evidently on his mind. "Oscar Ellis and Virginia Ogilvy-Pratt. The spouses," he declared. "One minute they probably think they're happily married, and the next they find out their other halves have not only been playing away from home but have also been charged with murder."

Quinn handed over a cup of tea, along with one of the fresh Danish pastries she'd purchased from a local bakery earlier that morning. There was one with a cherry topping on it for herself, and the other with little chunks of pineapple on it for her dad, as she knew that was his very favourite. "Mm-hmm," she said. "One minute it's all happy families, and the next..."

Chester admired his pastry, wondering how on earth he was going to tackle the flaky treat without too much of it ending up in his lap. "Yes? And the next...?" he said. "Are you going to finish what you were about to say?" he asked, when Quinn appeared as if she'd suddenly had the pause button pressed on her, sitting there with her mouth hanging open. "Hello? Wakey, wakey..."

"What? Oh, sorry," she said, coming back into the room, as it were. "I was just thinking about what happened to you. Because it still boils my blood that someone tried to kill you. And then, if we're assuming it's the same culprit, of course, *also* attempted to frame you for the murder of Mr Goodacre. And I won't rest until that certain somebody faces justice for that!"

Chester appeared well impressed, pressing out his lower lip and nodding approvingly. "Oi, that last bit gave me goosebumps," he remarked. "I like the way you said that, Quinn."

"Did you? Ah, I've been working on my dramatic delivery, so the feedback is appreciated," she said with a chuckle. "Anyway, my concern..." she added, not quite finished exploring her previous topic. "My concern is that the police are so consumed with the murder investigations. And rightly so, of course. But what if that completely overshadows what's happened to you, and your assault doesn't get fully looked into? It's important to me that it does, because I can't stop thinking that if things had turned out differently I could quite easily have been visiting you in either a prison cell, or God forbid, the morgue. For that reason, it's vitally important to me to find out who pushed you down the stairs. And also, *why* they pushed you down those stairs. Was it because you saw something you weren't supposed to...? Or did someone simply think you'd be an ideal patsy to take the fall for Major Goodacre's murder? And quite *literally*, in this case! I need *answers*, Dad. As I'm sure do you."

Chester had thoughtfully sipped his tea as Quinn was speaking, listening to her intently. "Wow, you're really good at this," he said. "I don't believe I've ever had the opportunity to witness you in full investigative action mode, even back when you were with the island's police, and I have to say I'm thoroughly impressed. For a moment, I was so caught up in your speech that it felt like I was watching one of those crusty, hard-boiled private detectives in a gritty American crime drama!"

Coming from anybody else, Quinn might have suspected she was being teased. But not from her dad. From the earnestness on his face, she could tell that he was being absolutely sincere and meant every single word of it. And she quite liked the comparison to the gritty, hard-boiled detective he mentioned.

"I think," Quinn said, after taking a quick nibble of her cherry pastry, "that I need some answers about what happened to you. And rather than relying entirely on the constabulary, who probably already have their resources stretched to within the breaking point, I'm going to do some more digging myself, along with my partner Toby's able assistance. What do you think?"

"I think that you've got a wee dollop of fruit topping stuck to your cheek," Chester observed. "Just there, beside your mouth."

Quinn collected the little dab of goodness and popped it into her gob, helping it find a happy home. "Thanks for that. But what about...?"

Chester's smile faded a bit as he considered Quinn's question. "Look, I'm behind you a hundred and ten percent, of course. You know that. But didn't the police warn you to stay away from the case? What are they going to say if you're—"

"Well, the police asked me to keep my nose out of it in any sort of official investigatory type of capacity," Quinn interjected. "But this isn't Quinn Flitcroft pissed-off *private eye* stepping on their toes, yeah? Rather, this is Quinn Flitcroft the thoroughly pissed-off *daughter* who wants to know who tried to kill her father and then frame him for something he didn't do."

"Hmm, I think you might be splitting hairs," Chester said in reply. "But, in answer to your question about what I think, then yes, I should absolutely like to know who shoved me down my own stairs! However, I think you were very likely going to crack on regardless, with or without my approval, yes...?"

Quinn offered the merest hint of a crooked grin, allowing her father's last point to float away without being answered directly. "Marvellous!" she said instead, clapping her hands together in a let's-get-this-show-on-the-road fashion. "First, I'll need to get closer to our prime suspects, Derek Ogilvy-Pratt and his object of illicit desire, Primrose Ellis, and find out what makes the pair of them really tick."

"Which might be challenging on account of them both being locked up at present?" Chester put forth.

Quinn was a glass-half-full sort of girl and didn't let minor inconveniences like this get in her way. "True," she had to admit. "Sooo..." she said, the cogs whirring in her head to find a solution. "I reckon I'll need to speak to those people *closest* to them..."

"The spouses? Virginia Ogilvy-Pratt and Oscar Ellis?" Chester asked. "Hmm, I'm not sure how willing they'd be to speak to an outside investigator just now?" he wondered aloud. "At least one who's not sympathetic to their side. No matter how talented and charming that investigator is."

"You forgot good-looking," Quinn pointed out, accompanied by an impish wink. "Anyway, after what those two have recently discovered about their spouses' philandering, I'm thinking they might be quite happy to throw their other halves under the proverbial bus. Or at the very least, talk to a talented, charming, and good-looking independent investigator."

"Oh. So you'll be taking Toby with you, then...?" Chester asked nonchalantly, already smirking about the delivery of his impeccable comic timing.

"Cheeky!" Quinn shot back, pushing herself up from her spot on the sea wall. "After that little remark, mister, you can wheel *yourself* back home," she playfully teased. "Now come along, you. I need to find two jilted exes to speak with!"

Chapter Fifteen

Oscar Ellis had officially disappeared off the face of the earth, or the Isle of Man at least, as far as Toby could tell. Because after the better part of a frustrating day spent attempting to track him down, both he and Quinn believed they were looking for either a ghost or perhaps somebody who could turn themselves invisible. He was nowhere to be seen.

As the owner of a large facility manufacturing electrical components for use in the aviation sector which employed over two hundred people locally, Oscar Ellis, and the Ellis family name, were recognisable on the island and, up until recently, generally well-respected by those who knew them or knew of them.

Oscar, for his part, had inherited the successful business from his father and, as a result, benefited from a lavish lifestyle which he shared with Primrose, his wife of over twenty years. Due to his outlandish and flamboyant dress sense, often consisting of brightly coloured suits that would give TV personality and former politician Michael Portillo a run in the garish stakes, he was considered by many to be something of a jolly eccentric. Often seen travelling around the isle in his mustard yellow 1920s Rolls-Royce, Oscar Ellis didn't give the impression he was the sort of man who'd enter incognito mode easily or willingly.

A bit surprising, then, that the island's two foremost investigators were unable to locate him at present. But as Quinn and Toby were to discover during their unproductive search, Oscar hadn't been seen recently at work, and his sprawling mansion house in nearby Castletown offered no sign of life. A subsequent whistlestop tour of his known haunts bore no fruit to speak of, and the phone numbers they'd obtained as contact information went unanswered. It was as if the man had simply vanished into thin air or just didn't want to be found.

And so, with that line of enquiry on hold for the time being, and with important questions still unanswered, Quinn and Toby were now making their way towards the next stop on their list—the Ogilvy-Pratt residence.

Toby, with his head resting against the passenger side window, appeared mesmerised by the vast expanse of open countryside, with rolling hills and cultivated land stretching out as far as his eyes could see. He watched, captivated, as a farm tractor trundled through a recently ploughed field with a pair of black-and-white border collies bounding happily behind like they were living their best life. Which they very probably were.

"You've gone quiet all of a sudden. Are you asleep over there?" Quinn asked without looking over, as she was trying to keep her eyes fixed on the narrow, winding road ahead.

"Nah, I'm awake. I was just taking a minute to appreciate the fact that there wasn't a high-rise tower block to be seen, or the sound of loads of honking car horns to be heard," Toby answered, peeling his cheek away from the glass. "I mean, I enjoy living in the bustling cities with the cut and thrust and all that, don't get me wrong. But there's something appealing about having, well... this," he said, sweeping his hand out in front of him, or as much as he was able without hitting the windscreen, at least. "All of this nothingness. It's just lovely."

"*Nothingness?*" Quinn replied. "You make it sound as if you're talking about the cold vacuum of space or something like that," she said with a laugh.

"Sorry, that's not what I— I mean I'd never..." Toby started to answer, slightly embarrassed now.

"Relax, I know precisely what you mean," Quinn assured him, reaching over and giving him a quick pat on the shoulder. "And I feel the same way myself. It's a gentler, quieter sort of life here, for sure. And that's not a bad thing."

During their twelve-minute or so car journey from Port Erin to Castletown, in which they continued to enjoy several miles of magnificent "nothingness," the two of them deliberated as to the potential whereabouts of Oscar Ellis. The prevailing theory, that they both currently agreed on, was that he had gone into hiding somewhere, not wishing to show his face after being humiliated by finding out his wife had been having an extramarital romp behind his back. And also, of course, that she was a murderer. Another theory put forth by Quinn was that Oscar had perhaps been implicated in the murders as well, and was AWOL only by virtue of *also* being locked up by the police at the present time. This latter scenario was a bit of a stretch, Quinn was happy to concede, but a possibility to consider nonetheless.

Soon, they moved on from the whereabouts of Oscar Ellis as Quinn drove into the street on which the Ogilvy-Pratt residence was located. Slowing to a crawl, Quinn looked past the slew of well-tended gardens to the various properties set back from the road, hoping to identify the particular home they were searching for. "Flippin' Nora," she said, admiring the grandiose houses. "After seeing the enormous size of Primrose Ellis's place, and now these bloody whoppers, I'm beginning to think you need a mansion in order to be a murderer on the Isle of Man."

Toby raised his pointing finger just as he spotted the words *Ogilvy-Pratt* engraved on a wooden postal box erected at the end of a fancy block-paving driveway. "That's the house, Quinn," he advised. "It's the one with the deep skid marks carved into the front edge of the lawn."

Quinn parked up on the opposite side of the road, taking those few moments to try and get clear in her mind what she wanted to achieve from their unannounced visit. It was distinctly possible that Virginia, if she was at home, might simply send the two of them packing with a flea in their ear. After all, emotions were likely charged at what must surely be an exceptionally challenging time for her. But Quinn needed to understand how and why her father had ended up in hospital with severe injuries, and she would spare no effort in finding the answers.

Toby unfastened his seatbelt, giving the house a once-over. "I think someone's at home, as there's a car in the open garage and a light on in one of the upstairs rooms," he observed.

Quinn climbed out of her vehicle with her notebook and pen retrieved and ready for action. "There's only one way to find out…"

Once across the road, however, the instant the toe of Quinn's shoe first made contact with the driveway, a yapping pooch from within the house erupted into life. Due to the shrill, high-octave pitch of the yapping, Quinn suspected this to be of the smaller, slightly less ferocious variety of canine. Still, she slowed her pace a bit, allowing Toby to take the lead.

However, Toby wasn't completely daft, quickly noting Quinn's progress had suddenly altered. "Ah, that's very kind of you. Let your partner face the angry dog first, eh?" he joked.

"But they like you!" Quinn insisted. "Remember a few months ago when we investigated the batch of fire alarms stolen from that warehouse in Glasgow? After the guard dog finished sniffing your leg, he took a real shine to you and even followed us back to the van once we were heading out to leave. They must sense you're a kind soul, yeah? A real dog lover, you are. What do they call it these days? An animal whisperer."

"Uhm, I don't know about that. I think that guard dog simply picked up the scent of the pork pie I was carrying in my pocket," Toby advised. "Toughest thing I ever had to do was give up that pork pie in furtherance of our investigation."

"Toughest thing?" Quinn asked, as she imagined there surely could've been things worse than that at one point or another.

"It was a lovely pork pie," Toby lamented. "Glorious, even."

"I'm very sorry for your loss," Quinn said with a chuckle. "Now, are you going to ring the bell?" she asked, once they'd reached the home's entrance.

Toby did as requested, pressing the button on the brass-plated doorbell, which quickly resulted in another volley of excited yapping from behind the rouge-painted front door. He moved his attention to the slate name plaque of the house, positioned above the bell, and read the inscription aloud. *"Thie as Moddey,"* he said, unsure if he was pronouncing the phrase correctly, whatever it might mean. "What's that in English?" he asked, looking over his shoulder for possible answers.

But Quinn shrugged, as her Manx language skills were a bit rusty. She was about to hazard a guess, taking a quick stab at translation, but the door abruptly opened just then, startling the pair of them as an ankle-high chihuahua lunged in their direction, snarling with menace. Appearing a short distance behind her dog was Virginia Ogilvy-Pratt, wearing a yellow rain jacket with a lead draped over her arm. One didn't need to be an investigative genius to suspect the woman and her pet were about to head out for walkies.

"Get back here, Hercules!" Virginia commanded the wee furry beast, the excitable thing now busy sniffing Toby's left trouser leg. Then, raising her head, Virginia regarded her two visitors with a scathing glance. "I told you over the phone that I've nothing to say, and I *meant* it," she declared. "So if you please, I'll thank you to vacate my doorstep."

On the basis that Quinn hadn't spoken with Virginia on the phone, she could only assume there was some kind of confusion afoot. "Mrs Ogilvy-Pratt, I'm Quinn Flitcroft and this is my partner, Toby Haddock," she said, introducing themselves. "I wonder if you might have mistaken us for somebody else?"

"Haddock...? Like the fish...? What a terribly peculiar name," Virginia remarked, as she attached the lead to her dog's collar.

"Ah. Sorry. It's just my name," Toby apologised, even though there was no need.

"You're not that tiresome girl from the local newspaper who's been pestering me all day?" asked Virginia, glaring at Quinn.

"No, Mrs Ogilvy-Pratt. We're not journalists, we're private investigators," Quinn responded, seeking to immediately distance herself from the caller who'd proved to be such a bother.

This information did nothing to pacify Virginia, however, as she slammed the door closed behind her in a huff. "Young lady. You'd have likely received a more welcoming reception if you'd told me that you *were* journalists. Now, come along, Hercules."

With that, Virginia stomped past Quinn and Toby, with her faithful companion offering the two interlopers another fierce, ear-piercing yap as a parting shot. "And I'd like you off my property forthwith," Virginia remarked over her shoulder.

Toby turned and took a tentative step in her direction, which served only to rile Hercules, who was lagging behind his owner and pulling at his leash towards Toby, eager for his pound of flesh in the most literal sense, it seemed. "There, there. Easy, boy," Toby said, slowly holding his hands out to show the little fellow that he posed no real threat. "Look, Virginia," he said, addressing her now, and dispensing with her convoluted surname, as he suspected he only had a very short window of opportunity in which to operate. "We just need to ask you a few questions about your husband, and then I promise you we'll leave you in peace..."

Virginia stopped briefly. "I've already fully cooperated with the police, and if you think I'm going to waste my time talking to you two bargain-bin private detectives, then I'm afraid you've got another thing coming," she advised. "Now, if you don't leave my property immediately, I shall have no other choice but to let loose my Hercules on you," she warned.

Toby struggled with the overwhelming urge to laugh at such an absurd threat, given the *under*whelming size of her dog. But not wishing to cause offence to either Virginia or the tiny tyrant by her ankles, he managed to successfully stifle it. And with his authority unchallenged, little Hercules marched proudly out in front with his head held up high, escorting his master down the driveway like the majestic beast that he was.

"Wait!" Quinn called out. "Virginia, please... I'm fairly certain that either your husband or his mistress tried to kill my father, and I need to know why. Scrap that, I *have* to know why."

Quinn's words wafted on the air and when they finally landed at their destination, Virginia slowed to a halt, at which point she stood motionless for a short period. Even wee Hercules appeared frozen to the spot by Quinn's revelation. Then, Virginia turned slowly. "Your father...?" she asked.

Quinn took this as invitation to proceed down the driveway to the pavement, where Virginia was now standing. "Yes. My father," Quinn said. "Look, I know you're probably going through an awful time right now, and the last thing I want to do is add to your distress. But my father was very nearly killed, and then not only that, but framed for a murder he didn't commit as well."

Quinn lowered her head, thoughts of what could have been still playing heavily on her mind. "Mrs Ogilvy-Pratt... Virginia," Quinn continued, looking up at her. "I need to try and understand why that happened. And I'm hoping that you might have some insight that could possibly help me achieve that end."

Virginia's frosty demeanour thawed as Hercules placed his hindquarters onto the ground, rightly sensing his daily walkies might be delayed for a short while longer. "You must be Chester's daughter? I've always had a soft spot for your father."

"Thanks, Virginia. He's a good, kind-hearted man, and someone I obviously adore. And to think somebody could have tossed him down the stairs like a ragdoll... well, it makes me sick to my stomach, as you can imagine."

Virginia offered an apologetic sort of look. "I can understand," she responded, not unsympathetically. "But I'm not certain what I can really do to help. I mean, what am I meant to tell you, dear? Wouldn't you be better off speaking with the police?"

"I have, and I'm sure they'll try and do what they can," Quinn answered. "But with a double murder to currently investigate, I suspect that'll have to be their priority and take up most of their attention." Quinn stepped in a little closer, being mindful not to tread on either of Hercules's tiny front paws. "I'd just need ten minutes of your time, Virginia. I hoped to ask you a few questions about your husband Derek. Questions that might—"

"Yes, that's fine, dear. But not just now, alright?" Virginia said, holding up her lead-holding hand and gently cutting Quinn off mid-sentence. She then employed her pointing finger, using it discreetly to motion towards her unsuspecting pet. "I've told him that we're going for a W-A-L-K," she said, spelling out each letter of the word. "However," she added, now talking in hushed tones. "Where we're actually going is to the V-E-T-S."

Quinn offered Hercules an empathetic smile, even as the wee fellow appeared happily oblivious at the present moment, sitting there on the pavement daydreaming about whatever it is that very small dogs dream about.

"I could come back tomorrow afternoon, if that would work?" Quinn proposed.

"That's fine. Although I'm still not certain what I can say that might possibly help you," Virginia answered, giving the lead a light tug, which served to call Hercules to attention, rising up on all fours again and staring lovingly at his mummy, poor innocent chap that he was. "However, given what you and your father have been through, I'll be happy to do what I can. Pop back and see me tomorrow lunchtime...?"

"Thank you. And yes, lunchtime would be splendid."

Walking back towards the car, Quinn breathed a huge sigh of relief. By getting Virginia's agreement to speak, Quinn hoped to gain some valuable insight into the mind of not only Virginia's husband Derek, but also possibly that of Primrose Ellis as well. And as someone who was the victim of their husband's infidelity, Quinn suspected Virginia wouldn't hold any punches once she managed to get her talking. Well, that was the hope in any case.

"That Virginia was a tough nut to crack," Toby remarked, once they were both inside the car with seatbelts fastened. "I didn't think we were going to have much luck with her at first."

"Yeah, I suppose her abrasive manner is understandable when you consider what she's recently gone through," Quinn offered. "I mean, imagine finding out your husband is cheating on you, *and*, if that wasn't bad enough in itself, he's *also* a lead suspect in a bloody double murder case. That's the sort of unexpected news that could really put a dampener on your day."

"Or maybe she's just like that all the time and it's her natural disposition?" Toby suggested.

"It could be that as well," Quinn conceded with a laugh. "But I'm allowing her the benefit of the doubt," she said.

"Anyway, so then what's the dog's excuse for being so unpleasant at first?" Toby put forth. "You said I was *good* with dogs."

Quinn turned the key in the car's ignition. She was just about ready for a nice cup of tea back at HQ. "Hmm. He was probably grumpy because he thought he was just heading out for a stroll and then clapped eyes on you darkening his doorway...?"

"Oi! That's hardly fair, as you're the one who forced me go to the door first," Toby said in protest. "It could just as easily have been *you* darkening that doorstep!"

"Well, let that be a lesson to you," Quinn countered.

"A lesson?"

"Yes."

"Okay, well what's the lesson, then?"

"Hold on, I'm still thinking," Quinn advised.

"And....?"

"I dunno. Always carry a pork pie in your pocket...?"

"Well, there's some definite logic there," Toby was happy to admit. "That's actually top advice, Quinn, and not just for when dogs are about!"

Chapter Sixteen

They say that time is a great healer. At least that's how the old saying goes. And, fortunately, that was proving to be the case for Toby Haddock, after days of abject pain, the severity of which he didn't like to burden those close to him.

Well, aside from his partner Quinn, that is, with whom he felt the need to provide regular reports on how he was such a "brave little soldier" in regard to how he was coping.

But by now, his sunburnt scalp had begun to heal, resulting in a remarkable layer of dry, flaking skin, giving the appearance of the world's worst case of dandruff. Or it looked perhaps like a snake shedding its skin, as Quinn's father had so helpfully suggested. Compounding Toby's current itchy situation was the fact that his hair was starting to grow back on his recently shaven head, a sort of light stubble now forming like that on a teenage boy's chin. And despite the cautionary words Quinn had given him along with threats to file down his nails, poor Toby couldn't help but scratch the top of his head, the scaly portions of which wafted down towards his shoulders like leaves in autumn.

At Bucket 'n' Spade Private Eyes HQ, freshly showered after her mid-morning jog, Quinn headed over to their temporary office (which was actually just whichever table at the ice cream shop happened to be available at any given time), convinced she was a little bit lighter after such an energetic outing.

Sitting herself down opposite Toby, she was greeted by a man who looked like he'd been suffering from a debilitating case of indigestion for most of the morning. "What's up with your face?" she said. "You'll scare all the customers away with that mug."

Toby sighed, cradling his face in his hands. "I've just been let go," he revealed, looking further despondent. "Sacked."

"Eh, for what?" Quinn asked, as a wave of guilt washed over her. "Barry's not fired you for coming over here to help me, has he? Because if so, I'll get straight on the phone to him and—"

"No, not from that job... From *that* job," Toby said, tipping his head towards the small queue of people waiting for an ice cream.

Quinn looked over her shoulder. "I don't follow," she said, not following.

"Doreen said she didn't need any more help from me behind the counter today," Toby told her, sitting there in an apron with an oversized ice cream on the front. "There were plenty of people on the beach. Which meant lots of customers here. So I thought I'd offer my services. But then, after only about ten minutes or so, Doreen told me I was a health hazard, and she didn't want the shop closed by the Environmental Health Unit on her watch."

Quinn didn't know if this was some sort of confusing and protracted joke that maybe just hadn't reached the punchline stage. "Wait, Doreen really said that...?" she asked, somewhat confused, as Doreen—her father's trusted right hand at the shop—was one of the friendliest, most accommodating of people she ever had the pleasure of knowing. "You're sure you heard her correctly?"

"I'm sure. Unfortunately, she received some complaints about me and was forced to take action."

"Complaints...?"

Toby offered a weary nod. "Yeah. I was serving up a couple of mint choc chip delights and according to the customer, a few wayward flakes of skin broke free of my head and ended up in their ice cream, apparently. I looked, but I didn't see anything."

"Well, people might expect a *Cadbury* Flake in their ice cream, chum. But I don't think they'd appreciate *sunburn* flakes," Quinn replied. She then paused, hoping to receive some appreciation of her comedic genius which she felt certain was about to arrive.

However, Toby knew what she was up to, noting that her left eyebrow was hovering expectantly just now, slightly higher than its right counterpart.

"You're doing that thing with your eyebrow," Toby informed her. "You know, where you crack a joke and you're waiting for me to laugh. But I'm sorry, I'm too emotionally damaged to do that right now. Because I don't believe I've ever had an official complaint lodged against me, nor ever been fired. Yet now I've had both, within the space of ten or twelve minutes."

"You've never been sacked from a job before...?" Quinn asked, sounding a little too surprised by this for Toby's liking, it would seem. Then, hoping to get his mind off his troubles, she quickly moved the conversation towards another matter. "I've just been speaking to one of my police contacts, who informed me when asked that Oscar Ellis hasn't been arrested. So, I guess it's more of a case of old Oscar simply not wishing to show his face around town just now."

"Do they not get fed up with you calling?" Toby asked.

"My police contacts? Nah. Well, maybe a bit," Quinn replied. "But somehow my credit seems to remain good with a few of my former colleagues."

"Well, I reckon I could apply some shoe leather to pavement, make some additional enquiries, and see if I can't track down Oscar...?" Toby offered, anxious to demonstrate his worth after his recent, unexpected dismissal. "Assuming you're still wanting to speak with him? After all, it's not like my services are required here at the shop today. Not anymore, anyway."

Despite his pouting demeanour, Quinn suspected her partner wasn't seriously depressed. She checked her watch, conscious of her upcoming appointment. "Yes, please do," she replied. "I'll leave that in your capable hands. Meanwhile, I'll pop out and see what Virginia Ogilvy-Pratt has to say. It might be a wasted effort, but you never know. Nothing ventured, and all that."

Toby removed his head from his hands and opened his laptop. "Sounds like a plan. And I'll likely still be here when you get back. Unless Doreen declares me a danger to the public and throws me out," he said with a comical and exaggerated frown.

"Didn't you just say something about hitting the pavement...?" Quinn asked, recalling specific words to that effect.

"Ah, I was speaking more in a figurative sense," Toby insisted. "Plus, I probably shouldn't really go out like this," he advised, motioning towards his bonce.

Quinn eased her chair back, giving the top of his head a quick inspection as she rose to her feet. "Hmm, it may look a bit rough just now, but I'd say it's definitely on the mend," Doctor Flitcroft was pleased to report. "I think I'd be more worried about frightening the children with that sour face of yours," she joked, right before making for the exit while the going was good.

To demonstrate there were no hard feelings, Doreen appeared a few minutes later armed with a mug of freshly brewed coffee and a warm toasted crumpet smothered in savoury butter. She set the small plate that was ferrying the crumpet down onto the table, strategically placing it so that the tantalising aroma would waft towards Toby's nostrils. However, Toby didn't flinch, and his unwavering gaze remained fixed on his laptop display.

"I've prepared you a crumpet, just the way you like it," Doreen felt the need to say, when Toby didn't acknowledge either her or the recent delivery.

But when Toby still didn't flinch, Doreen was starting to get the impression she had offended her part-time member of staff more than she'd thought. "Look, Toby, I'm genuinely grateful for all your help here and just wanted you to know there are no hard feelings, okay?" she added, although still nothing. "I've got some moisturiser in my handbag," she told him. "Maybe you could use some of it on your scalp, and you'd be good to go again behind the counter?" she suggested.

"Thie as Moddey..." Toby said to himself, looking up from his laptop screen and appearing disoriented, as if he'd just opened his eyes from a long afternoon nap. Then, spotting the familiar figure looming over him benevolently, "Oh! Hiya, Doreen," he said, noticing her standing there for the very first time, despite her having arrived a good thirty seconds earlier. "Ooh, a buttery crumpet!" he added, finally detecting it, along with its heavenly scent. "Thank you kindly."

Doreen playfully rolled her eyes. "I guess you were just caught up in the zone," she remarked, before spotting a customer waiting at the counter. "Oh, and it means *A House and a Dog*, if I'm not mistaken," she added. "Although it's been quite a few years since I've studied the language in school, obviously. But I'm pretty sure that's correct."

"What, now?" Toby asked, smiling politely and without much of a clue as to what Doreen was talking about.

Doreen signalled to the waiting customer that she'd be with them in just a tick. Then, addressing Toby again, "What you just said a moment ago. Thie as Moddey. I think it means 'House and a Dog' in the Manx Gaelic language," she said.

Toby jotted that useful piece of information down onto his notepad. "Very nice. Thank you for that," he offered. "And it's also, from what I've just uncovered on my laptop, the name of a Swiss holding company that paid Major Goodacre two hundred thousand pounds, interestingly enough. Though I don't have any idea as to why that should be just yet."

Doreen rubbed her hands together like she was twirling a stick between her palms and starting a fire. "The plot thickens..." she pronounced dramatically, narrowing her eyes, and pursing her lips. "Oh! I've always waited for just the perfect moment to say that!" she declared a short second later, accompanied by a giggle. "All I'd need to do now is jump into the back of a taxi and shout *'FOLLOW THAT CAR!'* to the driver, and I'll be a happy bunny."

Toby leaned back in his chair, impressed by Doreen's ability to effortlessly slip into character. "Well, if I should ever need to conduct a taxi-based pursuit anytime soon, you're definitely the first person I'll call," he said with a smile. "But what's also interesting, is that I've discovered who the beneficial owner is of this Thie as Moddey company..." he added teasingly.

"Derek Ogilvy-Pratt?" Doreen offered with a casual shrug, as if the answer was as obvious as the large embroidered ice cream on the front of both of their aprons.

Toby looked at Doreen as if she were a stage magician who'd just managed to saw her assistant in half while at the same time riding a unicycle. "Wow, you're really good at this sort of thing," he marvelled. "How on earth did you know that...?"

"Well, you're an active investigator," Doreen reminded him. "And you're busy digging into two murder cases where there are dual suspects held by the police. So while I'd like to say I'm some sort of genius sleuth, like Miss Marple, in reality, it was a fifty-fifty guess between the two people in custody."

And with that admission, Doreen quickly made her way back over to the counter where her customer's patience was currently being tested, as evidenced by the man's young son tugging on his arm, likely wondering why he wasn't yet in possession of the ice cream his father had no doubt promised him.

Toby returned his attention to his laptop, nibbling the edge of his crumpet while he reviewed the contents of the email he'd recently received. That email was from a former colleague who had recently relocated to Switzerland and was presently heading up a company investigating fraud on behalf of local banks there. As Toby knew from previous investigative experience, Swiss-based institutions were notoriously secretive about their clients to the extent that it was nigh on impossible to find out the beneficial owners of business entities registered in that jurisdiction. Of course there could be any number of legitimate reasons for structuring your affairs in such a private manner. But for somebody with a sceptical side to him, Toby couldn't help but think that there was an ulterior motive at play—like being able to transfer two hundred thousand pounds to a recently deceased Major, for instance, without anybody finding out it was you that sent it.

Fortunately, Toby's former colleague had managed to obtain, and then emailed through, several official company documents. She'd even taken the courtesy of highlighting some of the details of key interest to Toby, with those details revealing that Ogilvy-Pratt was listed as the sole director and 100% beneficial owner of the Swiss-registered company Thie as Moddey.

This information, in and of itself, was of uncertain value at present, as the police already had Derek Ogilvy-Pratt in custody. But if nothing else, it was another intriguing link between Derek and the murder victim which the police might find useful or at least of potential interest. But the main unanswered question on Toby's mind remained: Why was Derek Ogilvy-Pratt paying the good Major two hundred thousand quid, and what, if anything, did this have to do with his murder...?

Toby didn't have too long to dwell on this, however, as Doreen soon reappeared, tapping the tip of her pen against her two front upper incisors. She then leaned over, resting her forearms on the back of the chair opposite to him. "I might have been earwigging the other day," she confessed, immediately setting her stall out. "I mean when you and Quinn were talking about the list of the Major's business interests," she explained. "Although I don't feel so guilty for listening in..." she added, in a somewhat apologetic-sounding attempt to perhaps justify her actions. "Because, well, technically, we're all working in the same office space with you, right...? So, uhm..."

"Doreen, it's fine," Toby assured her. "What's on your mind?" he asked, grateful for any insight. Especially from Doreen, who was starting to prove herself as a natural at this game. Indeed, he was considering asking if she wanted to possibly swap roles. Once his scalp had cleared up, that is.

Doreen gave a quick glance over her shoulder, ensuring there were still no waiting customers at present, which there weren't. "From memory, you said Major Goodacre owned both the bowling club and the land it resides on," she replied. "But previously, he also owned great swathes of the surrounding area, correct?"

"You're good at this eavesdropping thing, too," Toby remarked. He meant it as a distinct compliment, as such a skill could easily come in quite handy when working in an investigative capacity. He just hoped Doreen took it that way, and didn't believe he was calling her a nosey parker or anything like that. However, Doreen didn't appear to be the slightest bit offended. "But yes, you're correct," he told her. "Although the Major subsequently sold most of the land a good while back."

"Right. Twenty or so years ago, I think I recall you saying. But that particular area, in and around the bowling club, is slap bang in the middle of Castletown, yes?"

"Okay. I'll take your word, as a local, for that. Go on...?"

Doreen stood herself upright, tapping the tip of her pen on her two front teeth again as she related her thoughts out loud.

"Well, Castletown is a beautiful location, with gorgeous views of the sea, plenty of fine restaurants and pubs and other places of interest, it's absolutely dripping with history, and it's even got its own medieval castle, Castle Rushen. For those reasons and more, I imagine the land that the bowling club resides on would be worth a pretty penny?"

"Okay. So what are you thinking?"

But Doreen didn't have all the answers, or at least none that were definite. "Dunno," she said. "But maybe the Major was selling the bowling club, resulting in that large windfall...?"

"But if that were the case, why would Derek Ogilvy-Pratt be purchasing it via a top-secret Swiss holding company? It doesn't seem to make any sense."

Doreen's shoulders slightly dropped. She still didn't have any definite answers. "You may be right. But you're the private investigator here, yeah? So get investigating!" she said. This was not intended as a dig, but more as a vote of faith and encouragement. "But be forewarned, I might be back over in several minutes with another theory for you," she advised with a friendly wink.

"Yes, ma'am," Toby replied, giving a smart salute to his newly acquired investigative partner. He was impressed by Doreen. She was smart, funny, and immensely likeable (when she wasn't busy sacking him, that is). Then, glancing at his mobile vibrating on the tabletop, "Ah," he told her, after unlocking the screen, "this is a message from my *other* investigative partner..."

> Quinn: Still sitting outside Virginia's house. Nobody home. I'll give it another hour. Any sign of Oscar?

On the basis he'd not even started looking for Oscar just yet, his focus having been temporarily applied to other matters, Toby decided he'd best come clean.

> Toby: Hey there! Nope. I just received some documents from Kasia in Switzerland. The company that paid the Major is called Thie as Moddey, and is owned by Ogilvy-Pratt. Just reviewing the rest of the docs Kasia sent me and will get on with Oscar next. Shout if you need me.

A CASE OF MAJOR MURDER

Quinn: Interesting! Okay, jolly good. Speak soon.

With Doreen's current theory fresh in his mind, Toby jumped back on his laptop, wondering if Major Goodacre had indeed engaged in a property/land transaction with Derek Ogilvy-Pratt. If so, it might certainly explain the two payments totalling such a large amount of money, of course. But one thing it didn't explain was the need for the cloak-and-dagger secrecy. Further, had the transaction then turned sour in some way, with the Major having to pay the ultimate price in the end? Toby had to wonder.

Fortunately, as an employee of a large organisation of insurance fraud investigators, one of the many resources available to Toby was access to the regional land registries, including that of the Isle of Man database. However, as Toby was aware, if a sale remained in progress and hadn't been finalised for any reason—including, as a pertinent example, one party in the transaction being murdered—then such an agreement was unlikely to have been registered prior to its conclusion.

Using the information available at his fingertips, Toby was able to quickly conclude that no such transaction had been recorded on the Isle of Man Land Registry. Or, for that matter, any transaction at all involving the sale of the bowling club. According to the official records, Major Vincent Goodacre was still, at the time of his death, the sole owner of the land upon which the bowling club resided.

On the verge of giving up on his current line of enquiry and shifting his attention to the whereabouts of Oscar Ellis as originally intended, Toby considered the matter for a few moments longer, clicking his tongue against the roof of his mouth as he often did when thinking. "Hmm," he said, a fresh idea occurring to him. He then extended the search parameters on the database, now looking for any relevant details on the wider area of land surrounding the bowling club—specifically, the pieces of land that were originally gifted to Vincent Goodacre by his uncle and then subsequently sold on.

What Toby was hoping to uncover, precisely, he wasn't quite certain. But he was intrigued by the possibility of who might have purchased the land from the Major all those years ago. As he scrolled through page after page of historical transactions, Toby half expected to see the name Thie as Moddey pop up at any moment. He wasn't sure why. Perhaps it was just his investigative sixth sense, he thought.

Unfortunately, as he was soon to realise, that wasn't going to be the case. Because, according to the official records at hand, several parcels of land in central Castletown were sold by Major Goodacre to an individual, rather than a Swiss corporation. Toby took a closer look at one of the records in question, expanding the sale document with the tips of his fingers in order to zoom in on the signature section. "Frank *Smellie*...?" he said, reciting the name out loud to himself. "Why was I expecting to find any sort of *normal* name in this investigation?" he asked, struggling to suppress a laugh and failing miserably.

With a momentary lull in customers, Doreen made her way over to Toby's table-cum-office once more. "What's tickled you?" she asked, noting the look of mirth on his face.

"Oh, don't mind me, I'm just being silly here," Toby admitted. "Quinn would probably tell me off for being immature by laughing at all the bizarre names I've encountered since being on your quaint little isle," he said. "Anyway, what's up? Have you brought your next theory with you?"

But rather than deliver another theory, Doreen instead placed a white tube on the table in front of him. "Here's that moisturiser I mentioned earlier. Back when you weren't listening to me," she said. "I found it in my handbag, and I reckoned it would do wonders for your flaky head."

"Oh! Well then my scalp thanks you kindly," Toby responded. "Cheers, Doreen. Here, but before you disappear again, Doreen. You've lived over here for a few years, yeah?"

"One or two, yes," Doreen answered. "In fact, all my life."

Toby flicked his eyes to his laptop screen and then back up at Doreen. "In that case, I don't suppose you've ever heard of somebody by the name of Frank Smellie?" he asked, managing to say it without laughing this time, although only with great effort.

A CASE OF MAJOR MURDER

Doreen freely let out a chuckle, however. "Sure. That's the sort of name that doesn't go unnoticed on a small island," she said.

Toby waited patiently for her to elaborate in some way. "And?" he said politely, when that didn't immediately happen.

"Ah, sorry," Doreen replied. "I'm not familiar with any Frank, specifically. But I do recognise the surname, as it's a rather difficult one to forget," she said. "Hmm. You know, I'm pretty sure Derek's wife was a Smellie before they got married. In fact, now that I think on it, I'm certain it was. So, I'm guessing that Frank was her father, or uncle, maybe?"

"Eh? Virginia Ogilvy-Pratt's maiden name was Smellie?" Toby asked, surprised by this new piece of information. "Wow. Well as much of a mouthful as Ogilvy-Pratt is as a surname, at least it's a bit of an improvement over Smellie...?" he considered.

"That's very true," Doreen agreed. "Virginia, and Derek as well, for that matter, both went to my school. And as you can imagine, a girl with the last name of Smellie was subjected to the most horrible of... of... Toby, are you okay...?"

But Toby, for his part, didn't appear to be okay right now at all. In fact, he presently had one eye pointing straight ahead, while the other was angled slightly off towards the door, as if each eye had a sudden falling out with each other. It was somewhat of a disturbing sight, really, as Doreen would have been able to attest. "Toby...? Toby..."

Toby held one finger aloft, signalling to Doreen that he was somewhere deep in thought. Gradually the blood started to drain from his face, however, leaving him a ghostly shade of pale.

Just as Doreen was about to give him a poke to see if he was still conscious, Toby's right eye returned to its normal position, realigning itself with the left one. "Holy... shit..." Toby said, as he pushed his chair back.

"Whatever is the matter?" asked a concerned Doreen. "You're not having some kind of episode, are you...?"

"No, no. Nothing like that," Toby assured her. "Doreen, can I possibly borrow your car?" he asked, jumping up from his seat abruptly and anxiously reaching for his mobile phone.

Despite Toby's obvious agitation—or perhaps even because of it?—Doreen rather liked the sound of where this might be going. "Hang on, is this one of those *FOLLOW THAT CAR!* adventures I was talking about earlier?" she enquired, getting fairly excited at the prospect.

But Toby didn't understand what Doreen was on about, really, as his focus was elsewhere at the moment. "What...? No," he said absently, quickly scrolling through his list of contacts in search of Kasia, his former colleague who'd since moved to Switzerland. Once located and the call placed, he looked directly at Doreen, all traces of his prior mirthful demeanour having vanished. "Can I have your car keys? Because I have to leave now!"

"They're in my handbag, Toby. Why? What's going on?"

Toby placed his phone against his ear. "Come on, Kasia. Please pick up..." he said, directly before Kasia did precisely that. "Kasia, it's Toby Haddock here and I need your help with something," he said with great urgency, and without any preamble. "Kasia, this is important," he told her. "In fact, you could even say it's a matter of life and death..."

Chapter Seventeen

Quinn was having serious regrets about the large coffee she had treated herself to from the local, recently opened gourmet coffee shop. It wasn't that the beverage wasn't lovely, because it was, as the currently empty container sitting in her vehicle's cupholder would attest. Rather, it was more that her swollen bladder was starting to severely protest the volume of liquid presently contained within it.

Compounding her discomfort further was the fact that she'd been sitting outside of Virginia Ogilvy-Pratt's house for well over an hour without the opportunity to enjoy a desperately needed comfort break. Quinn glanced at the digital clock displayed on her dashboard, wondering if she'd turned up at the wrong time or if Virginia simply had little desire to meet with her and had been too polite to say so. But as Quinn had been to the front door and knocked three times already, all she could really do for now was to continue to sit and wait. At this point, she was counting down the minutes and trying to figure out if it was logistically possible to have a wee in the same coffee cup that was responsible for her current physical discomfort in the first place.

Fortunately, however, that tricky proposition didn't progress past the planning stage as a dark green Land Rover soon appeared into view, driving up the street in Quinn's general direction and then turning into Virginia's driveway.

Quinn, parked on the opposite side of the road, watched on in relief as Virginia climbed out of her vehicle with Hercules under one arm and a shopping bag held in her other hand. Quinn gave Virginia a minute or two to get inside so it didn't appear like she was there to ambush her, using that time to review a short list of questions that she'd written onto her notepad. Those questions being designed, she hoped, to aid in revealing any information that might prove valuable regarding her father's assault and his subsequently being framed for murder.

Once sufficient time had elapsed, Quinn made her way across the road to Virginia's front entrance and raised her index finger to the bell. But Hercules had already quickly alerted his owner to Quinn's presence with a series of yaps and clawing at the inside of the door.

"Hercules!" Virginia's voice could be heard from within. "I've told you before, that's not how we greet our visitors!" she admonished, just before opening the front door. But when she clapped eyes on who her visitor was, Virginia didn't appear to be quite so genial. "Oh," she said, looking Quinn up and down with the sort of frosty glare you'd offer to a door-to-door salesman peddling a job lot of second-hand encyclopaedias that nobody ever wanted. "Oh, it's you again."

For most people, receiving that sort of standoffish reception would have them spinning around on their heels and making a sharp exit. However, in Quinn's line of work, it was fairly normal and one she was reasonably accustomed to. Granted, if she was calling on a relative or an old friend and was greeted the same way, then that would have been a different story.

Unfazed, Quinn flashed Virginia her most cheerful smile. "Yes, you suggested that I should pop back today," Quinn said nonchalantly, opting to make no reference to the fact that Virginia was over an hour late for their scheduled meeting.

Virginia shepherded Hercules away from the front door and sighed. "Well as long as you're standing there, I suppose you may as well come in," she offered, although not sounding very pleased about it.

Quinn paused on the doorstep, aware that her mobile phone was ringing in her pocket. "Thank you," she said, reaching for her phone, but only so that she could set it to silent mode and return it to her trouser pocket so it wouldn't further disturb their time together. "Should I take my shoes off?" she asked as she stepped inside.

"Don't bother," Virginia answered, wrinkling her nose. "If you track anything in, I'll just have my girl clean it later," she said. She then directed Quinn through the hallway and on into the tastefully appointed living room, where there wasn't so much as a cushion out of place.

"You have a lovely home," Quinn offered by way of friendly small talk. "Ah! I've always been a fan of Clarice Cliff," she added, spotting a set of colourful ceramics on display in an oak cabinet. She had seen a film about Clarice Cliff a few years prior, so was pretty familiar with the artist and her distinctive, recognisable work, and she was pleased this knowledge should become useful just now. "Have you collected for long?" Quinn asked, hoping the 'shared interest' tactic would relax her defensive host.

And it appeared to do the trick. Because before she knew it, Quinn was having her ear talked off about the positive attributes and various notable features of the 1930's Art Deco vase that was the star piece in Virginia's prized collection. However, there were only so many ceramic pieces that Quinn could feign interest in before her bladder exploded.

Visiting the loo was another regular tactic that she deployed while on an active investigation. From experience, Quinn found it caught people off guard, and also provided an opportunity to have a good nosey around areas of a person's home you wouldn't ordinarily be able to see. And this time, there was also a genuine and rather urgent requirement to use the facilities, as well.

"I'm sorry to ask," Quinn said, squirming slightly where she stood. "But could I possibly use your loo?"

"The lavatory? Oh, yes. Yes of course. Head upstairs and it's the second door on your left," Virginia advised. "While you're busy in there, shall I fetch you a coffee or tea?" she asked.

After already demolishing a large coffee and feeling decidedly wired from the resulting caffeine overdose, the last thing Quinn wanted was another coffee. However, it made it more difficult to chuck a guest out if they were drinking something the host had so kindly prepared for them. For that reason, Quinn accepted the offer, while selecting the less-caffeinated option this time. "Ah, a tea would be absolutely marvellous," she said.

Quinn proceeded upstairs with Hercules following not too far behind, likely wondering where this trespasser thought she was going in his domain. She approached the first door on the left, opening it and having a quick peek inside. "Oops," she said, making out like she'd opened the wrong door in error, even though she knew precisely what she was doing. Then making certain she wasn't being observed (by a human, rather than Hercules, as she was confident Hercules wouldn't be able to report to his master what he was seeing), Quinn repeated this process again, having a quick nosey inside another room before she eventually reached the door that her bladder had been crying out for.

Interesting, she thought, as she finally settled herself onto the home's porcelain throne. Because what looked to be the master bedroom had only one single bed in it, she had noticed, as did the other, slightly smaller room she had just investigated. From this, assuming there was no other master bedroom located elsewhere in the house, Quinn deduced that the Ogilvy-Pratt residence had not been a happy marital home for quite some time.

After concluding what was a quite glorious pee and feeling at least half a stone lighter, Quinn seized the opportunity to sneak a peek behind another door in the hallway that she hadn't yet tried. She eased it open, conscious that squeaky hinges weren't a stickybeak's best friend in circumstances such as this. Taking a step in and peering around, Quinn could see this was a study, or perhaps a room used as their office, judging by the presence of a mahogany writing bureau positioned under the window. There, resting on the polished surface were a stack of documents that she'd relish the opportunity to have a good rummage through if there were more time. But conscious of her extended bathroom break, Quinn reckoned she'd better soon get back to her host.

"Good grief, this woman likes her dogs," Quinn muttered to herself, spotting at least ten framed photographs of Virginia and Hercules in a variety of poses on one wall of the room alone. "But none of her husband..." Quinn further observed before deciding it best to make haste. But before she'd fully stepped out, Quinn couldn't help but notice a jacket draped over an exercise bike in the far corner of the room.

Indeed, it wasn't just a jacket there, as there were other articles of clothing draped over the device as well, giving the impression it was used as a clothes horse rather than as an instrument for good health. The reason the dark jacket caught her attention, however, was the fact that there was a silhouette of a chihuahua on the back, its outline created by dozens and dozens of sparkly white sequins. "Oh... kay...?" Quinn said, not too much a fan of this particular fashion statement. "Each to their own, I guess."

Quinn gently pulled the door behind her, taking care to close it without making too much noise, again with the ever-present fear of creaking hinges or possibly loose floorboards in mind.

"Did you get lost, dear?"

Quinn jumped back, clutching her chest, startled at the sight of Virginia at the top of the stairs with her arms across her chest. "What...? No, I– erm, that is.... Hercules!" Quinn said.

Virginia glanced down at her ever-loyal companion currently standing faithfully by her side (at about ankle level). "Yes? What about him?" she asked, arms still folded.

Quinn was used to working under pressure, but try as she might her brain didn't appear to be delivering the goods as quick as she'd like. She shifted her weight nervously from one foot to the other, looking to the wall on her right where she noticed yet another framed photograph of Virginia posing with her beloved pooch. "I– erm... I think I spooked Hercules when I came out of the lav," Quinn said, intrigued to hear what kind of nonsense her brain was coming up with, even as she was speaking it. "And he darted into that room," Quinn added, pointing to the doorway she'd just walked through. "I was worried he'd get locked inside somehow. So I shooed him out, and I was just, uhm, closing the door to, you know, make sure that didn't happen...?"

Virginia offered a thin smile. "Your tea is going to get cold," she advised.

Quinn followed Virginia downstairs and back into the living room, where she accepted the offer of a seat in a lovely wingback chair positioned near to the fireplace. Between the intake of too much caffeine and her recent fright upstairs, Quinn could feel her heart thumping against her ribcage.

Virginia placed herself down on a nearby sofa, sitting with a rigid back and her hands resting on her knees, exuding an air of formality like she was hosting the vicar for a fancy brunch. "You had a few questions for me...?" she asked, picking up her floral bone China cup and taking a dainty sip from it.

It was at this point that Quinn realised she'd left her notepad on the passenger seat of her car. "Yes. And thank you," she said, deciding to freestyle rather than face Virginia's possible wrath for having to duck out and go retrieve it. "I understand you know my father?" Quinn asked, to get the conversation started.

"Chester? Yes, he's a good man. A real gentleman."

Quinn enjoyed hearing people say nice things about her dad. "Yes, he's lovely," she agreed. "So you can understand why I'm so upset that somebody tried to hurt him, and then..." she began. But her thought process was being interrupted on account of her phone vibrating incessantly in her pocket, as it had been for virtually the entire time she was there. "Sorry, what was I saying...? Oh, yes," she continued, picking up right where she had left off. "That somebody tried to hurt him. And was attempting to frame him for a murder he didn't commit."

Virginia shook her head in apparent solidarity, making her elegant diamond drop earrings swing back and forth like little pendulums on a clock. "A terrible business," she insisted. "You'll be sure to pass on my very best wishes?"

"Thank you. Yes, of course," Quinn told her. "Anyway, you may or may not know, but one of the reasons the police suspected my father was the presence of a handwritten note placed inside of Mr Goodacre's blazer pocket."

"A note?"

Quinn took a sip of her own tea before carefully placing her cup down onto the side table. "Yes, it was a note suggesting my dad owed Major Goodacre seven thousand pounds in gambling debts. Which he didn't."

"So the police interpreted the presence of such a note as being a motive that your father would benefit greatly from the Major's demise?" Virginia put forth.

"Precisely! Unfortunately, my father's memory of the evening in question is still hazy, most likely due to his nasty fall. But as the police believe your husband and his, erm... his lady friend, Primrose... were responsible for both of the murders, then it's a fairly logical assumption that at least one of them was involved in the incident with my father as well. I'm just trying to understand why."

But Virginia was gazing down at her feet just now, giving the impression that she was listening, but wasn't overly interested in what was being said, really. "And you have a question...?" she asked, without looking up.

Quinn was about ready to reach into her pocket and toss her phone into the nearby fireplace, as the silly device hadn't stopped vibrating since she'd sat down. "Yes. Yes, I do," she said. "Did your husband ever talk about my dad? Maybe something suggesting there was ill will between the two of them...?"

Virginia considered the question only briefly. "No, not that I recall," she said. But then it seemed as if she'd suddenly changed her mind. "It's definitely possible," she insisted. "Just not that I'm able to specifically remember off the top of my head."

This time around, Quinn did reach inside her pocket, as her next question required access to her phone's camera roll. "Okay. If you don't mind, I'd like to show you a photograph of the handwritten note I mentioned," she advised, removing her phone that was still vibrating. Quinn pressed the cancel button, cutting off the latest attempted call (which she could now see was coming from Toby) so that she could easily access her saved photos.

With the photo in question shortly located, Quinn rose from her chair, taking a few steps over towards the sofa so she could hold out her phone for Virginia's inspection. "Does this look like your husband's handwriting?"

Virginia leaned forward, squinting her eyes as she scrutinised the image. "How did you get this?" she asked, throwing Quinn a suspicious look. "Is this not police evidence?"

"Uhm... technically, yes," Quinn admitted. "I mean, sort of."

"Well I don't recognise the handwriting, if that's what you're asking me," Virginia responded.

Quinn held the phone in front of Virginia's face for a moment longer, just in case this might somehow assist her identification. Which it didn't. "So, you definitely don't recognise it?"

"No," Virginia said impatiently. "And your phone is vibrating again. So if you need to go, please don't let me keep you...?"

Quinn turned her phone around so she could view it herself again, at which point she could see that it was Toby attempting to get through to her once more. "He's a persistent little bugger," Quinn joked as she returned to her seat, noting there were now thirteen missed calls according to her phone's notification display. Quinn veered around Virginia's somewhat less-than-subtle suggestion to wrap things up, as she wasn't nearly finished just yet. Instead, Quinn tried to form a mental inventory of the outstanding questions she'd written down in the notebook that was still sitting in her car, eager to address each of them in turn.

"If we could just..." Quinn started to say. But the image of her notebook in her mind's eye was being edged out, for some odd reason, by the view of Virginia's exercise bike/clothes horse she had seen several minutes earlier. In particular, the dog-shaped sequin design on the back of the dark jacket found there.

"Yes? You were saying?" Virginia pressed, making no effort to disguise the obvious, deliberate glance at her watch.

Quinn didn't respond right away. Instead, she stared vacantly, feeling dazed as a loud buzzing noise in her head—a noise that wasn't her vibrating phone—jarred her as if being attacked by a pneumatic drill. Quinn had a strange, niggling feeling she'd seen that sparkly, sequined pattern somewhere previously, although she couldn't remember where. But after a few moments it suddenly dawned on her. It was, she now felt certain, the very same pattern she'd seen on the jacket of the hooded woman captured by the onboard camera of the graffitied fishing vessel. The same hooded woman who was most probably the final person to see Major Vincent Goodacre alive.

As fast as it had come on, the clattering abated and Quinn felt groggy, slowly moving back into the present as if she was coming to just after surgery. With a mouth drier than a sailor's hardtack biscuit, Quinn reached for her waiting cup of tea with one hand while opening up the messages on her mobile phone with the other. It appeared that Toby had given up on calling, opting to send her an urgent text instead.

Toby: Quinn, I'll explain later but GET OUT OF THERE NOW!

Quinn placed her phone down on the side table, screen down, giving the outward impression that all was well with the world. Forcing through a pleasant smile, Quinn looked at Virginia, still sitting there with a rigid, straight back and sporting a prim and proper expression like a Victorian headmistress.

"Ah. I couldn't help but notice your lovely, sparkling earrings," Quinn said, eventually breaking the silence. "They're very pretty," she remarked casually. "Were they a gift?"

Virginia gave her a peculiar look. "And what does that have to do with your enquiries?" she asked.

Quinn waved away Virginia's response, as if her own question hadn't been especially relevant to their discussion. But then...

"Oh, it's just that I like diamonds, Virginia," Quinn said with a satisfied sigh. "So you can imagine how excited I was, when I found one at the foot of the stairs leading up to my dad's flat. Yep. Almost missed it. But there it was, all magnificent and sparkly, lying there caught up in the carpet."

Virginia instinctively cupped the base of her ears, placing a protective shield over them. "Have you been drinking, girl?" she snapped, as she rose up from her chair. "Regardless, I think we're done here. And I'd appreciate it if you'd—"

But Quinn wasn't quite finished, cutting Virginia off before she could complete her sentence. "You know, it's very interesting. Because I couldn't help but notice that you've also got one of the small stones missing from your left earring. That's an amazing coincidence, isn't it...? Hey, here's an idea, Virginia. Why don't we see if the stone I found at my father's flat matches the one you're missing? That would really be something, wouldn't it...?"

The colour in Virginia's cheeks immediately turned a furious shade of crimson. Firmly on her feet, her polite, accommodating demeanour was now entirely vanished as she stormed across the room in the general direction of her house phone positioned on the sideboard behind Quinn.

"Oh, are you calling for the police...?" Quinn asked, after turning to look and see where Virginia was going. "Good idea. Maybe they can help you locate your missing—"

But Quinn didn't have an opportunity to finish what she was saying, as Virginia's lead crystal paperweight made sure of that.

Quinn dropped her teacup and slumped to the floor, unconscious before her battered head made contact with the carpet.

"You stupid, stupid girl!" Virginia shouted, now standing directly over Quinn's motionless figure, watching as a stream of blood slowly made its way down the side of Quinn's head. "And don't you dare think about bleeding on my new antique Persian rug!" she warned through gritted teeth, reaching for and placing an old newspaper under Quinn's head.

"I'd had *everything* worked out," Virginia continued, talking merely to herself at this point, and now pacing back and forth. "Dirty Derek and his wandering libido were going to spend the rest of his miserable life rotting behind bars, along with that wretched little floozie of his. And then you try and spoil all my hard work. Well, I can't have that, you meddling little brat."

Virginia lowered herself carefully down to one knee, listening as a barely audible groan escaped from her unconscious victim's mouth. "I'm sorry about this," Virginia added, stroking Quinn's hair like she was at the vet's and about to say a final goodbye to the family's aged pet. "But if you'd just learned to mind your own business, I wouldn't have to do what I'm about to do now."

Virginia offered a quick, tight-lipped smile before raising her left arm high above her head, the crystal paperweight secured in her hand refracting the sun's rays coming in through the front window and producing a rainbow splash of colour against the ceiling. She gripped the paperweight so hard that her knuckles had gone completely white.

"Remember, my dear, this is all *your* fault, not mine. And if you hadn't been such a bloody Nosey Nellie, then I wouldn't have to be doing *this*..."

Chapter Eighteen

For a creature with a diminutive stature similar in size to, say, a grey squirrel or perhaps a mildly overweight guinea pig, Hercules couldn't half produce a cacophonous racket when he wanted to. A series of throaty barks were followed by a menacing snarl as he tried to snap at the hands wrapped firmly around his middle, just agonisingly out of reach of his jaws. Toby burst into the Ogilvy-Pratt living room with his arms stretched out in front of him, holding the pooch like it was a ticking time bomb that could explode any minute. "Virginia, drop that thing in your hand and drop it now!" he shouted.

A startled Virginia looked over, finding a man standing very unexpectedly just inside the doorway. It took her a brief moment to realise who it was. "You! What are you doing with my Hercules? You put him down this instant!" she demanded.

Toby took several guarded steps forward, lifting his arms all the way up so that the pooch was now held towards the ceiling. "Drop it, and move away from Quinn *now!*" Toby warned, indicating to her with a sudden, sharp movement that her beloved pet was in imminent danger of being let go from a great height at a moment's notice if she refused to comply. He had no intention of actually doing such a thing, of course, as he was no monster. But Virginia wouldn't have any way of knowing that.

Virginia froze, considering her next move as the gears turned inside her head to formulate some kind of excuse or explanation. "She, em... she tripped and fell!" Virginia offered, though with no effort made to lower her weapon-holding hand, still appearing poised and ready to strike like a scorpion's tail. "I – I was checking on her to make sure that—"

"Drop that thing now, Virginia! We *both* know she didn't fall!" Toby answered.

Virginia's sinister stare gave way to a congenial smile, unsettling Toby in the process. "Are you saying I did this to her...?" she asked, appearing like butter wouldn't melt in her mouth.

Toby took another step forward. "I already suspect you killed Major Goodacre and Cindy Shuttleworth, so you can understand why I'd be entirely sceptical when you say Quinn *tripped and fell*," he said. "Oh, and by the way, I was very intrigued to learn that the Smellie family own quite a bit of land in Castletown. Smellie was your maiden name, Virginia...?"

The fact that Toby knew this information appeared to catch Virginia off guard. "So?" she snapped. "What's that got to do with anything? My father owns land. Big deal!"

"Well, what about the fact that you also paid Major Goodacre two hundred thousand pounds through a secret Swiss holding company that you own? Why was that, Virginia? Did the Major object to the recent planning applications to develop the land? Is that why you murdered him...?"

Virginia's paperweight-holding arm started shaking. Now in a furious rage, any pretence of her innocence was thrown firmly out of the window, or perhaps into the fireplace. "You and your bloody idiot friend!" she yelled, snarling just as her dog had done a few moments earlier. "You've ruined everything for me!"

Virginia then looked up at the lead crystal paperweight, pulling her arm fully back in order to maximise all of the force she could muster. "It wasn't supposed to end this way..."

For Toby, his perception of time slowed to a crawl. As Virginia cocked her arm, he knew precisely what she was going to do and where she was going to aim the heavy item in her hand. Without even stopping to think what he was about to do, he launched a bewildered Hercules across the room like a rugby player executing a spin pass.

Virginia, for her part, watched as her darling pet soared in the air towards her like a garden gnome shot out of a cannon. In that split second, she broke off her attack, dropping the hefty object

A CASE OF MAJOR MURDER

in her hand as she tried desperately to intercept Hercules's flight path and collect him safely into her arms, which eventually she did, tumbling backwards.

Seizing his opportunity, Toby quickly moved forward, kicking the paperweight clear and out of the reach of Virginia, who was now sprawled on her back, legs akimbo, a whimpering Hercules clutched into her bosom. "Ah, and that would be the police sirens you can hear. I called them on my way over," Toby informed her, taking up a defensive position in front of Quinn's feet, shielding her body from any possibility of a further assault.

The sound of sirens intensified as several emergency vehicles hurtled up the road—three police cars, as well as an ambulance—likely leaving those in the neighbourhood to wonder what the dickens was going on. The lead police car drew to an abrupt halt on Derek Ogilvy-Pratt's prized lawn, adding another impressive skid mark to accompany the one deposited by the previous police vehicle to visit the property.

To Toby's immense relief, the officers surged into the Ogilvy-Pratt house mob-handed, along with two paramedics. However, the two EMTs made a beeline heading straight towards Virginia, who was still stretched out on the floor with a yapping Hercules clutched to her chest.

"No!" Toby shouted, placing a hand on the shoulder of the paramedic closest to him. "She's the *murderer*, and there's nothing wrong with her at all!" he told them. "It's *her* you need to attend to!" he advised urgently, pointing to Quinn, his voice raw with emotion. "Please help her!" he pleaded, horrified at the sight of the blood-soaked pages of newspaper under Quinn's head.

"Oh, Quinn. Quinn, please be okay..."

***

With his mummy in handcuffs and in the back of a police car being whisked away to Castletown Police Station, Hercules was handed over to a neighbour who'd wandered outdoors to witness the unfolding spectacle taking place next door. Completely unharmed during the recent drama inside his home, Hercules had even worked up quite an appetite during the excitement if the bowl of food he was presently demolishing in record time was anything to go by.

Also about to be whisked away was Quinn, being wheeled on a gurney towards the ambulance as Toby walked alongside with his hand wrapped tightly around hers. Fortunately, by this point, the EMTs had managed to stabilise her, and she was now thankfully conscious and talking.

Despite the suggestion to save her strength, a woozy Quinn still had the gumption and wherewithal to relay to the police the details of the critical evidence she'd discovered while inside the house—that being the garish jacket with a distinctive design on the back, and the diamond earring with a missing stone. With this crucial evidence directly implicating Virginia in at least one of the murders, as well as the assault on Quinn's own father.

Along with the fishing boat's video recording, in addition to what Toby had uncovered with Doreen's helpful input, things weren't looking too rosy for Virginia right about now, one might fairly suggest. And that was *before* the police had even factored in the attempted murder of Quinn from several minutes ago.

"Will you go and tell my dad what's happened?" Quinn asked, looking up at Toby with blood-soaked hair matted to her cheek.

"You don't want me to come to the hospital...?" Toby asked.

Quinn gave his hand a gentle squeeze. "Of course I do," she told him. "But will you please check in on my father first? I just don't want him to find out what's happened to me second-hand, and getting upset. You don't mind, do you?"

Staring at his partner, and good friend, lying there helpless, battered and bruised on a stretcher, was simply awful. Trying desperately to keep his fragile emotions in check, Toby looked at her earnestly. "No, I absolutely don't mind. I'll head to your dad's flat straight away," he promptly assured her. Toby then released Quinn's hand so the medics could load her into the back of the ambulance. "I'll bring you an ice cream!" he shouted through the closing doors, though immediately wondering to himself if that was a stupid suggestion he'd just made, or a brilliant one.

Toby stood watching as the ambulance eased away a bit more sedately than how it had first arrived. Indeed, he took consolation in the fact that it hadn't roared furiously away, figuring this must mean its crew didn't view Quinn as being in any pressing, immediate danger.

And with only one injured party requiring an obvious trip to hospital, the crew of a second ambulance that had subsequently arrived were now in the process of packing up. That is, until one of the crew spotted Toby. "Hi there. My name is Natalie," she said, deploying her best bedside manner (or roadside manner, as it were). "Can I dress that wound for you...?" she asked, holding up her first aid kit for Toby's consideration, as well as confirmation of her professional credentials.

Toby smiled, uncertain as to where the kind offer of medical assistance was being directed. But when Natalie didn't move or lower her first aid kit, Toby glanced over his shoulder and quickly realised there was nobody standing behind him. "Oh. You mean me?" he asked, though shaking his head, as he was still confused by her offer. "No, I'm fine," he promised. "But thanks."

But Natalie the caregiver was nothing if not persistent. "You do know you've a nasty gash on your left hand?" she suggested.

"Eh? I do?" Toby asked, surprised by this piece of information. He wasn't particularly good with the sight of blood ever since he crashed his BMX bicycle into a bramble bush as a child, but he dared a glance down at his supposedly damaged extremity. "Oh... I *do*!" he said, confirming the EMT's observation.

Natalie had already removed a dressing and a tube of antiseptic cream, ready to attend to Toby's injury. "Don't worry, I'll take care of it," she said. "So how did this happen?" she asked, opting to keep her patient talking, as she could see he was queasy.

Toby could feel his legs starting to buckle, so he looked off into the distance somewhere to prevent himself from being able to view what was going on. "Oh, that?" he said casually. "Well, I was involved in a serious altercation with a vicious murderer. I'm a private investigator, you see."

"This may hurt a tiny bit," Natalie cautioned, as she set about cleaning the wound. And then, "A private investigator, is it? That certainly sounds exciting."

Toby puffed out his chest and offered a proud sniff. "I suppose I just like helping people," he said, the unsung hero that he was.

"So how did you hurt your hand, exactly? It looks like a bite."

Now able to feel the bandage being applied to his hand, thus covering up any sign of the wound, Toby bravely looked down at it. "Well, the vicious murderer had a dog. A dog I had to subdue during the scuffle," he advised, bending the truth a fair amount. Then, using his free hand, Toby held it out flat like he was measuring the height of a child trying to get onto the rollercoaster at the fair. "It was at least *this* big," Toby added, with his hand about halfway between the height of his chest and his belly button.

"Incredible. What breed was it?" Natalie asked.

"Erm, I'm not sure, exactly. But it was dark in colour. Black as pitch, you could say! And it had *enormous* teeth, with an evil glint in its eyes, like... like *hellfire!*" Toby said gravely. "It pounced on me when I was wrestling with its owner," he explained.

Natalie started laughing, which did nothing to bolster Toby's ego. "Is that right?" she replied. "Only I thought the 'vicious murderer' was a sixty-something female, and I could've sworn I saw the police coming out of the house with a teensy weensy, beige-coloured chihuahua when we arrived?" she said. "Anyway, we're all done here and you're good to go. But if you have any discomfort, then do seek further medical attention, as you may need a tetanus shot, or even a rabies shot, as having a bite like this can possibly result in some potentially serious side effects."

"Oh? What should I look out for?" Toby asked.

Natalie fastened up her first aid kit now that she was finished with her patient. "Swelling. Discomfort. And seeing imaginary demon beasts and that sort of thing," she cautioned.

Toby bowed his head in appreciation of the impressive piss-taking at his expense. "If I see another imaginary hell hound, I'll be sure to head straight to the emergency room," he joked. "But on a serious note, thank you for this," he added, holding up his bandaged hand. "And if anybody asks, I'll be sure to tell them it was merely a bloodthirsty chihuahua!"

Chapter Nineteen

Three days later...

The population of the Isle of Man breathed a collective sigh of relief when the police made the announcement that Virginia Ogilvy-Pratt had been formally charged with two counts of murder—that of Major Vincent Goodacre, and Cindy Shuttleworth. Additionally, there were charges as well for the attempted murder of both Chester and Quinn Flitcroft.

The incarceration of such a calculated and cold-hearted killer was welcome news indeed. But there were likely none on the isle more grateful for Virginia's eventual capture than her husband Derek and Derek's lover Primrose Ellis. Both of whom had otherwise been facing the prospect of decades behind bars. Armed with the compelling dossier of evidence provided by Quinn and Toby, the police moved swiftly to release the pair of them, with their reputations restored, at least to a certain degree. (And they didn't get off entirely scot-free, because while the law might no longer be after them there was of course still the small matter of a furious, jilted husband—one Oscar Ellis—that the two of them would have to contend with.)

Furthermore, faced with the overwhelming evidence against her, Virginia Ogilvy-Pratt didn't, as it transpired, have either the stomach or the inclination to fight the damning charges levied her way, instead opting to make a full and frank confession.

Part of this evidence included what Toby, with Doreen's helpful input, had uncovered through records at the land registry. In those, he'd discovered that Virginia's father, Frank Smellie, had purchased several parcels of land surrounding the bowling club, some twenty-three years earlier—at a time before Virginia was married to Derek. That land, of course, having been purchased from Major Vincent Goodacre.

It was upon discovering this information that first led Toby to wonder if it was the wrong Ogilvy-Pratt that had fallen under the cloak of suspicion. His fears were confirmed when he spoke with Kasia, his associate in Switzerland, who had emailed copies to him of the company documentation for Thie as Moddey—the entity that paid the Major two hundred thousand pounds. From the scanned copies that Toby reviewed, he could just about make out the name Ogilvy-Pratt as the beneficial owner in the small print, and incorrectly assumed this to be Derek.

However, as soon as he'd become aware of Virginia's family's interest in the land, Toby had phoned Kasia, asking her to take a gander at the original documents in her possession for a clearer view. It was at this point that she was able to inform him that it was a V Ogilvy-Pratt listed as the beneficial owner rather than a D Ogilvy-Pratt. A minor detail, one might think, but crucial to the investigation and information that prompted Toby to rush over to the Ogilvy-Pratt residence, thus preventing Quinn from becoming Virginia's third victim as a result.

What wasn't initially clear to the constabulary, though, was why Virginia had recently paid two hundred thousand quid to Vincent Goodacre. But the answer to that little mystery became more apparent when one started reading through the list of outstanding planning applications for the area around the crown green bowling club, as Toby suggested they should do. In them, it was clear that a large commercial development had been earmarked for the property owned by Virginia's father—something he'd no doubt hoped was a possibility, and very likely the reason he had purchased the land from the Major to begin with.

These new plans for the heart of Castletown, once approved, would have resulted in quite a significant return on investment, with the property developers prepared to pay a handsome price for the land. And that was money that most certainly would have filtered down to Virginia, helping her to build a new life without her "gallivanting pig of a husband in it," as she had so eloquently stated to the police.

A CASE OF MAJOR MURDER

But there had been only one minor—or, more aptly, Major—fly in the ointment. And that was Major Vincent Goodacre, who expressed concern about the effects that some vulgar commercial development might have on the established look and feel of the area. And while happy with what he'd earned from the sale of his land originally, the Major, perhaps naïvely, had never imagined the property might be put to such use in the future or in the present, having feared—prior to his untimely demise—that it would spoil the traditional, historic nature of the community that he so loved. As such—and especially being the owner of the bowling club which sat directly next-door to the proposed commercial development—the Major became determined to object to the local planning consent, even managing to rally other area residents in support of his noble cause.

"So I tried bribing him," Virginia had bitterly admitted to the police. "I sent him one hundred thousand pounds to begin with. But he was furious. Claimed he couldn't be bought off! Can you imagine? What a load of rubbish. I assumed he was bluffing, of course. Simply holding out for more money. So I then sent him *another* hundred thousand, even appealing to his sense of altruism, telling him he could make use of the money for one of those charities he was always so fond of. But that didn't convince him, either. He kept bloody sticking his oar in, threatening to derail a multi-million-pound windfall. In the end, there was really only one solution to stop him from scuppering our plans."

Unfortunately for the Major, it was this reasoning that led to his eventual death. And once the deed was actually done, it was at that point Virginia had decided it might be a wise idea to pin somebody else for the murder just committed. As such, a fake letter purporting to be from the Major landed on the doorstep of Primrose Ellis, suggesting he was aware of her illicit affair with Derek. Virginia timed the delivery of this 'letter from the grave' so the pair of them, Primrose and Derek, would realise that the Major's knowledge of their affair would be viewed as a potential motive for them to wish him dead. Landing them both in a spot of trouble as a result.

"It was a bit of mischief-making on my part," Virginia claimed with a grin as she'd spoken to the interviewing detective. "I could just imagine the panic they'd be in once Primrose received that letter." Virginia had to pause at that point on account of the fit of giggles she experienced picturing that very scenario. "It was payback," she'd continued. "Payback to my fool of a husband who thought I knew nothing about his wandering eye. And Primrose wasn't the first, either. She was just the latest in a long line of heartless homewreckers. And the thought of her and that idiot Derek rotting in jail while I was off sunning myself in warmer climes was a most pleasant outcome indeed, in my opinion." It was at that point in the police interview that Virginia's demeanour had softened a bit, catching the officers by surprise. "About Chester Flitcroft," she'd said. "You must tell him I never planned to do that to him. But I spotted him standing at his window and I couldn't take the risk about what he'd seen that evening. It was simply in for a penny, in for a pound at that stage."

What became obvious to the police was that, in Virginia, they were dealing with an intelligent and shrewd individual, and one who spoke of murder in the same casual manner as one might discuss a recent visit to the shops. What remained initially unclear, however, was precisely how and why Cindy Shuttleworth, a young woman with a large part of her life still ahead of her, found herself on the receiving end of Virginia's ire and wrath.

"She was a distraction," Virginia replied when presented with that very question. "Cindy found out about my husband's affair. And I then overheard Derek talking with his mistress over the phone, discussing how they'd decided to pay Cindy off and make the problem go away." Again, Virginia broke into a fit of laughter at that point of the interview. "Just how stupid were they?" she'd said. "If you pay a blackmailer once, then you're bloody paying them for *life*. And where does my loving husband get most of his money from? From *me*! So if I hadn't done something about it, then my bank account would've been drained for years to come. I'd had everything planned to perfection, and I didn't need Cindy Shuttleworth upsetting my apple cart."

A CASE OF MAJOR MURDER

Fortunately, the Virginia Ogilvy-Pratt crime wave had come to a conclusion, with her now behind bars. A position where she could expect to remain, very likely seeing out the rest of her days firmly locked up. For the seasoned team of officers working on this case, Virginia was, without question, the most dangerous criminal on the isle they'd ever encountered or would probably encounter again.

But what also sent a chill through their collective spines was the thought of what Virginia could have gone on to do had she not been apprehended when she had. Clearly, she was a woman who'd think nothing of taking a life if anybody dared to stand in her way. Would this have been a pattern that might've continued into the future, with another dead body being discovered each and every time Virginia had been in some way inconvenienced? Fortunately, this was no longer a concern, thanks in large part to the determination of both Quinn Flitcroft and Toby Haddock.

The people of the Isle of Man owed a debt of gratitude to the duo whom Derek Ogilvy-Pratt had originally ridiculed, referring to them disparagingly as "Bucket 'n' Spade Private Eyes." Ironic, then, that without this pair, Derek Ogilvy-Pratt, along with his present girlfriend, would still be incarcerated with the prospect of a hefty prison sentence awaiting them.

***

There were many benefits to having a sandy beach within just a stone's throw of your front door, that's for certain—carefree days spent relaxing on a portable, fold-up deck chair, the prospect of a quick dip anytime you liked in the brisk, invigorating, briny waves, or just the enviable position of having a picture-perfect postcard seaside view from your living room window. And for Chester Flitcroft, this was his idea of paradise. He adored seeing the tourists and locals alike arriving each morning to secure their spot on the sands, eager for another day of fun and frolics enjoying simple pleasures—with those pleasures often not requiring an electrical plug or a Wi-Fi connection to appreciate them. And if those new arrivals decided that ice cream was in order at any point in their day, then he (once recovered from his injuries, of course) and his trusty crew of associates would always be ready, willing, and able to dispense the delectable frozen treats as they had been for many years prior and a fair few years yet to come.

But as much as he enjoyed seeing the hordes arrive, there was still something special, Chester reckoned, about the most magical moment of the day. And that moment was when the last of the visitors vacated the beach, leaving the soft sands as the playground of those neighbouring residents fortunate enough to call this charming little village directly by the sea their home. Previously, before his injury, as the sun started to set—casting a warm orange hue over the bay—Chester would often lock up his shop and wander across the road alone to have a seat on the very edge of the promenade wall, enjoying a glass of wine or two while the foraging seabirds wheeled about above him, always in search of an easy meal.

And while he had always appreciated those lovely moments of quiet solitude alone, Chester was as equally thrilled now, on this particular evening, to share this special time of his with his favourite and only daughter...

Sitting near each other on a warm summer's evening, Quinn relaxed in a beach chair as did Chester in his wheelchair, with the two of them observing a solitary kayaker returning leisurely to shore as if they hadn't a care in the world.

Quinn glanced across at her dad, and then down to the base of his chair. "Here, are your wheels sinking into the sand...?" she asked. "Is it my imagination, or do you look a bit more lopsided than when I parked you up?"

Chester waved away her concerns. "I'm fine," he said. "Besides, if I am a bit wonky, then I'm sure a glass of wine will straighten me right up," he advised, with his own particular brand of curious logic.

The pair of them sat for the next several minutes in silence, appreciating the quivering red and yellow reflections flickering on the surface of the incoming tide. On either side of the bay, dark, hill-shaped silhouettes formed from the headlands as the sun decided it had put a solid shift in for the day and was disappearing before it would need to come back the following morning and renew the cycle all over again.

"It's quite magical," Quinn remarked, sounding almost emotional about the evening spectacle unfolding before her.

Chester reached over, wrapping his fingers around Quinn's hand. "It's something I'll never tire of," he agreed. "Now if only we had that glass of wine to accompany it..."

Quinn looked over her shoulder towards the ice cream shop, where the only sign of life was a young couple out pushing their pram along the promenade walkway. "I guess Toby got waylaid on his journey back from fetching your bottle of red. Either that or he's cracked it open on his own, eh?"

But Chester didn't answer, instead staring solemnly out to sea just now.

"Dad? Everything okay?"

Chester released his daughter's hand in order to adjust the cushion behind his back for lumbar support. "What? Oh, yes," he replied. "Sorry, I was just thinking about what a cold, calculated, nasty piece of work that Virginia Ogilvy-Pratt is."

"She is that," Quinn concurred.

Chester took a deep breath and then let out a sigh. "I've known Virginia most of my life," he reflected. "I can't say we were ever good friends, or anything like that. But as you're well aware from growing up here yourself, living in a small village like this, you certainly get to know most folk in your community in one way or another. And the thought that she'd sneak up into my home and try to *kill* me is... well, it's bloody chilling, is what it is."

Quinn could only nod in agreement.

"And I wouldn't mind so much, but I wasn't even a witness to her attacking the Major like she thought I was! Or at least I don't believe I did. It's difficult to say, of course, as I don't recall much of anything from the night in question," Chester advised. *"And,"* he continued, "to have the callous forethought to return to the Major's corpse right after pushing me down my stairs, and then plant a fictitious note to implicate me in his murder over some unpaid gambling debt...? I mean, blimey, you nearly have to hand it to Virginia, because that's some quick thinking in a stressful situation."

"You sound almost impressed?" Quinn answered.

But before Chester could opine one way or the other on this suggestion, the chinking sound of glasses alerted the two of them that someone's arrival was imminent. "A-ha! I think the barman is on his way," Quinn announced, placing a hand to her ear.

Before Toby had even stepped one foot onto the sand, he was already happily chuckling away to himself. "Honestly, you pair look like you're waiting in the doctor's surgery," he joked upon arrival, handing each of them an empty glass. "You've got your father in his wheelchair on one side, and then there's you, Quinn, with that monstrosity of a bandage wrapped around your head, on the other."

"If you don't pour that wine, Toby," Chester playfully growled, "then the list of patients waiting to visit the doctor is about to increase by one, if you take my meaning?"

Toby didn't need to be asked twice, diligently filling their wine glasses like an expert sommelier. Then, with his own glass also attended to, he settled himself down into his own beach chair to appreciate the fading light. "Ah! I could most definitely get used to this," he said.

"Well I'm glad you finally made it. We thought you'd got lost there for a bit," Quinn teased him.

"Oh, not at all. Barry from work phoned me," Toby explained. "Turns out he needed me to conduct some surveillance work at a fish processing plant in Peterhead, over on the northeast coast of Scotland."

Quinn didn't mean to, but she couldn't help laughing. "Oof, I'll be able to smell you all the way from here," she commented.

"You won't be leaving that soon, will you?" Chester asked, his disappointment fairly evident, having grown quite accustomed to young Toby in his life. "You'll stay a few more days?"

Toby scrunched up his face in a funny sort of way. "Em, yeah, about that," he said. "I may have just told Barry I've had enough of insurance fraud surveillance operations. And I quit!"

Quinn wasn't sure if he was being serious or not. It was often difficult to tell with Toby. "What? You quit...?!"

"Yeah. Not too long ago I was stuck in a skip for days on end, and next it sounds like I'm going to be up to my neck in fish guts and whatnot. Nope! No thanks. It's time for a change, I reckon."

"So what are you going to do, son?" Chester asked. "I thought you liked being a private investigator."

Toby sat himself completely upright (which wasn't easy in the cloth, hammock-like saddle of his foldable beach chair) before adjusting himself to look directly at Quinn and her father lined up next to each other in their doctor's waiting room. "Well," he advised, planting his feet into the soft, still-warm sand, "I heard this rumour that a new detective agency was setting up business on the Isle of Man."

Quinn flashed him a smile, hoping that what she thought he was talking about was what he was indeed talking about. "Oh, is that right? And the name of this new detective agency wouldn't happen to be Bucket 'n' Spade Private Eyes, would it?"

"Eh...? No, why?" Toby responded, acting entirely confused by Quinn's suggestion. "Actually, I met this bloke when I was heading to the butchers yesterday. Nice enough fellow. And what this fellow informed me was that..." he started to say, clearly making things up as he went along, before quickly abandoning the obvious ruse and offering Quinn a grin. "Of *course* it is, partner! If you're up for a new adventure...? Granted, I'm not expecting there to be any additional murders that'll require our investigative skills anytime soon. But I imagine there should still be plenty of other work to keep us busy? At least I certainly hope so, as I no longer have a job. So, whaddaya say?"

"Me and you as partners in our own private detective firm?" Quinn answered, thoughtfully rubbing her chin as she pondered the various pros and cons of such a proposal, although with little on the negative side of the scale to be considered, really.

"Oh, and we might need to also draft Doreen in from time to time," Toby interjected. "Because she's bloody good at this detecting lark!"

Chester, who'd been in listening mode up until this point of the discussion, felt the need to chime in here. "Oi, I'm not letting you nick Doreen from me!" he said. "Not unless you're prepared to put a shift or two in behind the counter at the shop."

Toby leaned over Quinn with his hand extended to Chester, eager to strike that deal. "No problem, Chester. But Doreen said I'll need to wait until my scalp fully heals before I'm authorised to dispense anything intended for human consumption."

A moment later, after giving it the briefest of thought, Quinn raised her wine glass. "Ah, why the hell not," she decided. "After all, what's the worst that could happen?" she put forth. "Right. To Bucket 'n' Spade Private Eyes!"

"To Bucket 'n' Spade Private Eyes!" came the collective toast, followed by the sound of wine glasses clinking to formalise the new enterprise.

"And we already have our first job," Toby was keen to point out. "THE CASE OF THE HMS TODGER!" he declared, christening the name of their fledgling business's opening investigation.

Quinn, Chester, and Toby kicked back, reflecting on what had been a rollercoaster of emotions over the last few weeks. Indeed, there was every possibility that the wine bottle was already in imminent danger of needing to be replaced. And sure, setting up a detective agency on an isle that prided itself on a modest crime rate was, Toby and Quinn both realised, a calculated gamble. But they were both intelligent, capable people, the two of them, and if it didn't work out, they knew they could return to their previous hectic lives flitting from one city to another, never staying long enough to call any particular place a proper home.

But sitting on a beach at dusk, with two of her favourite people, one on either side of her, Quinn Flitcroft knew there wasn't any place on earth she'd rather be right about now.

"Ehm, Quinn...?" Toby asked a short time later, sounding like he wanted to pose a potentially awkward question and possibly wasn't quite sure if it was the best idea. "Would you mind if I asked you something personal?"

"Is it about whether you should head up to the flat and obtain another bottle of red?" Quinn suggested.

Toby noticed that they'd already drained most of their first bottle in record time. He began clambering out of his beach chair, which again, wasn't the easiest feat after getting so settled into it (plus with a few glasses of vino now on board as well). "Okay, I'm on it!" he promised, now standing upright. "No, but what I was actually going to ask you..."

"Yes?" Quinn asked.

Toby tilted his head, first one way and then the other, but then figured he ought to simply come straight out with it. "Well, I was just wondering," he said. "What was the reason you were kicked out of the Isle of Man police force...?"

"Oi, I was not kicked out!" Quinn insisted. "Well, not technically, at least. You see, I left because..." she started to explain, but then changed her mind. "You know what? That's another story for another day, my friend. Now, when you head upstairs to go and get us another bottle, how about you grab that huge bag of Monster Munch Pickled Onion I left next to the microwave?"

"Oh? What did your last slave die of?" Toby protested, acting as if an awful burden had just been placed upon his shoulders, though in truth very pleased to go and fetch the snack.

Quinn pointed to the big bandage wrapped around her head. "Don't forget I'm injured and need looking after!"

"Me too!" Chester added, holding up his now empty glass with his good, unbroken arm to signal he was ready for a refill.

Toby offered a flourish of his hand, happy to look after his two preferred patients. "In that case, one bottle of wine and a bag of Monster Munch Pickled Onion coming right up."

"Excellent," Quinn said. And then, a short moment later, "Just one more thing, Toby!" she called after him.

Toby, who was approaching the steps leading from the beach to the promenade walkway at this point, spun around. "Yeah?" he asked. "What is it?"

"There's still one important thing we need to decide!" Quinn stressed. "Which one of us is going to be Bucket, and which one is going to be Spade!"

THE END
But they'll be back...

Printed in Great Britain
by Amazon